To Jeanne

The GENTLENESS of STEEL

Enjoy the read

Ron Ludlow

The GENTLENESS of STEEL

ANNE LUDLOW

Matador
9 Priory Business Park,
Wistow Road, Kibworth Beauchamp,
Leicestershire. LE8 0RX
Tel: 0116 279 2299
Email: books@troubador.co.uk
Web: www.troubador.co.uk/matador
Twitter: @matadorbooks

ISBN 978 1838593 506

British Library Cataloguing in Publication Data.
A catalogue record for this book is available from the British Library.

Printed and bound in the UK by TJ International, Padstow, Cornwall
Typeset in 11pt Minion Pro by Troubador Publishing Ltd, Leicester, UK

Matador is an imprint of Troubador Publishing Ltd

For those who have lost themselves
and hunger for freedom

and for my husband who set me free

England, 1950s

S HE STOOD WITH her back against the wall. He was holding her lightly by the wrist, his other hand resting on her shoulder. Softly, he stroked the slope of her neck with his thumb. That look was in his eye. Raising his hand up to her nape, he massaged it for a moment and then slipped his fingers through her long auburn hair and gently began entangling it, rolling it up in his hand until he held all of it in a tight ball. Bending his head down until his face was an inch from hers, his cool blue eyes bored into her and he whispered, 'Who is he?'

Sharply, he wrenched her head forward into his chest, then snapped it back to hit the wall and she felt the heat of rising blood rushing to it. Shock froze her.

'Who is he?' he asked once more. Again, he hit her head against the solid brickwork, a little harder this time. The third time, he used his full force. Stars flashed before her eyes and blessed blackness overtook her, expelling fear as she felt herself sinking into welcome oblivion.

SOMETIME LATER HER eyes opened. She was looking at a sea of short, sandy-coloured grass; it was a while before she recognised the sitting-room carpet from this angle. Not knowing how long she had been unconscious, she lay still and mentally checked her body. The bitter taste of blood was in her mouth. She was not ready to come to life, so remained motionless and stole a few moments of dark peace to think.

Their relationship was barely a year old, but after only a few weeks he had begun to assert control over her. Until now it had just been small cruelties: a slap if she had looked at a man with the wrong expression; friends she was no longer allowed to see; her money taken because she was too spendthrifty. She had tolerated it because there was no one else and she needed someone to love and to love her. She didn't want to be alone. Everyone said how obvious it was that he adored her.

The clock on the mantelpiece ticking away the seconds, and Bill's breathing, heavy with a slight rasp, were the only sounds.

Opening her eyes, she saw that his feet, clad in black leather shoes, were just in front of her. His long legs and powerful torso appeared larger looking up. He was sitting in the armchair, not looking at her, so she closed her eyes and hoped he would think her still unconscious.

There was no other man.

Something in her breathing must have changed, because suddenly he yanked her from the floor and began punching her around the room. Having no control over her flesh and bones, she sped through air before crashing into walls and furniture, her limbs flung wild. All the while he questioned her. She tried denying it, but he became more violent, so she remained tight-lipped.

The beating felt endless, and with each thump of his fist against her flesh another piece of her spirit was crushed and destroyed. The pain of this was far worse than the physical damage. She wished that one of the blows would be fatal, so that the terror would stop. It wouldn't matter if she died; no one would miss her.

OVER THE YEARS violence became a normal part of every day. The energetic, animated person she had been was slowly erased and blind fear replaced every rational thought. They were married and had two children. A boy, quiet, thoughtful and intelligent. A girl, spirited, brave and adventurous, just like she used to be. They were the ones who reignited a tiny spark inside her. She built a steel cage in which to keep and nurture the spark, to grow it strong until the time was right.

January 1965

ELEVEN YEARS LATER she lay on her back in bed, arms rigid, barely able to breathe. Her body ached from keeping so still. In the darkness she made out the sharp angles of the wardrobe and dressing table, the curve of the chair in front of it. A weak beam of light from the window landed on the clothes she had placed there the night before. Adrenaline pulsed through her veins, forcing every muscle into a tight knot, while her heart beat so loud, she feared it would wake him.

The plans were all made; it should happen like clockwork. But what if things went wrong? What if Lilly made a noise? What if he woke? There was no choice, no going back. Terror had spread from her to the children and invaded their lives. They had to leave; they had to escape.

She turned her head, just a little, to check the time. Three minutes since her last look; a couple of hours before she could make her move. She could not go until he was in his deepest sleep.

Many times, she had risen at two in the morning, crept downstairs and walked about the house, touching things, thinking how life could be without him. Once she had stood over his peacefully slumbering frame with a carving knife in her hand, her anger raging. Oh, how she'd wanted to kill him, and known that she could. But she wouldn't have got away with it, and what would have happened to her children with her in prison and them in care? Defeated again, without him raising a finger, Adie had walked away and replaced the knife in the kitchen drawer.

To her neighbours she seemed aloof, thinking herself above them. She was slim and attractive with an adoring husband and she never gossiped with the rest of them. When she didn't leave the house for days, they never enquired after her. They didn't know she thought herself beneath them. A failed daughter, wife and mother.

There was nothing to do but be still and wait. She tried to distract herself with happy thoughts, recalling her father and their Sunday mornings, when he would take her for riding lessons at the nearby stables and they would trek across the rolling hills near their home. She allowed her mind to languish in the memories of wildflowers and an occasional glimpse of a fox or rabbit, and how he had made her laugh with his funny faces and mimicking of characters they both knew. These were calming thoughts that slowed her racing heart, so she kept running through them like a film stuck on a loop. But after a while the loop broke and her mother's voice cut through the serenity.

Get out of my sight, you ugly brat; you've done it wrong again. You will never come to anything.

She battled to retrieve the calm vision of those rolling hills, but the picture went black and the spiteful voice kept returning. Her mind would not obey. Instead her heart started to pound, louder and louder. With a start she was awake and looked first at the man beside her, then at the clock. It was 2.30. Time.

Putting on her clothes, she made every movement precise and measured. Even so, each rustle caused internal panic; she told herself she had done this many times before, on countless sleepless nights, and not woken him. That was the easy part.

She crept to Sam's room. He was awake, waiting for her. She had felt guilty involving him in her plans for that night. But she needed a friend, a confidant, someone who knew the true problems that they would face. Even at the age of ten, Sam was the only person who could fulfil that role. He got straight out of bed, already clothed, his face pinched and strained. Sam knew the dark side of his dad; had tried to protect her from him many times before. He understood, for certain, what would happen if they were caught.

Silently, he followed his mother to Lilly's room. His little sister was in a peaceful sleep, unaware of the changes that night would bring. Gently, Adie picked her daughter up and her eyes opened in wild panic; then, on seeing her mother, she smiled and started to speak. Adie's hand shot forward to cover her daughter's mouth. Lilly was standing now, swaying slightly, sleep still upon her, a puzzled look on her face. Placing her finger against her own lips, Adie indicated for her to be silent.

'Shh! Don't say anything; we are going on an adventure.'

Lilly understood about adventures. Adie had often invented stories and adventures for her children; her method of taking their minds away from the ordeals of their life. While Adie threaded her daughter's arms through the sleeves of her dressing gown, Sam got her winter boots from under the bed.

'Is Daddy coming on our adventure?' whispered Lilly.

'No, just us.'

'Oh! That's good,' she breathed.

They crept down stairs bent on giving them away, each one creaking under their trembling feet. Adie's ears strained for any sound from the bedroom. If he caught them... Panic threatened to break out of her clammy skin. *Just make the next move forward*, she told herself. *Keep thinking about the next thing, nothing else.*

In the hall, buried deep in the under-stair cupboard was a bag of essentials she had been squirrelling away. Crouching on hands and knees, she reached inside for the bag, unaware of the presence of an old saucepan on a shelf above her. Its handle was sticking out and, unwittingly, she caught it with her head. As it crashed to the floor, the sharp sound completely undid her. Rapidly she left the cubbyhole, without the bag, cracking her head on the door jamb and leaving herself woozy. Danger alarms were sounding in her head. Any moment she would hear his voice, and at its sound she knew they would all be paralysed with fear. Failed again. Grabbing Lilly under one arm, and her handbag from the hall table, she ran the two steps to the front door. Opening it, they rushed through, then slowly, quietly, she closed it behind them.

The moon was shining, full, clear and radiant. It flooded the housing estate with silver light, reflecting in frozen puddles and glinting from piles of shovelled snow, offering no cover should he look out of the window. Winter had taken a cold, hard grip.

They slipped and skidded along the icy footpath. Reaching the Morris Minor, with hands shaking, Adie fumbled as she tried to locate the keyhole to unlock the driver's door. Once in the car she began to unravel further, her body quivering. With trembling fingers, she reached out across the vehicle to unlock the passenger door. Sam snatched it open, reached inside to unlock the rear door and almost pushed his sister in. When Adie tried to start the engine, she misjudged the choke and it failed.

In a voice taut with fear Sam said, 'Mum! Get it together, we have to go now; we can't go back. Mum! Do it.'

His voice steadied her enough to start the car and pull away, her foot jerking nervously on the clutch. The windscreen was iced over, and she was unable to see, but there would be no one on the road at this hour. Suddenly there was a glare of headlights and she swerved to miss a passing car full of youths. They shouted abuse and made rude gestures. She could just make out raised fists through open windows.

This startled Lilly. It was as if she had awakened from a dream and was suddenly aware of reality. Sensing that her mother was not in control, she began to panic, screeching high-pitched words without meaning. Eventually, unable to cope with her daughter's distress, Adie snapped at her, but this only made Lilly worse. Sam clambered into the back seat and put his arm around her, calming her until she whimpered quietly and Adie prayed her daughter would not have one of her asthma attacks.

Adie's heart went out to her son. Would he always have to be older than his years? There had been other times when his young arms had comforted Adie herself.

Gradually the ice cleared from the windscreen and, as they drove on, front gardens began to dwindle, semis became terraces and tower blocks loomed. A drunk wandered off the kerb and she had to swerve again. In shop doorways the homeless slept, huddled in their cardboard boxes. They made their way through one of the rougher boroughs of South-East London, into revealing street lights. She hoped it would be for only a short while.

As she drove, her mind strayed. Sometimes, when Bill was in the full throes of his wickedness, he would tell her things, evil things he had done to others. Recoiling in fear and dread, she would then do his bidding. Now she couldn't help thinking about what would happen to them when he caught them, as he surely would. He had caught her so many times before. She forced herself to take a grip, reassuring herself that she was doing the right thing. They were running for their lives, all three of them.

It was her intention not to stay too long in this area. She wanted to find a job in the North, far away down country lanes into darkness, where they wouldn't be found. Darkness had always felt more comforting to her than the glare of street lights. Some people believed that other human beings would help if they knew someone was in trouble. Adie had not found this to be the case. Instead she found that people tended to shut their doors, turn a blind eye and wait for the problem to go away.

It was a one-hour drive to the bedsit she had rented through the *Daily Mirror*'s small advertisements, from someone called Norman. A very long hour. In the back seat the children were asleep. Every so often an unconscious sob escaped from Lilly, each one causing Adie's heart to fracture. Now, as she pootled slowly down the squalid high street, looking for the correct number, her fear and doubts returned. Again, she had to tell herself it would all be worth it.

E VENTUALLY SHE FOUND the number and pulled up at the kerbside. Staring up at a narrow, three-storey Victorian terrace, reluctant to wake the children, she sat quietly for a moment and took stock of their situation. It had taken her just over two years to save enough money to make their escape. She remembered clearly the moment she resolved to leave; it was the first time she saw terror on her children's faces.

Mrs Duncan, the woman she worked for as a cleaner, had asked her if she would stay on and help prepare for a house party she was giving. Adie had arrived home late, about seven in the evening, expecting the children to still be up and looking forward to putting them to bed. She placed her key in the front door and entered the house. Instantly, something in the atmosphere raised the hairs on the backs of her arms. Silence, and a sickly smell of fear in thick air. Containing her instincts and adopting a casual air, she took off her coat, placed her handbag on the hall table and walked into the front room. Bill was in his armchair, a cup of tea on the side table and a newspaper in his hand.

'Where are the children?' she asked.

'All tucked up in bed. I thought you'd be too tired tonight, so I did it for you.' He smiled up at her.

Her stomach turned over. 'I'll just pop up and say goodnight to them.'

Turning on her heel, she left the room quickly, afraid that he would stop her. Upstairs, she went to Sam's room first. He was lying on his back, staring up at the ceiling. She knew he was not all right but, stupidly, asked him if all was well. He nodded silently. She asked again, noiselessly mouthing the words.

Beckoning her to come closer, he whispered, 'Daddy says to tell you I fell down the stairs.' Uncovering himself, he pulled up his pyjama top, revealing blue and red smudges covering his ribs. 'It's worse for Lilly,' he whispered.

She remembered locking down her anger at this point; sewing in another layer of hate. She could not react; it would have been worse for all of them.

Kissing his forehead, she gently stroked his hair and told him, 'I love you, sweetheart.'

Leaving his room with guilt overwhelming her, she wanted to promise him she'd do something. She wanted to make it better, to tell him it would never happen again, but she could say none of those things, guarantee none of those things. Instead she took silent steps to Lilly's room.

Her daughter turned away as she entered, curling up in a tight ball. Adie sat on the bed and stroked her back. The child flinched at her touch.

'It's Mummy,' she said, speaking softly.

Lilly unfurled and turned to look at her. Her little face was ashen with shock and she couldn't speak.

Adie hugged her for a few seconds and then asked, 'Did Daddy hurt you?'

Lilly screwed up her eyes as she lifted her nightdress. Adie balked and shut down, unable to react. She hugged Lilly, and tried to convey words of comfort and hope in that embrace. Then, as she had with her son, she kissed her and left the room, closing the door quietly behind her.

Until then she had thought it was just her own fear she had to contend with. She stood at the top of the stairs, and at that moment something inside her turned. A furnace had been ignited; it might falter, but would never go out until they were free.

She returned to the living room, intending to behave as if nothing was wrong. Then Bill raped her, his unspoken way of telling her that he knew she knew, and there was nothing she could do about it. The rape was not accompanied by his usual level of violence, and instead of closing her eyes she looked directly into his through the whole episode. That seemed to unhinge him a little. When he finished, he pulled up his trousers and walked out of the house.

She remembered being tempted to grab the children and run there and then, but knowledge stopped her. How many times had she tried that before? Going to the police was a waste of time. They always told her that if she didn't go back to her husband, her children would be taken into care. She had no family to run to, only her cousin Bridget. She'd been there once, but Bill had turned up and threatened Bridget and her husband, and after that they didn't want to be involved. She had no friends; Bill had alienated them all throughout the years. It was just Mrs Duncan, the woman she cleaned for, and if she had known, she would've sacked her for sure; she would not have wanted to be involved with the scandal.

So, Adie had sat in her torn, mucky, dishevelled state, thinking; and realised she had to have a proper plan, one that relied on no one else, and enough money to make it work. Slowly, things had started to happen. Mrs Duncan was so pleased with her work that she recommended Adie to her friends, and soon she had cleaning jobs for six days of the week, paid cash in hand. After each morning's work, Bill would take the money from her as soon as she arrived home, but he didn't know how much she earned, so she creamed some off the top of every payment, hiding it in the lining of her shopping trolley.

She remembered feeling it would take forever, at this rate, to have enough to leave. Then, Mrs Duncan gave her a raise, and her other employers followed suit. This extra money went straight behind the lining.

When Bill lost his hod-carrier's job, another fight being the final straw for his employer, she saw her opportunity and told him not to worry; that she'd get some work cleaning offices in the evenings. For some reason he'd agreed. Adie had thought that perhaps it made him feel more secure if her time was occupied. She'd cleaned offices five evenings a week, and although her wages were paid weekly, she was still paid in cash.

THE THOUGHT OF money jolted her back to the present. Her savings would not last long. In less than two weeks, after paying for the room and having the number plate changed on the car, she would run out. She hoped to have moved far away by then, and to have a job. But right now, all of that seemed impossible as she sat in the car outside their temporary lodgings.

She knew they were on the top floor: one large attic room, two beds and a sink. Toilet to share, down one flight on the landing. She had not seen the room; circumstances had not allowed a trip to London. It was just a line advertisement she had seen in the *Daily Mirror*. When she had called the number, Norman, the landlord, had been willing to make all the arrangements over the telephone and agreed that she could send him a postal order. It was cheap; Norman asked no questions and said she could pay weekly. It would have to do.

She was glad it was dark when they first entered the room. The children were too tired to take a good look. When she had managed to settle them together in one of the beds, and they were once again asleep, she sat in an upright chair at the cup-stained, cigarette-stubbed table, and awaited the arrival of a dreary dawn. There was no sleep in her; her mind was still alert and functioning on all levels. She could not stop thinking about what was left to do, running over again and again her actions for the next day.

First, she would go down to the shop she'd noticed on the corner, to get them some breakfast. It was close by and the children would be able to see her from the window. Maybe the people in the shop would know of a garage she could use. She needed to find one of those backstreet garages, to have the number plates changed on Bill's car. She was praying that, with his history, he would not be inclined to report them to the police. After that would come the task of finding a job. She had looked at *The Lady* magazine lying around in Mrs Duncan's home; that seemed to be the one to list ads for live-in housekeepers. Then she would have to sort food as there was no kitchen or cooker in the room. And, lastly, clothes, at least for Lilly, who was still in her nightdress.

W HAT WAS LEFT of the night passed quickly and at seven she woke the children so she could make the most of the day. As they came to full alertness and the realisation that last night had not been just a bad dream, she tried to encourage them.

'Come on, this is going to be a big adventure,' she said, full of enthusiasm.

'I don't like this room,' Lilly said, her lips pouting and eyes roving, penetrating every telling stain.

'But it's only for a short while. Just until I can find us a new home.'

'Without Daddy,' Sam said, looking down at his sister and smiling. For a moment she was still, the pout held on to. Then, slowly, she returned his smile and hugged him. Not another word of complaint was spoken. It was a moment that strengthened Adie's resolve.

From the window, she pointed out the corner shop to the children and explained that she was going to leave them in the room while she ran down the road to get breakfast.

With no coat, by the time she arrived at the shop she was frozen. Inside it was warm and smelt of newly baked bread. It was busy, mostly with men on their way to work, buying their cigarettes and newspaper for the day. She stood at the back of the queue, arms folded around herself, her eyes searching the shelves behind the counter for things she needed. Everyone was dressed for the cold day and she felt out of place in her jeans and jumper. When it was her turn, the plump, turbaned Asian man and his wife, who appeared to be the owners, gave her broad, friendly smiles. Still unconsciously hugging herself, she returned their smiles, not noticing the glance they gave each other. Selecting milk, warm bread, butter, strawberry jam, toothbrushes, toothpaste, soap and a small towel, she was carefully counting out the money to pay when she noticed *The Lady* magazine.

'Oh, and that too,' she said, nodding in its direction.

The Asian man took her money as his wife packed her things into a brown paper bag. They seemed a friendly couple, so Adie asked, 'Is there a garage nearby? You know, one that does small jobs, not too expensive.' Her voice sounded out of place in this guttural region, and inwardly she shrank as she noticed people looking her over.

'There's one around the corner. Just follow the railway arches to the bottom,' the man said quickly, keen to attend to his waiting customers.

'Thank you.'

With her bag of supplies she was relieved to be outside again, and began a brisk walk back to their room.

'Miss, miss.'

She heard someone calling from behind, but chose to ignore it; they couldn't mean her.

'Miss, miss.'

She glanced back and saw the woman from the shop trotting towards her, waving her hand. Adie stopped and waited, and when the woman caught up, she had to lean on her arm and pant for a few moments before she could speak.

'That garage,' she said, handing Adie a piece of paper with directions on it. 'Make sure you ask for Steve; don't deal with Alf, he is not a nice man.'

'Thank you,' Adie said, taking the directions and beginning to walk away.

'Wait.' The woman beckoned for her to return. From around her shoulders she removed her shawl and shoved it into Adie's arms.

Adie tried to give it back to her. 'I can't, it's yours. You'll need it.'

'I have many, it's nothing,' she said, dismissing Adie with a gesture of her hand.

Realising that now was not the time to be proud, Adie accepted the offering and thanked her gratefully. Giving Adie a worried frown, the woman waved a dismissive hand and returned to her shop.

B ACK IN THE room, Adie found dusty cups, plates and cutlery on a shelf. She washed and dried them, and they ate their bread, butter and jam. Then once again she had to leave the children alone while she took her car to the garage.

The hastily drawn map took her down a narrow side street, not much more than an alley. On one side, archways formed a support for the railway above. Each archway contained a small business: coal merchants, blacksmiths, carpenters, local builders; there was much activity about the place. On the other side, a scrap metal dealer with its towers of twisted material ran the length of the lane. The road was in such bad repair that the ruts and potholes were unavoidable, and try as she might, at one point she noisily scraped the undercarriage of her car.

'You wanna mind the 'oles, luv!' a voice shouted.

'I could drive it for you if you're strugglin',' another chimed in.

Grimacing at the sound of grinding metal, she ignored them and drove on. For a moment she was troubled and began to feel intimidated by the surroundings. Then she looked at them, and told herself that these men were industrious, working; they probably had families to support and she was not to be afraid of them. They were pussycats compared to Bill.

The garage was at the dead end of the lane. It was larger than any of the other businesses, encompassing two of the arches and a lean-to building. She parked in a corner and walked towards one of the arches. A flash of welding torches caught her eye and she could hear the sound of banging against metal. Reaching a little doorway, she looked inside; there was a desk covered in paperwork, marked with oily fingerprints. On the walls were large posters of women pouting their lips; thrusting their naked breasts; arching their bodies. Listening to The Rolling Stones – 'Little Red Rooster' competing with the general racket, she waited for someone to approach her, conscious that she was being appraised.

'Marks out of ten? What do you reckon?' one of the men shouted above the din.

'Nine,' came the reply.

'Nah! Six. Too skinny,' bellowed another.

'Yeah, no tits.' Another voice.

'I'd rather do 'er than you,' was the next comment.

'You don't wanna mind them, luv. It's just their bit of banter. Harmless, really. What can I do you for?'

The voice had come from close behind her, momentarily startling her. Turning, she saw a man whose shirt would not button over his hanging belly, and whose sweaty odour was overpowering.

'Are you Steve?'

'Nah.'

'Are you Alf?' she asked, maintaining a strong composure.

'You've found me, darling. So, what is it you want me for?'

'Oh, actually, it's Steve I wanted to talk to. I'll come back later.' As she turned around to head for her car, Alf took hold of her elbow.

'But I heard you ask for me. You don't want to be frightened of me; I'll do anything you want for a little payment. Now, you show me your car and tell me what you want. I know we can come to an arrangement.' Giving her elbow a little squeeze, he guided her to the car. 'Now, what's the problem?' he asked, soft-voiced and stooping lower to look into her eyes.

'There's nothing wrong with my car,' she said, truthfully. 'It's something personal I have to discuss with Steve.' With this lie she extracted herself from him, raised her eyes to look directly into his, and in a clear voice asked, 'Do you know when he'll be back?'

'Dunno, luv, dunno. What's so special about him?' His eyes scanned her from head to toe, hovering over her chest and mouth.

Recoiling, she climbed into her car. 'No, that's fine,' she said. 'I'll call back later.'

Turning out of the garage, she began to pick her way back up the lane. Twice she scraped the bottom of her car on the rugged road and admonished herself for not taking better care. She felt close to tears and tried to tell herself that it was not such a bad problem, that she would just have to go back later. Unable to console herself, she couldn't stop the tears. It was not because of Alf that she cried; it was fear. Fear of what she had brought them to, fear of the past, fear of going back, and fear of the future. She scraped the bottom of her car for a third time, and then, when she was nearly at the junction, a car turned into the lane, blocking her exit.

Gulping her tears down, she waved angrily at the driver, shouting at him to reverse. He shrugged his shoulders, palms raised, indicating that he could not reverse into the busy traffic of the main road. Looking down, she tried to get her car into reverse gear, but for some reason it would not go. She kept repeating the actions, and each time the gearbox of the Morris Minor protested with an angry crunching sound.

Then there was a tap on the window. 'Would you like me to do it for you?'

'No,' she shouted back, far too loudly. Then she burst into tears, and was embarrassed but could not stop herself.

The man tapped on the window again. She looked up and saw that now another car was waiting behind the first one.

'Let me do it for you; I promise I won't bite.'

His voice was kind, not mocking, so she unlocked the door and made to get out of the car.

'Move over into the other seat; it's far too cold to get out. And anyway, you don't want this lot to see you crying,' he said, indicating the men working nearby.

In her diminished state she did as she was told. It was not as if he could drive away with the road blocked. Smoothly, he manoeuvred her car out of the way, then parked his own in front of hers, allowing the waiting car to pass.

She was still sat in the passenger seat blowing her nose when he tapped on the driver's window again. She leant across and wound it down. Placing his hand through the window, he introduced himself.

'Hi, I'm Steve and I run the garage at the other end. You have a leak of some sort. It'll probably be all right for a short while, but you'll have to get it done. I expect it was caused by driving up this lane too fast.'

Inhaling deeply, she managed to stop this bad news from making her cry again.

'Is it all right if I sit in here with you for a minute?'

She nodded her reply.

He seemed so kind that she found herself telling him a brief version of her story, and about needing another number plate. He listened, silent until she had finished. Then, after thinking for a moment, he told her the story of his wife, and how she had escaped with her children from a violent man.

'So, here's my plan,' he said. 'I personally will carry out the work. I suspect the leak is just your radiator. The number plates won't be a problem. I won't charge for the leak, just the number plates; I feel like the leak is my fault anyway for not being there and you having to put up with that slob Alf.'

'Thank you so much. Shall I drive the car down to you now?'

'No, we'll leave it here for now. I'll drive you home and deliver the car to you in three days. Will that be all right?'

'Yes, of course. Are you sure?'

'Yeah, I'm sure. There's nothing I hate more than men treating women badly. These kids of yours, did you manage to bring any of their stuff?'

'No, in the end I couldn't risk bringing anything, just ourselves. I'm hoping to go shopping later today to buy them some clothes at least. Poor Lilly is still in her nightdress.'

'A boy and a girl, you said; ten and seven?'

'Yes, that's right.'

'C'mon.' He got out of the car, indicating for her to accompany him. 'We'll go see my missus now; she's always got too much for the kids. I've got four now, what with her original ones and then our own.'

'Oh, no, really, that's too good of you. I can't,' she said.

He waved away her words and beckoned her to follow.

'But I must go back to my children; I've left them for far too long as it is.'

'That's no problem. We'll go past your place and pick them up.'

'But surely we can't land on your wife at such short notice?'

'She'll be fine. Salt of the earth, she is. If I told her your story and she found out I'd just let you go, I'd be for the high jump. Now, come on, let's go and get your kids.'

Steve was as good as his word. That evening they were delivered back to their room, having eaten a cooked meal and been supplied with spare clothes and books to read. He and his wife had even apologised that their house was not big enough to accommodate them. Their kindness fed Adie's parched soul and softened some of its bitter edges.

———*—*—*———

F OR THE SECOND morning, Bill reached out across the empty bed and a little trickle of dread crept down his spine. If she wasn't back by midday, he'd go to the police.

Yesterday, even before he'd got out of bed, the silence and stillness of the house told him she had gone. Once up, he'd wandered slowly about their home, looking in wardrobes and drawers. The door of the hall cupboard had been slightly ajar. Intrigued, he'd rummaged in its depths, knowing this was her hiding space for Christmas presents and such.

The discarded bag told him she had taken no clothes, food, or even Lilly's asthma medication. In fact, nothing at all for the children. A smile came to him then. He realised that either she would be back very soon, or his story of an unstable, possibly dangerously insane wife running off with his precious children would be plausible.

She had left him before, of course, but never in the middle of the night. Once she had returned voluntarily without him even needing to look; women couldn't survive on their own. She had been to the police before, but they had always persuaded her to return. Whatever the situation she had always been back by the following day.

There had been many women before, all short term. They were disposable in one way or another. Adie was different. There was goodness in her on which he fed. He needed her for that. The first time they met it was like he had been struck. Not just by her looks, but by something that emanated from her and spoke to him. He had been instantly obsessed and tried to walk away, but his legs had become stone. The vulnerability of it turned him pale and weak, and ever since he'd had to beat down this pathetic exposure.

She served him in ways that no other human being had done. When he was with her, he had better control over the hated voices in his head, so that they didn't rule him all of the time. His very survival depended on her.

With his temper and his history, he'd never held a job for long. When she had first started the cleaning work, he had been frightened that her confidence would grow, and she'd leave him. But in the end, he'd encouraged her to get more work, wanting her to be too busy and exhausted to think of anything else.

Looking after his children while his wife worked was not a man's intended role, but it didn't bother him what people thought. The important thing was to be with his son and daughter as much as possible, knowing she wouldn't leave without them. He'd always thought of her as virtuous, but now he saw that she had a cunning side.

He would find her, no matter what. Nothing would get in his way, even if he did have to go to the police and play the part of the charming, worried, family man. He would get them to return her; she was, after all, his property.

The police station was at the far end of the High Street, which would make it a long walk through the town, but Bill was glad of it. It would give him time to think, to fully immerse himself in the character he was going to be when he spoke to the sergeant on duty. But before he did that, he needed to run through the events of that morning, so that each moment could be filed away and stored in his memory until it was needed. That need would come when he took payment for his suffering.

REACHING THE HALFWAY point along the High Street, he stopped and sat on a bench, lit a cigarette and took a long, deep drag. It was time to change persona. He had bathed, shaved and put on fresh clothes. Nothing too smart; a working man's look. He didn't want to seem too capable; he wanted the policeman's sympathy. By the time he'd finished his cigarette he had absorbed his adopted role.

As he climbed the steps to the entrance of the police station, he mentally checked his face and stooped his great height and shoulders just a little. It wasn't easy for him to appear vulnerable.

Inside, a sergeant stood behind the counter checking through some paperwork. Bill waited, chin down, looking at his hands as they nervously worried each other, remaining respectfully back until the officer looked up and said, 'Yes, sir, what can I do for you?'

'It's my wife, sir,' Bill blurted out. 'She's gone, taken the kids. Been two days now.'

The sergeant sighed and raised a hand. Bill ceased to speak; he had expected this reaction.

'Had an argument, did you? I expect she's gone to her mother's, so I should look there first. She'll be back;

they always come back. Now, I'm afraid we here in the police force do not have the time to go chasing after errant wives, so while you have my every sympathy with your predicament, I suggest you go and look a bit harder for her. Just say you're sorry, even if it wasn't your fault – they like that.' The sergeant lowered his head to his paperwork.

Bill persisted, took a step forward, placed his fingertips on the counter and looked at the sergeant with appealing eyes. 'Sorry, sir, but you don't understand. She went in the middle of the night, you see. She took no clothes or food for the kids, and she took my car.'

The sergeant frowned and opened his mouth to speak. But before he had a chance to say anything, Bill, with a measured crack in his voice, continued. 'And she forgot to take Lilly's asthma inhaler. This is the second day she's been gone, and I know my little girl will be stressed; she always has an asthma attack when she's stressed.' Bill had now worked himself up, and managed to produce a few tears. 'I've been worried about her, you see – my wife, I mean. She hasn't been very stable lately, forgetting to do the cleaning and that. Sometimes I've had to cook the tea and put the kids to bed while she just sits there, staring into space. I tell you, she's not right in the head, and I'm worried. What if Lilly has an attack? What will she do without her inhaler? She could die. And my wife, what if she's gone insane? What if she's dangerous?'

The sergeant lifted the flap in the counter and came through the gap to give him some comfort. He showed Bill into a side room, sat him down at a table and offered him a cigarette. Bill accepted it with a shaking hand.

'Stay there; I'll get you a cup of tea.'

Bill waited, motionless until the sergeant returned with a mug of steaming tea. Dragging on his cigarette, he ran his other hand through his hair and stared at the table, aware of the scrutiny from the sergeant, who finally spoke.

'So, have you looked for her? What about her family and friends – she could have gone to one of them, right?'

'She hasn't got any family, they're all dead, and no friends. Like I said, she's not very stable; she doesn't seem to make friends. I've tried to encourage her, taken her out to meet people, but she just wants to stay in, sat in the chair and staring, not even watching the telly. I don't know where to look for her.'

'Right, this is what we are going to do,' the sergeant said. 'You are going to give me all the details and then I'll put someone on to it. You will go home and stay put, and when your wife returns, as I expect she will, you will let us know immediately, do you hear me?'

'Yes, I will. Do you really think she'll come back? Only the kids are meant to be back in school after the Christmas holidays.' Bill looked up, adopting a hopeful expression.

'I expect so; they usually do. It was probably Christmas that took her over the top – you know, makes people think about family and get emotional.'

'You may be right.'

'The main reason I'm taking this on is because your daughter is asthmatic. Still, I expect it will be a waste of police time, so just make sure you let us know if she returns.'

Half an hour later Bill was on his way home, smiling to himself with satisfaction and proud of his acting skills.

Next, he had to visit the school. He wished he could see Adie's face when the police found her – she would never believe that he had gone to them for help.

L AWRENCE AND JONESY were in the pub mulling over old CID cases; ones that would probably never be solved. They often shared time over a drink at their local. Sergeant Jones was a worldly sort with a bulbous drinker's nose, a heavyset body and a cigarette permanently dangling from his lips. He was non-judgemental and accepting of most human flaws. Basically, if he could heal a wrongdoer rather than charge him, he would. And Lawrence knew he had a good nose for the real nasty ones.

There was no doubting that Detective Inspector Lawrence Appleby was odd. As if being mentally astute, teetotal, a non-smoker and immaculately dressed wasn't enough, he held a black belt in ju-jitsu. These quirks made his colleagues feel uncomfortable in his company, but not Sergeant Jones. Jonesy was Lawrence's extra pair of eyes and ears. He updated him on everything that presented at his reception desk, but didn't always get passed on to CID. Also, Jonesy kept him informed about stuff his colleagues did not tell him.

Lawrence had been raised a Catholic and, although lapsed, his priest was a frequent visitor to his home. His parents had expected great things from him – to become a doctor like his father, or lawyer, maybe. But Lawrence always wanted to be a detective, right from when he was a boy and filled the wartime days of his childhood reading detective stories. His only regret was that he had never allowed himself to get married and have a child.

Lawrence was still thinking about the past when he realised that Jonesy had moved on to new cases. He liked to know the latest. Most of his colleagues didn't waste their time on trivia, believing it all to be just menial stuff for the uniforms to deal with. But he had often picked up a hint, a sniff or even a lead from talking to Jonesy. Right now, Jonesy was on his second pint and in full flow about a man who, earlier that day, had reported his wife missing.

'He reckoned she was off her trolley. Driven off without the kid's inhaler in the middle of the night. He sat crying in my interview room, saying she might be a danger to her nippers. We're out looking for them now, of course.'

'She must have been desperate to go off in the middle of the night like that,' Lawrence said, picking up his lemonade.

'Yeah, maybe. Or run off to her lover. Has no friends or family, apparently.' Jonesy grew silent and dragged on his cigarette.

The faces of many desperate women Lawrence had interviewed in the past flashed through his mind. Their blind fear haunted him. They never had friends, and if they had family, they were not allowed to see them.

'There was something not quite right about him,' Jonesy continued, almost as if talking to himself. 'But I can't quite put my finger on it.'

—⚔⚔⚔—

Later that night, back in his flat, faces stopped Lawrence from sleeping. Parents, good people. Their shock, their horror and complete devastation. The look on a father's face after he had identified his daughter's body. Daughters who had been wives, who had reported violent husbands and been sent home and told to be good. Those faces would live with him forever.

During his long career he'd seen many despairing women, often with children in tow. Some broke away, usually to the arms of another man because they didn't have the means to support themselves. Typically, they ended up back with their husbands, resigned to regular beatings and whatever other humiliations their men imposed on them. It was the ones who went back and ended up dead; they were the ones Lawrence could not forget. He would not give up on them. Their faces woke him in the night.

On their third night in the room, shortly after the children had gone to bed, Adie could no longer keep her eyes open and fell into a deep sleep. She was woken by her arm being vigorously shaken.

'Mum, Mum! Wake up!'

In an instant she was conscious and looking into her son's face. She stood up too quickly and, with a wobble, sat back down on the bed.

'Where's Lilly's inhaler? She's having an asthma attack.'

'I packed it in the...' She couldn't remember where she had packed it. Standing once again, she glanced at Lilly and saw that her lips had a blue tinge and her short breaths wheezed their way out. In panic, Adie rummaged through her handbag, then tipped its contents onto the floor and sorted the items. It was not there. Then her mind cleared, and she could see the inhaler in the bag that she had left behind.

'Mum, what shall we do? She's getting worse.'

'Sit her up,' instructed Adie, still on her knees searching amongst the debris for the lavender oil she always carried. Finding it, she sat on the bed and put drops of the calming oil on her daughter's nightdress, then undid a few of the top buttons. Sam knelt on the floor next to his sister and held her hand.

'It'll be all right, sweetheart,' said Adie in a soothing voice, although inside she wasn't so sure. 'Now, come on; try to slow your breathing down. Think about the pretty new home in the country we're going to have.'

Lilly's tiny chest was rising and falling at a rapid rate and her frightened eyes looked to her mother for further guidance.

'What will our home look like?' asked Adie. 'Picture it. Will it be a cottage?'

Lilly nodded her answer.

'And will it have lots of pretty flowers in the garden?'

Again, the nod came.

'And a big tree for Sam to climb?'

'Yeah, and maybe we could build a treehouse,' Lilly's brother joined in.

They carried on like that, building their perfect home, planning their new life, until eventually Adie saw that her daughter's breathing was slowing, and her lips were returning to their normal shade of pink.

'And you'd like to go horse riding, wouldn't you?' she asked, hoping Lilly would speak her reply. 'What sort of horse would you like to ride?' Seeing that she was still too frightened to talk, Adie answered for her. 'One of the camel-coloured ones with the white mane and tail, or is it the black-and-white one? I can't remember the proper name for them.'

'Palomino or piebald,' Lilly answered, smiling through a whispery voice.

Thirty minutes later, and, after Adie had assured her that she would not leave her side, Lilly was asleep. Sam had fallen asleep on the floor and he barely stirred as his mother lifted him onto the bed, alongside his sister.

After covering them with the woollen shawl given to her by the lady from the shop, Adie once again sat by the window, staring out at the cold night with a thin, moth-eaten blanket around her. Thoughts sped through her mind. How could she have been so stupid to have left Lilly's inhaler? This room was damp and mouldy; she had to get them out of here as soon as possible. They couldn't see a local doctor – it was too much of a risk, and may arouse suspicions. She was not sure if a chemist would sell her an inhaler, and if he did, would he want details of their doctor?

For a moment she pondered returning to the house and sneaking in when Bill was out. She would go in, get the inhaler and leave; he wouldn't even know she had been back. As fast as she thought it, she dismissed it. Round and round her thoughts went until, eventually, she had fallen into a kind of sleep.

———✳✳✳———

S HE WOKE, STRICKEN and unsure why. A pain shot through her neck, which had spent hours in an awkward position. Then she heard the rasping. Dashing to the bed, she saw that her daughter was blue, her eyes wide, and she knew they needed to get help. Sam was in a deep sleep. She nudged him awake while putting on her shoes and coat and wrapping Lilly in the shawl. Sam put on his clothes over his pyjamas. A strange calm shrouded their inner panic.

'We'll get a taxi to the nearest hospital,' Adie said.

Sam led the way down the four flights of stairs. Outside, the cold air shocked them, and she felt Lilly's body stiffen in her arms. Although she knew it would be ineffective, she tried to warm the air her daughter inhaled by holding her face close to her. At the kerbside she glanced quickly to and fro, desperate to see a black cab. Sam spotted one, but it did not have its light on. Even so, he ran into the road to wave the cabby down, and Adie was afraid for his safety. But the driver spotted her with Lilly in her arms, and pulled up to the kerb.

'The hospital,' she said, as they climbed into the back.

'No problem, love. Should only take a couple of minutes this time of night.'

They sat in silence while the cabby concentrated on driving too fast and Lilly's breathing became shallower. In a very short time, they turned a corner and she saw the lights of Accident & Emergency.

'No need to pay me,' the cabby said. 'I could do with a bit more in my favour if I'm gonna get to heaven.'

Adie's crooked smile thanked him and they clambered out of the cab.

'I hope the nipper will be all right,' he shouted after them, as they ran to the doors.

Inside, a nursing sister instantly saw their plight. Taking Lilly in her arms, she indicated for Adie to follow. Adie grabbed Sam's hand and they trailed after the nurse, determined not to be separated.

They were led into a cubicle where there was oxygen available.

'Come on, sweetie,' the nurse said, as she gently laid Lilly on the bed. 'We'll soon have you feeling better.' Smoothing the curly tendrils back from Lilly's forehead, she placed the oxygen mask over her face.

Adie took a step forward, wanting to be at her daughter's side, but the nurse stopped her, firmly gripping her upper arm. Sam took his mother's place next to his sister.

The nurse studied Adie's face for a moment before letting her go. Briskly, she checked Lilly and said, 'Doctor will be with you shortly', then left the cubicle.

Pulling up another chair, Adie joined Sam at Lilly's side. The three of them held hands. They did not speak. The wait seemed to go on forever. Lilly's colour returned and she gave her mother a faint smile, a little squeeze of her hand, then closed her eyes – not sleeping, but resting her exhausted body. Sam had already dozed off, his head having fallen forward onto the bed.

The hospital was quiet at this hour and Adie's nerves were taut enough to snap. She used to cherish a little bit of silence and solitude; now she had to live with judgemental thoughts picking through her every action. Maybe their broken lives were her fault. Look at where they were now, here in this hospital; that was her fault. Taking them to live in a damp room; that was her fault. Her children deserved a better mother. Maybe Bill wouldn't be violent with another woman. She tried to reason with herself, but wicked pessimism was running through her. If only she could empty her mind.

But she couldn't, and it took her back to the night she and Bill met. It had been a couple of months after her father had died in a road accident. Friends had dragged her out for the evening, believing it was what she needed. They went to a pub. Bill was there, tall and charming, older than her, but still looking good with his (what she thought of then as) smiley blue eyes. He had flattered her, flirted with her and made her feel good. If only she had walked away from him then, but, being vulnerable, she was perfect prey for his manipulation. Having spent the first twenty years of her life relying on her father's protection from her mother, she was, unknowingly, looking for another male protector. What had happened to the man she'd met then? Was it her fault he'd turned so nasty?

The doctor arrived, followed by the nursing sister, and she hauled her thoughts back to the present. He was a mature man, perhaps at the end of his career. He said nothing but moved directly towards Lilly to check all her vital signs. Satisfied, he removed the oxygen mask and she opened her eyes. He smiled at her and ruffled her already tousled hair.

Sam raised his head, blinking his eyes as they adjusted to the light.

Turning to Adie, the doctor held out his hand. 'Mrs…?'

'Lewis,' she replied.

'The sister and I have been talking and we believe this person to be you.' He handed her a telex printout. 'And now that you have confirmed your name, I see it is you.'

---

*S*USSEX *C*ONSTABULARY *A*RE *searching for a mother and her two children. They left the Bartenden area in the early hours of Monday morning driving a black Morris Minor, registration plate CHL 791, with red interior.*

Mother, Mrs Adie Lewis, dark hair, 5'4", age 31, of slim build. Daughter, Lilly, long, fair, curly hair, 7 years old, suffers from asthma. Son, Samuel, dark hair, 10 years old.

Mother left home with her two children, taking her husband's car. She left without her daughter's asthma medication or any other basic needs. It is believed she may be mentally unstable. Due to the above situation she may seek the assistance of a hospital. We ask you to inform us should she attend your facility.

'SHOULD I INFORM the police?' the doctor continued. Adie was dumbfounded, open-mouthed and silent. Had Bill gone to the police? Unbelievably, he must have.

It was Sam who jumped in with an emphatic, 'No!'

'Why not, young man?'

'Because sometimes Dad hits Mum so hard I think he's going to kill her. And he goes in Lilly's bedroom and frightens her.' Sam's voice started loud, full of rage, and then it trailed off as he said, 'And he hits me and frightens me too.'

The doctor put his hand on Sam's shoulder to quieten him. 'Sister, will you arrange some breakfast for these two youngsters, and some for Mrs Lewis, while I have a chat with her?'

He indicated for Adie to go with him, but she stood her ground, not wishing to be separated from the children.

'I assure you that I will not inform the police or anyone of your whereabouts without telling you first.'

Unsure if she believed him, she felt she had no option but to go with him. She did not want to seem unreasonable or, worse, unstable. They left the cubicle and, a short distance down the corridor, entered a small office.

'I would like to hear your story. You could start by telling me if what your son said is true.'

Adie was about to speak when a nurse entered with tea, toast and cereal on a tray. To her embarrassment, her stomach grumbled. The doctor smiled at her and then she told him their story – briefly, but the whole thing, from her father's death, to meeting Bill, to now.

When she finished talking, he said, 'The sister and I have made sure that no paperwork has been completed with regard to your visit here today. In a moment she will bring several inhalers for you. I hope that in a happier future you will not need them. When you are ready, if you like, we can show you an exit from the hospital that is the furthest from the one you entered by. Or, we can fill in the registration forms and I can call Sussex Constabulary if that is what you want.'

Adie chose the first option.

When they returned to the cubicle the sister gave her three inhalers. Adie placed them in her handbag. The children were looking at her with eager faces. Lilly had a moustache of milk on her upper lip; it made Adie smile.

'OK. Are you ready to go?' she asked them.

Scrambling down from the treatment bed, Lilly declared she was ready, then had to steady herself as she experienced a giddy moment.

'Not so fast,' the doctor said, taking hold of her.

The sister left the cubicle and returned a moment later with a wheelchair. 'You can ride in here, just to the exit. You should be all right by then.'

With the nurse pushing Lilly, they marched off at a brisk pace down several corridors, through many sets of double doors and past numerous ward entrances. Eventually, they arrived at a heavy, single blue door. Passing through into a dimly lit, warm room, the smell of disinfectant left them to be replaced by a whiff of oil. Inside there was a continuous whirring noise.

'Her giddiness seems to have abated,' the doctor said as Lilly rose from the chair.

Shaking his hand, Adie told him, 'I do not know how to thank you.'

'You can thank me by making good your escape,' he said. 'I have worked too long in this dense borough. Seen too many beaten women and children. Seen some returned to their husbands only to end up in our mortuary. I am too old to obey rules that do not work.' His eyes were tired and sad. 'Stay safe,' he said, letting go of her hand. He turned and was gone, so that she was left staring into the space he had left behind.

The sister tapped her on the shoulder, and they made their way, ducking under heavy pipework, towards a door that led outside. Finding themselves in a narrow alley, the sister pointed the way to the main road and wished them luck. Then she, too, was gone.

Looking up to the narrow strip of sky between the buildings, Adie saw that dawn was breaking.

'Come on,' she said, picking up Lilly and marching off up the alley. Sam fell in behind her.

WHEN THEY EMERGED from the gloom of the tall buildings, the rumble of traffic and bustle of people assaulted them. Adie tried to get her bearings, but it was not a road she recognised. Seeing a bus approaching with *Egon Arches* on its sign, she asked Lilly, 'Can you run?' Lilly nodded and Adie put her down, grabbed both children's hands and they ran towards the stop. As they approached it the bus began to slowly pull away and all three of them had to scramble aboard the open back. They sat on one of the long seats and Lilly curled up on her mother's lap. The rhythmic sound of the bus engine as it slowly changed up through the gears was soporific and Adie's tired body sank into the seat.

'Where are we going, Mum?' Sam asked.

'We'll get off at Egon Arches; that's where the car is.'

The conductor approached them and took their fare. When she had moved on and was out of earshot, Adie continued. 'I want to see if Steve can get the car ready a day early. The sooner we head north the better; as far north as we can go, as far away from here as possible.'

'But what if the car isn't ready? Didn't Steve say it would take three days?'

'Yes, he did, but I'm hoping he's managed to do it earlier.' She thought for a moment, then spoke again. 'We have to go back to the room to get our things. We'll do that as soon as we've spoken to Steve.'

The bus trundled on, stopping every few hundred yards to let people on or off. It felt as if the journey would go on forever. The clothes they wore were ill-fitting. The coat Steve's wife had given Adie was too large and kept slipping off her shoulders; her hand shook each time she adjusted it. Other passengers seemed to be looking at them, curious expressions on their faces.

Eventually, they arrived at Egon Arches and the three of them picked their way down the rutted lane. It was still early, so there was no calling out from the men as there had been during her previous visit. When they neared the double arches of Steve's workplace, she was relieved to see him there. He looked up and saw them approaching.

'What's happened?' he asked.

She explained their predicament and their need to get away.

'The car's not ready yet. I've done the leak, but it's the number plate. I have to wait for the right situation, if you get my meaning. There's supposed to be one turning up this afternoon, but that's not guaranteed.' He stopped talking and rubbed his chin in concentration.

Adie was physically and mentally exhausted, out of ideas. Lilly clung to her leg, and even Sam was drooping.

Then Steve's face reanimated. 'Right, you and the kids can stay in my staffroom. It ain't very nice, you know, what with blokes using it.'

Interrupting him, she said, 'We have to go back to our room now, to get our things. I'm worried the police will trace us there, so we have to vacate it.'

Steve thought again. 'What if I drive you over to your room?' he said, taking in their exhausted appearance. 'Because I am going to have to chase up this number plate to get any chance of finishing the car today. You could get your gear together and I'll pick you up on the way back.'

'Thank you,' was all she could say.

Spreading his arms, he herded them towards his car. 'It's open, get in; I'll be with you as soon as I can.'

ALL WENT TO plan, and when Steve returned to pick them up from their room and they were back in his car, he winked at Adie and reached beneath his seat. With a boyish grin on his face, he slid a number plate out, winked again and returned it to its hiding place. Never before in her life had she done anything that even remotely broke the law; now it seemed she had not only stolen her husband's car, but obtained illegal number plates for it. Instead of worrying about this, she was relieved.

Back at the garage, Steve showed them the staffroom and apologised for the state of it. It had no windows and the smell of sweat and cigarettes hung in the air. Some black plastic-coated chairs surrounded a filthy table with an overflowing ashtray and several dirty tea and coffee mugs. Adie did not care about the dirt.

'Is Alf still working for you?' she asked.

'You'll be pleased to know that Alf has left, and I've got a new trainee to take his place. Ray!' he shouted over the din of the workshop. A lanky youth in tattered jeans and a leather biker jacket came to his bidding. 'Nip down the road, will you, and get three lots of fish and chips and three cans of Coke.' He stuffed a five-pound note into the youth's hand. 'Is Coke all right or do you want lemonade? I'd offer you tea, but you've seen the state of the cups.'

'Oh, there's no need. You've done enough already,' Adie said.

'Coke or lemonade?' he asked the children.

'Coke,' was their happy reply. It was gone lunchtime and they must be hungry; she could not deny them. And anyway, she had a long journey ahead of her, probably through the night, and no resistance left for things of little consequence.

'Stay here. Eat your fish and chips when it comes, and I'll see you when the car is done.'

With that he closed the door, shutting out the noises of the garage. In this claustrophobic room, lit by a single bare light bulb, fear and doubt engulfed Adie again. Here she was, in a filthy room with her children, one poorly. They had no home, only a little money, and were relying on the help of strangers. What sort of danger was she putting her children in now? Her hands started to shake. She tried and failed to hold them still in her lap. Sam noticed, placed his hands over hers, and held them still for her.

After about twenty minutes Ray returned with their fish, chips and Coke. They ate in silence, and then the three of them could stay awake no longer.

I T WAS 4.30 in the afternoon when Adie was woken by Steve's wife.

'All right love?' she asked softly.

The depth of her sleep had left Adie groggy and she could only nod in return.

'Steve sent the boy round and he told me you were here, so I brought down some clean cups and a teapot. Thought you'd need a good strong brew. Now, I've made it milky and sweet for the kiddies; that's how mine like it.' She woke the children and they sat with hands cradling warm cups of tea. 'I've got to go now, get back to the kids

– you know how it is. Anyway, I hope you get on all right.'
She headed for the door.

Quickly, Adie rose to her feet. 'I can't thank you and Steve enough for everything you've done.'

'No need, love; been there myself, so I couldn't turn my back on you, could I?'

The car was ready, but on Steve's instructions they did not leave until after the rush hour. In the passenger seat Adie noticed three small packages wrapped in tinfoil, and a flask. She was about to thank Steve, but he spoke first.

'If you thank me again, I'll give you away to the police myself!'

He repeated the directions to Barnet, where she was to join the A6 and follow it north.

———※———※———

L AWRENCE HIT THE alarm button before it sounded. Rising naked from his bed, he drank a glass of water and began his morning routine of physical exercise. A night of interrupted sleep had left him hollow-eyed, but as soon as he started the movements his body and mind settled, absorbed in perfecting his technique.

He was early as he walked the dark streets towards the station. It was foggy, but this didn't bother him; he could have walked this route blindfolded. Turning the last corner, he saw the entrance lights of the station illuminating its red brick.

'Telex from Greenwich Station,' said Jonesy, waving it at Lawrence.

Having stopped at the reception desk, Lawrence wanted only to have a quick glance at the overnight entries in the casebook.

'Remember that Mrs Adie Lewis I told you about? Seems she may have been spotted carrying her daughter into the A&E of Greenwich Hospital. Receptionist says she saw them go in but didn't see them leave. Apparently, there's no paperwork, and they're not there now. I'll give the boys at Greenwich a call, see what else they know.'

'Good,' Lawrence said over his shoulder, on the way to his office.

At his desk he took out the files of the women and children he'd let down. The ones whose murders he'd not prevented, and whose murderers he had not found. He couldn't give up, even when ordered to by his superintendent. Some of the files were more than ten years old, but Lawrence couldn't let them rest in unsolved graves. Slowly he thumbed through them; the details were all familiar to him. The conversation with Jonesy last night had stirred him up and made him drag these unfortunates out this morning. If only he could settle just one of them, maybe he could sleep. But he stared at them blankly, guiltily, knowing he had nothing more to offer them. Then he opened the bottom drawer of his desk where they lived, patted the pile into a neat oblong and returned it to the 'don't waste time' drawer.

Looking at the pinboard that held the paraphernalia of his latest case, he tried to concentrate on that. Noticing that some of the photographs of the crime scene had not arrived in his office, he went back to Jonesy to enquire as to their whereabouts.

'It was her,' Jonesy said, as Lawrence approached. 'But she made off as soon as the daughter was better. She got the medication and left through a boiler room.'

'Did they find the paperwork on her?' Lawrence asked.

'Nope. When the local bobby's questioned the receptionist, she said there had been an error because the night receptionist was not at her desk when they came in. Looks like they might have a lead on the car, though. One of their informers got the sack from his job, wants to shop his old boss. He used to work at a garage that handles all sorts of illegal work. Apparently, the latest car to be worked on was a Morris Minor fitting the description given by the husband. It's been given a false set of number plates.'

'Seems like this Mrs Lewis is pretty clever,' said Lawrence.

'Yeah, she's sharp all right,' said Jonesy. 'You know what, though?' he continued, in his thinking voice. 'That husband of hers, he's still bothering me... there's something about him.'

Lawrence forgot about the photographs. When Jonesy was bothered by someone, it bothered him. 'What does he look like?'

'Tall, blond, thickset sort of fella. Blue-eyed, the sort women would go for. Something didn't fit about him. That donkey jacket didn't look right on him for a start. His hands didn't look like they did any hard labour.'

Jonesy was still looking up to the ceiling, thinking his slow, methodical thoughts, when Lawrence left him and returned to his office. He opened the 'don't waste time' drawer and took out the files. Had he allowed his mind to become stale over the years? Here was a possible lead and he had almost ignored it. Going through the files, he scrutinised every page, picking them over in fine detail as he had done many times before. Of the eight files there were only two that had descriptions of a possible suspect; neither of them fitted. Lawrence put the files back together and was about to slide them into the drawer, when a photograph slipped out and landed, face up, on the floor.

It was a black and white picture of a young man. The fellow was probably blond, and if he was blond, he could be blue-eyed. Tall, judging by the two other men in the photograph, but very thin. Lawrence knew which file it went in. This was the bereft boyfriend of a murdered young woman. The case was fourteen years old.

He opened the folder to refresh his memory. The woman had received a blow to the face, probably from a fist, causing her to fall and hit her head against a heavy piece of furniture. It was this that killed her by triggering a brain bleed. For a while the young man had been a suspect. In the end, his story about popping out for a packet of cigarettes, and returning to her home to find her dead on the kitchen floor and the house ransacked, was corroborated by the shopkeeper, and eventually believed by the police.

Lawrence continued to go through the file, inspecting each piece of evidence minutely. When he picked up what he thought was the last piece of paper, a scrap, torn from a notebook, was left lying on the buff folder. He turned it over to reveal what could have been Jonesy's handwriting. It said, *There's something about this chap, but I can't put my finger on it.*

Lawrence took the photo and the scrap of paper to the reception desk. 'Jonesy, is this your writing?'

Taking it between his forefinger and thumb to examine it, Jonesy held it high, and gave it a little wave as if drying wet ink. 'Bit flimsy; must be years old. Where did you get that from?'

'Never mind that. Is it your writing?'

'Looks like it.'

'And could this be the fellow who reported his wife missing yesterday?' Lawrence placed the photograph on the desk.

Jonesy took his time. He picked up the picture and took it to the window. 'I remember this one. His girlfriend was murdered about fifteen years ago.'

'Fourteen,' said Lawrence.

'It could be him. He'd have put a lot of weight on, though.'

'So, what's his name, your crying husband?'

'Er, Bill Lewis.'

'William Lewis, that's what it says in this file. Are you going to inform him of the progress we've made?'

'He said he'd call in later today, to see if there was any news.'

'Got the address?' Lawrence asked.

Jonesy confirmed he had.

'Good – let's go and see this weeping father at home.'

B ILL SAT IN his armchair, smoking, waiting. Knowing the police would bring Adie home to him was pleasing; he was satisfied with the way things had turned out. He was aware that she feared suffering the same illness as her mother; once she knew they thought her mentally unstable, she would be more malleable.

He needed to make plans for how it was going to be in the future. She obviously had more money than she was letting on – that needed sorting. He'd have to drive her to work and pick her up, make sure she had no free time. The children needed thought, too. Lilly was under his control, but Sam was a different matter. The boy needed the man beaten into him. And of course, he'd have to frighten Adie a bit; her respect level had to be raised.

He thought about his wife's unbreakable spirit. He was obsessed with it. No matter how much he tormented her, she clawed her way back. It was good to know that he would again be able to relish watching her rise from her degradation, and his anticipation was piqued at the thought of knocking her back down. Unlike other women, she didn't beg him to stop. Her silent endurance excited him, hooked him like an addict. He knew he must never completely break her. She was clever, beautiful, and now he had learnt that she was cunning too. He had to carry on owning her, could not go back to existing in his world before her. Adie was not disposable.

Previous women had been of no consequence. Compared to Adie, they were nothing, with their simpering and crying. If he'd hurt them too much, it was because they'd driven him to it.

Standing, he paced as pictures of damaged female flesh flashed across his mind until they stopped at one. He lit another cigarette, pressed the heels of his hands hard against his temples and forced his thoughts back to his wife. He must be more careful with her, not hurt her too much. It wouldn't be long; she would be home soon. It could all be done, and he was happy.

An assertive knocking on the front door broke his thoughts. He peered down the hallway and through the frosted glass he made out a police uniform. He was going to see them at the station this afternoon; why had they come here? Had they found Adie so soon?

The knocking came again. Bill ruffled his hair, undid a few shirt buttons and rubbed his eyes until they were red. With a pounding heart, he opened the door. In front of him was Sergeant Jones and another man who was not in uniform, but his face was familiar.

'This is DI Lawrence Appleby. Can we come in? We have some news.'

Bill stood aside and the two men stepped into the hall.

'Shall we go in here and talk?' said the plain-clothes one, walking into the front room.

The man's smooth accent and cool confidence caused sweat to bead on Bill's brow. Quickly, he wiped it away. Now he recognised this bastard: he was the one who'd nearly undone him before, when that silly bitch smashed her head on the dresser. Christ, what was he doing here?

'So, we nearly caught up with your wife and children last night,' said Sergeant Jones. 'She and the kids turned up at Greenwich Hospital Accident & Emergency. It appears

Lilly was having an asthma attack, just as you said she would.'

'What do you mean, nearly? Why wasn't she detained at the hospital?' Bill was furious, but he dared not show it.

'Well, she's clever, your girl. As soon as your little one was better and she'd got the medication, she and the kids slipped away through a boiler room.'

'What about the paperwork, did that give an address?'

'No – nothing.'

'What?' Bill's anger was just below the surface, ready to burst through his skin. The stupid bastards – how could they lose her? What if she was never found? Dread crept through him.

'Receptionist says it must have been forgotten in the emergency. Anyway, I doubt your wife would have given a traceable address; it's beginning to look like she's determined to get away from you.'

Bill buried his head in his hands. She would not get away. He could not allow that to happen. But where should he start to look for her?

Sergeant Jones continued. 'We have another lead. We've found the garage in Lewisham where she had false number plates fitted on your car.'

'She did what?' Bill's surprised face lifted from his hands. Inside, his world was crashing; it seemed Adie would not be coming home so easily after all. And what was that bloody detective doing, sitting looking at him the whole time? Why didn't he say something? Bill could feel himself beginning to lose control. There was a moment of silence, during which he steadied his thoughts, keeping his anger and frustration inside.

'Not very lucky with women, are you?' the detective said, speaking for the first time.

Now Bill knew why he was here. Through a sob heaved from his chest he said, 'No, I'm not.'

'Why do you think your wife left you? Could it be she was frightened of you? Maybe you hit her?' the detective asked.

'I love my wife. I would never do anything to hurt her.' Bill's voice was trembling.

'Do you love her in the same way you loved Maureen? In the same way you never hit her?' the detective continued.

Bill wouldn't deny that Maureen had been his girlfriend; all he had to do was stick to the story. They couldn't make the charge stick then, and they had even less chance now. Playing the broken man, he said, 'Why are you doing this to me now, bringing up Maureen when I am at my lowest? It's very upsetting on top of my wife going mad and leaving me. I told you what happened then, and I was believed. Now my Adie has gone, and I just want her and the children back. How are you going to find her now?'

'We'll inform every constabulary across the country to keep a lookout for the car. She'll turn up,' said Sergeant Jones.

'Are you working, Mr Lewis?' asked the detective.

'No, sir, I'm waiting for the weather to break, then I can get back on the building sites again.'

'That's all for now, Mr Lewis. I presume we will be able to contact you here with further information?' said Sergeant Jones.

'I'm not going anywhere.'

'If you should decide to go anywhere at all, you must inform us of your whereabouts.'

The two men left, and Bill slumped back in his chair. Shit, it was all coming apart. The stupid bastards had let her slip through their hands. Adie was getting away from him; he'd have to go after her. He could trace that garage – how many garages could there be in Lewisham? Lots. It didn't matter, he would go to every one of them until he'd sniffed out the crooked one. Meanwhile, that detective was making him uneasy. He didn't know how they might prove anything, but he wasn't going to the gallows for any woman. He'd find that garage, beat the information out of the owner, and be on his wife's trail.

***

B ACK IN THE car, Jonesy said, 'I don't know, he seems pretty cut up. Maybe he is the genuine article.'

'Genuine con artist, if you ask me,' said Lawrence.

'What makes you say that, then?'

'He said his story about Maureen was believed. If he was innocent, he would have said it was true, and not once did he ask after his daughter's health. That wife of his has taken desperate measures. This isn't a woman who has left on a whim. Put someone on him. I want him watched day and night. If he goes anywhere, follow him. All his movements are to be reported back to me.'

Bear with me, Lawrence silently told Maureen, *we'll get him.*

M ost of London's commuters had gone home by the time Adie and her children left Steve's garage. Because they had slept in the afternoon the children were awake and excited as they started their journey. They fired an incessant list of questions at their mother and chattered endlessly about their new life, full of hopeful dreams, not realising the problems that lay ahead of them. She didn't want to dispel their enthusiasm, but she didn't have the answers. So, they talked to each other, building a new world of ease and happiness.

She drove for three hours, stopping somewhere near Leicester in a quiet lay-by. They had their tea and sandwiches, and then, shortly after they resumed their journey, the children fell asleep.

When all was quiet Adie's mind began to stray. She felt exposed now that they were out in the world on their own. At the same time, she felt immense relief to be putting further distance between them and Bill; to not have to wake every morning wondering what 'crime' she would commit against him. No matter how hard she had tried there was always something she had done that would warrant a reckoning. The thought that at night she would not have to lie next to him, feeling her flesh crawl, gave her a moment's pure joy.

As she drove through the night, feeling no need for sleep, she tried to think about practical matters, getting a job and accommodation, but her father kept invading her thoughts. It felt as if he was sitting in the car with her. There were so many questions she wanted to ask him. It was too late now. He'd been a kind and gentle man, the only one she could trust. When she was a teenager, she'd asked him why he had not taken her mother to see a doctor. He'd replied that he could not endure seeing her locked up in an institution. He'd had a great capacity to love.

She recalled her earliest memory from when she was about three years old. It was the day her father had returned from work to find her injured. Pieces of broken glass had sliced into the soft bones and tissues of her knees as she'd crawled about the grass making a daisy chain. It had happened in the morning. Her mother had made her stay in the garden all day with no food or drink. 'You'll have to wait until your father gets home,' she had spat, slamming the door shut.

All day Adie had sat on the lawn, blood congealing around the penetrating glass. At 6.30 her father came home. She recollected him being silent as he put her in an old pram – it was impossible for her to walk by then – and pushed her to the doctor's house.

The doctor had smiled at her, telling her how brave she was for remaining silent as he removed the glass and stitched the skin. In between his smiles she remembered angry words directed at her father. She felt sorry for him. Years later, when she asked why the doctor had been angry, he told her that she was diagnosed with severe malnutrition.

These gloomy thoughts troubled her as she drove on in the dark. Trying to lift her spirits with visions of the happy future envisaged by the children failed. She could not see how she was going to support them, put food in their mouths and a roof over their heads. Sometimes, it seemed as if the only way forward was to find another man, but her inner voice screamed against it.

Stopping in a lay-by, she tried to sleep. But her mind was like the driving – twisting and turning, up and down in endless darkness – so she resumed her journey along the icy roads, mentally exhausted.

That's the way it was until dawn began to break. It started with a tiny glimmer of orange on the horizon, and for some reason that glimmer spoke to her, lifting her spirits. Watching the light turn to gold against the snow-laden hills touched her innermost senses. Jealously, she guarded that moment, glad the children were still asleep. The light created some sort of elation in her. And, somehow, she felt as if they had done it. As if they had finally escaped, were free at last. A magical space surrounded them, and she let it remain, just for a little longer. In truth she felt as if she was going mad, switching from destitution to jubilation in a moment, so she stopped herself.

Waking the children, she told them to look out for a roadside café. After passing two that appeared unsuitable, they arrived at one with red vinyl tabletops and wooden chairs. It was scruffy, but warm and clean. A man with Elvis sideburns, who seemed to be the manager, was not interested in smiling at his customers. The other customers were truck drivers, absorbed in their tea, newspapers, cigarettes and breakfast. No one was interested in Adie's family. Prices on the menu were cheaper than in the South, so she ordered full English breakfasts for two and an extra plate, milk for the children and a pot of tea.

Lilly and Sam were looking out of the window, watching a farmer and his dog moving sheep. Adie searched through the situations vacant pages of *The Lady* magazine, pen poised ready to encircle any relevant advertisement, only to become deflated when she realised that the live-in jobs were for single nannies or housekeepers. There was nothing that included accommodation for a family.

The children were still occupied watching the farmer, so she grabbed a couple of local newspapers off the counter and continued her search. There was nothing in the regular papers, just ads for part-time shopworkers and office clerks based in town. Then she picked up the *Farmers Weekly*. The situations vacant page was full of jobs that were either live-in or with a cottage as part of the remuneration. She knew she was fantasising, but it soothed her to think of a simple life, with fewer demands and more freedom for herself and her children. A job with a cottage would solve so many problems. Indulging her fantasy, she scanned the page. There was nothing for her; all of the jobs were for farm labourers and the live-in jobs for housekeepers. She could be a housekeeper, but they were unlikely to take on two lively children. As her fantasy dispelled and she went to close the magazine, a small advert at the bottom of the page stopped her. It was for a housekeeper and general assistant; the wages were small, but it included independent accommodation. There was a telephone number to apply. It was a possibility. Not stopping to think, she told the children to stay put, acquired some change from the Elvis lookalike, and went to the red phone box situated just outside the café.

Knowing the likelihood of them taking her on with two children was slim, she decided to call anyway; she had nothing to lose. When she reached the phone box she procrastinated. Then, after a few seconds, feeling foolish and full of doubts, she dialled the number. It rang for a very long time and she was just about to replace the handset when a woman's breathless voice came on the line. Pushing her coins into the box, she heard, 'Beckdale Farm, Doris speaking. How may I help you?'

'I'm interested in the position advertised in the current *Farmers Weekly* for a housekeeper and general assistant,' Adie explained, her voice coming out reedy and weak.

'Are you married?' Doris enquired, a little less breathless.

Adie was taken aback by this question, having expected to be asked about relevant experience. 'No,' she replied, wondering if she had heard correctly.

'Good.' The woman's voice took on a brisk, businesslike tone. 'Because we've only got one position. Some people have been thinking we need two people because the advert says, "housekeeper and general assistant", but we only need one and we don't need a man. Can you come this morning? I'll speak with you first and if I think you're worth putting in front of Thomas then you can go and see him during his lunch break. I don't wish to sound rude, but I know what he wants. So, can you make it this morning or not?'

'Yes, but there is something I should tell you. I have children. Will that be a problem?' Now she had said it, she waited, deflated, ready for rejection.

'Not at all, dear, the village school is just a mile away up the hill.'

'Erm, what time should I be there?'

'You'll need to be here just before lunch break, so that will be 12.15.'

Hurriedly, Doris gave directions to the farm and Adie scribbled frantically, filling up the white edges of the *Farmers Weekly*.

'Have you got all of that?' Doris asked.

'Yes, got all that,' said Adie, hoping she sounded efficient.

'Good – come straight down the farm road to the house, then follow the pathway at the back of the house, that way you won't miss the office.'

Instantly the line went dead, the abrupt voice was gone, and Adie was left staring at the handset. Despite herself, she giggled. She was not frightened of being tested; her life had been one long test. But after a few seconds her giggles left her flat, and she wondered if she was wasting her time. She knew nothing of farming. Perhaps she should have stayed in London and tried to find work there. But that was what Bill would have expected her to do; he would not think of them living on a farm. It was why she came north, hoping to lose the three of them in the remoteness of this landscape.

BILL SPENT A short time slumped in his chair, thinking. Then, decision reached, he quickly packed a small holdall with a few essentials, a photograph of Adie and the children, and a wad of money he'd kept hidden; his share from the sale of some stolen goods. After taking a quick look about the house, he left and headed for the railway station, walking at a brisk pace.

At this time of day, the Lewisham train stopped at every village. The other passengers were either elderly, or mothers of young children. Most seemed to be travelling just a few stops. Bill was uncomfortable; he could feel them looking at him.

When they stopped at Pett Bottom a middle-aged woman got on. She was carrying a large cloth bag, made heavy by its contents of freshly ironed laundry. She sat opposite him with a work-weary sigh. Bill knew it was freshly ironed by its smell; it was the smell of his childhood.

He could see his mother now, slaving over the washing board, scrubbing other people's dirty linen, while his father sat huddled in the corner, weak and useless. The man's hands shook every time he rolled a smoke, which was often as he always lit the new cigarette from the old one not yet extinguished.

Bill had been told that his father had returned from the war in this state, and that he should be happy he had returned at all; many had not. He would have preferred it if his father had died in battle; at least then he could be proud of him. Instead, the man was just a figure of ridicule who could not support his family and at times was even afraid of his own son.

Bill crossed his legs, folded his arms and tried to shove his childhood back where it belonged, but the aroma penetrated deeper. He looked around, thinking to move to another seat, but for some reason he was transfixed.

Every Sunday morning, they'd gone to church, where he'd had to endure the sympathetic eyes of the congregation. Bill hated them; he didn't want their pity. His mother seemed grateful for it. All her time and energy wasted on a man with no hope. Nothing left for her son. Bill remembered trying to get her attention. It never worked, so he had played pranks on his father by making loud crashing noises behind him, speaking orders with a Japanese accent or pretending to be choking to death in front of him. This sent the old man into a panic, often ending in a fit. His mother would come running to comfort her husband and shout at Bill to get out of the house.

Outside he'd run feral, joining up with gangs of older boys. As he grew, he found he could bully his way to the top and become gang leader by instilling fear with savage acts of cruelty.

It was during his thirteenth year that he began to hear voices in his head. He was terrified of them, believing they were from God and that he must be angry with him. These first voices had instructed Bill to attack his teacher. He'd tried to deny them, to silence them, but they became stronger and he found himself crouching in a corner, hiding and weak, just like his father. He couldn't let that happen; he'd have to obey them. He struck his teacher and was expelled from school. His mother told him to leave the house and never return. He was glad to go.

Surviving by hanging out with a mob who committed burglary and sold drugs, the violence of these young men was, in a way, good for him. It released some sort of inner frustration and the voices in his head abated.

He first experienced sex and the love and hate of females at sixteen. It was a different way to get his kicks. This was not just about raw violence, but an exciting mix of physical pleasure, emotion, torture and power. These girls were nothing like his mother. He soon learnt that he was handsome and exciting to them, so when he grew tired of one, which happened quickly, he could easily find another. He continued like this for many years, but as each year passed the thrills became less. Gradually the voices returned, striking their terror deeper into him, until he was almost bursting with the desire to kill.

Then he'd met Adie and focused all of his angst on her. She was like first prize. God must be happy with him. Beautiful, clever and classy – he'd known then that if he could train her right, he would never hear the dreaded voices again.

But now she was gone. And he was on the train. And the voices were whispering inside his head. He needed to stay in control; to get away from this woman with her laundry, then he'd be all right. He'd have to hang on until he was in Lewisham. Once there, he'd look at the telephone directory, make a list of garages and begin his search.

B ACK IN THE café, Adie told the children the good news and they were eager to be under way. Her next instruction, given with one of her rare stern faces, to be on their best behaviour while at the farm, dampened their enthusiasm.

She paid their bill and asked the man with the sideburns if he had a ladies' room. 'Toilet out back,' was all he said. In the cramped facilities they attempted to wash and tidy themselves before setting off to find Beckdale Farm.

The children sensed their mother's nervousness and sat quietly in the back seat of the car. A part of her felt she was being foolish, wasting her time. What did she know of farming and these new surroundings? But then, she told herself, she was on a learning mission; what else could she do with her time, except try to find a job and a place to live? One minute she told herself she was crazy, that she should, right now, be pleading at the door of some sort of Christian charity and the next she shook the thoughts away and made herself concentrate on the road.

The lanes were narrow, buildings were scarce, and the countryside was devoid of people. At first the route had been in sync with the directions in her head, but after a while the surroundings did not relate, and she needed to check her hastily scribbled instructions. Glancing at the passenger seat she saw that the magazine was not there; it must be on the floor. It was not. She stopped and they searched the car to no avail. She'd probably dropped it somewhere near the café.

Angry at her own stupidity, she drove onwards, searching her memory, trying to visualise the scribbled writing at the edges of the page. They climbed the winding roads bordered first by thick hedgerows and then drystone walls. Green fields rose on either side of them until they passed the treeline where they broke out onto snow-laden rocky hillsides. The wind had blown the snow into drifts against the walls leaving some parts of the road clear and other parts covered in deep blankets of white. Adie had to pick her way through this bleak landscape. It was an alien world to them, and she was lost. Feeling disheartened, not able to speak to the children, she drove on, pretending she knew where she was going.

Reaching the crest of a hill, she stopped the car and studied the view in front of her. The lane meandered down the fell until it disappeared into a wall of trees that stood like dark monoliths against the blue sky. A memory triggered in her mind, although she could not pin it down. Putting the car into a low gear, she cautiously navigated the descending slopes until they reached the trees. Passing through their dark tunnel they left the snow behind them and the view opened out onto a wide valley. Further down the hill she could see a humpbacked bridge, and now she knew she was on the right road.

When they reached the bridge the car bounced off its mound, they left their stomachs behind, and the children burst into peals of laughter. Relieved, Adie smiled to herself.

Finding the entrance to Beckdale Farm on the other side of the valley felt like a small triumph. She recalled that Doris had told her to drive down the farm road; fortunately for Adie's car, it was fairly smooth and dry. Passing a paddock with horses, she mentally ticked off the route. A large pond, then tall hedgerows that could not be seen over, a bend, then a view across the river and valley.

She was concentrating hard when the children squealed with excitement, and instinctively she slammed on the brakes.

'Look at the swans,' said Lilly. 'They're running on the water.'

'They're not running on water, silly, they're running to take off,' Sam corrected her.

'They are running on water,' argued Lilly. 'Can we watch them for a minute, please, Mum?'

Adie glanced at her watch and realised they had the time. It was a beautiful sight. As they looked on, little splashes of water flew up from beneath the swans' orange feet as their legs moved faster. Then their graceful necks extended as they rose and beat their wings in unison, to fly down the valley. They were so engrossed with watching the swans that they did not hear the tractors approaching. There was a tap on Adie's window, and she found herself looking into a deeply lined face, topped with a much-used waxed hat.

'Madam, will you be blocking the road for long? It's just that some of us have work to do.' His voice was deep, clipped and well schooled.

'I'm so sorry,' she said.

In her haste to clear the road, her foot slipped off the clutch with a thud, and she stalled the engine. Glancing at the man's face, she noticed an amused raised eyebrow, but no smile. Moving her car to the side of the road, she allowed the tractors to pass. The man who had tapped on her window was driving the first. His corduroy trousers were tucked into expensive knee-high leather boots. As he passed her car, he gave a curt nod, but did not look in her direction. She had a nervous feeling that she was looking at Thomas. Driving the second tractor was a man with collar-length white hair that protruded from his flat cap. Giving her a wide smile that made his eyes wrinkle at their corners, he raised his hand in thanks.

The tractors entered a field, enabling her to continue towards the farmhouse. Glimpsing its roof of pitches and dormers above some trees, the children squealed with excitement. Rounding a bend, the whole house came into view. Surrounded by curvaceous borders and winding pathways, Adie thought it had a friendly appearance. At each end of the property, large chimneys promised open fires, and in the centre, there was a heavy, unpainted oak door.

As instructed by Doris, she parked in front of the barn and told the children to stay put until she returned. But as she made to leave the car she was surrounded by several dogs and quickly retreated to the safety of her vehicle. They milled about, barking and wagging their tails. The children wanted to play with them, but Adie made them promise to stay in the car, reasoning that although the dogs looked friendly enough, they were strangers.

Then a piercing whistle assaulted their ears and all the dogs, except one, loped off in the direction of a five-bar gate. Adie counted six of them. First to the gate were four tall, elegant pointers; they jumped it and disappeared behind a barn. The fifth dog, a tan-and-white Jack Russell, trotted behind the others, in no particular hurry. Upon reaching the gate he flattened his belly to the ground and stretched his legs far out in front and behind him, then dragged himself, inch by inch, under the lowest bar, creating amusement for Lilly and Sam.

The sixth dog, a black-and-white Welsh border collie, sat staring at the car with her head cocked prettily to one side. But Adie was taking no chances; the dog must be a working animal and would want to round her up, along with a few nips. They sat, Adie and the collie, each watching the other with curiosity. Maybe a minute passed before the sound of the whistle came again. The collie stood up, looked towards the gate, then at Adie, and sat back down, having decided to disobey the command. Again, the whistle came, this time more urgent, with three blasts on the trot. With that the dog stood up, a hoity height to her chin, watched Adie a few seconds more, then turned and trotted off in the direction of the gate, cleared it in one elegant, balletic leap and disappeared behind the barn.

Finally able to leave the car, and afraid she had been made late, Adie hurried to the back of the house and took the winding path through the garden. Eventually she came to a large shed with a window and a stable door: the farm office. As she approached, a woman who she assumed was Doris opened the top half of the door and, pointing to it, waved a teapot at her. Gratefully, Adie mouthed, 'Yes please.'

'Come in, dear, shut the door and keep the warmth in. Sit there,' Doris said, gesturing to an old leather wing-backed chair, its stuffing beginning to burst through cracks in the upholstery.

Doris, Adie noticed as she put the kettle on a small coal stove, was round; her chin, neck, bosom and belly merged into one. Setting cups and saucers on a table that doubled as a desk, she said, 'I don't like those chunky mugs people drink out of these days, do you?' But before Adie had a chance to answer, she added, 'Sugar?'

'No, thank you.'

As they waited for the kettle to boil, Doris told her about the work. She went to great lengths explaining how everything had to be polished with beeswax, and that she would have to prepare meals for all the staff, even late at night if they were lambing. And then she said something about a full breakfast for everyone every day, and the fact that she would also be responsible for provisions, the management of the household accounts, and occasional other duties. At this point Doris stopped talking. Adie, however, had decided she could do all of those jobs and she had become distracted, thinking about the surroundings and not paying attention to Doris's words. It was only after a few seconds of silence that she caught up with the phrase 'occasional other duties'.

Intrigued, she asked, 'What would they be?'

While pouring tea, Doris clarified. 'Sometimes on a farm it's all hands on deck; times like lambing, haymaking or farrowing. Then there is the fruit and vegetable garden, or, if too many puppies are born and the bitches are not coping, some might need to be bottle-fed. All sorts of jobs, dear. Are you adaptable?'

'Yes, I can't see any of that being a problem.'

To Adie all these tasks seemed simple enough and she could see no reason why she would not cope. Doris asked about her work experience and she found herself exaggerating, even making up stories about her past employment; anything that might persuade this woman to believe she was fit for the job. In her mind she could see the children playing in these wide open spaces. For some reason these surroundings gave her a feeling of security. It looked like a simple, uncluttered life; hard work, maybe, but rewarding, surely.

'You have two children and no husband, I understand?' Doris asked.

'That's right,' Adie said, feeling guilty and ashamed. This was the part that troubled her. How was she going to explain their situation to a prospective employer?

'How old are the children?'

'Sam is ten and Lilly seven.'

'Were you married?'

'Yes, but he's dead. I mean, no he's not.' Her conscience was tripping her up.

'Which is it, dear? Dead or alive?'

'We have run away from him. Travelled a long way from down South. He was treating me badly and I could live with that, but then he started on the children and we had to get away. Now I have to find a job and somewhere to live. At the moment we have neither. I am desperate.'

She stopped herself before she said any more. Feeling ashamed of the pleading tone to her voice, she lowered her eyes, fully expecting to be told that her circumstances were unacceptable.

There was a silence that became uncomfortable. Adie looked up at Doris, who was tapping her chin in thought. She was about to apologise for wasting her time, when Doris held up her hand and stopped her.

'I know exactly what Thomas will say about this situation.' As she made his speech, she gave a surprisingly good imitation of the voice of the man on the first tractor. '"There is room enough for everyone as long as everyone understands, children included, that farming is not a job, it is a way of life. And as long as everyone knows their place, plays their part and does their job, then we will all rub along just fine. But beware anyone who thinks they are going to get away lightly and not pull their weight!"' This last part was said with a deep, pompous flourish, and both Doris and Adie exploded into guilty laughter. 'He's OK once you get to know him,' Doris said. 'Takes himself too seriously and has forgotten how to be happy. Anyway, people with children know more about hard work and commitment than most.'

Adie felt a little bolstered; it seemed Doris had taken a liking to her.

'Are you fit, strong and healthy, dear? Only there's quarry tiles to be polished and we don't have too much in the way of modern equipment. And the boot room gets filthy in winter. It all gets too much for me and I've got a bit of meat on my bones; there isn't much of you, is there?'

'I am far fitter and stronger than I look, and relish a bit of physical work,' Adie assured her.

'Well, if Thomas decides to take you on, I won't be around to help out. Normally I only work a couple of hours a week doing the bookkeeping and I shall be very happy to revert to that immediately. Right, well, if you've drunk your tea, we'd better get a move on, otherwise they'll have finished their lunch.'

And with that she left the office. Gulping down her tea, Adie closed the stable door and trotted after her.

It turned out that Farmer Thomas Elliott Lambton was indeed the man with the leather boots and clipped tongue. Adie was told to wait at a distance while Doris introduced her candidate. He leant against the wheel of his tractor, looking at the ground and nodding. When Doris stopped speaking, she took a step back from him. Farmer Thomas continued his study of the ground. The man in the flat cap was there, and as the three of them were left waiting, Adie felt uneasy. To her, Farmer Thomas's behaviour seemed rude. Bored with looking at the top of his hat, she took a peep at the man in the flat cap. He winked at her, and in the next second, as if he knew about the wink, Farmer Thomas dismissed him to get on with his work. Then he curtly dismissed Doris, and beckoned Adie to come forward.

First, he ran his eyes over her from head to toe, as if surveying a farm animal. Then he studied her face openly. She held his gaze; his eyes were both sad and hard in equal measures.

After what seemed an age, he asked, 'Are you capable of hard work? There's not much of you. You do not look or sound like a housekeeper and we don't have nine till five and weekends here, you know.'

She was frustrated with their doubts in her ability to work hard. Feeling that this man wanted to intimidate her with his stares and silences and his rudeness, she did not once let her eyes flicker from his. 'You should not be fooled by my appearance. I can assure you that I am fit, strong and able.'

He continued to look directly into her eyes, but she would not be daunted.

'Do you have any knowledge of farming or animals? Have you ever driven a tractor? Fed a lamb? Do you mind the dirt? How worldly are your children? Do you overprotect them, or do you allow them to flourish?'

She knew her face was red with fury. But she could tell he was testing her. She did not mind the questions about farming, but she resented him questioning her mothering skills. 'I have never driven a tractor or fed a lamb. But I am confident that these are skills I can easily learn. As for dirt, do you mean the dirt of changing a baby's nappy, or a child's sickness, or the clearing away of my own afterbirth? Or do you simply mean the earth in all its forms, which I do not see as dirt? As for my children, I can assure you that they are worldlier than you could possibly guess. There is nothing more that I wish for them, than to flourish. But I will protect them with my life if I have to.'

Finally, he turned his head from her and looked away across the valley. 'Should you wish to take on the challenge of this position, you may begin this afternoon.'

—⟶⊹⟵—

AFTER CONSIDERING ADDRESS and ownership, Bill had whittled the list of garages in the phone directory down to four. He had visited two. They were not the ones. By the time he got to the third one, down a rutted lane alongside a raised railway, it was getting dark.

Bill had been waiting in the cold, but he didn't mind; he had a feeling about this one. Since most of the other workshops in the lane were closed for the day, it was easy for him to find a hidden corner from which to observe. The lights of the workshop acted like a homing beacon. Bill had counted three men. Two of them were preparing for the end of the day, tidying and putting things away; the third was sitting behind a window, head down, presumably doing his paperwork. After about twenty minutes the two men pulled down a large shutter, closing off the main workshop. They left via a door that opened within the shutter. Both climbed onto a motorbike and threaded up the lane, past Bill.

Lighting a cigarette, he strode out towards the garage. He could see the man still working at his desk. Tapping on the door within the shutter, he opened it and walked into the small office.

'We're shut, mate,' the man said.

'Didn't know if you could help me; I'm in a bit of a fix,' said Bill.

'Like I said, we're closed. Come back tomorrow.'

The man had not raised his eyes from the figures he was adding up. Saying nothing, Bill slid the photograph of Adie and his children between the man and his paperwork, closely observing any reaction. The man froze for half a second, then stood, handing the picture back.

'I can see you're not the fuzz. What can I do for you?'

'That's my wife and kids. She ran off, taking my car. Apparently, she had some work done on it, in this area. The car is a Morris Minor. Have you seen it, or them?'

'No, mate – crikey, I'd remember a looker like that. We don't get many of them here.'

The man indicated for Bill to take back the photograph. Bill did not, but detected a slight tremble of the man's hand. Turning around slowly, he scanned the shelves, stacked untidily with motoring paraphernalia. He noticed several number plates, sticking out from between two books. Staring at them he dropped his cigarette. The man tried to make a dash for the door, but Bill swung around and threw his full might behind a punch to the temple. Hitting his head hard against the reinforced glass window, causing a small circle of it to shatter, the man slumped to the floor. Blood ran from his temple, past his ear, and formed a dark stain on his overalls. Bill pulled him up by the collar and threw him back into his chair. Grabbing his number plate, he shoved the edge of it hard against the man's Adam's apple.

'How did she pay you for it? Have you had her – have you?'

The man raised his hands in submission, unable to speak. Bill eased the pressure on the number plate.

'She had money. I never touched her. She had money,' he croaked.

'Where has she gone?'

'North, up the A6.'

Bill returned the pressure to the man's throat, leaning forward, spitting in his face as he spoke. 'That's not enough – where up North?'

'Cumbria was all she said. I swear it. She didn't know any more than that herself.'

Bill dropped the number plate and, clamping a hand either side of the man's head, forced him to look at a framed photograph of his own family that sat on the windowsill above his desk. 'You'd better pray that I find my family,' he said. 'If I don't, I'm coming back to get yours. Do you understand me?'

The man nodded.

Bill picked up the picture of Adie and the children from the floor and slid it into his pocket. 'Where's your money?' he commanded, pulling the man out of his chair.

The man fumbled in his overall pocket. Withdrawing a key, he opened the drawer of a filing cabinet, took out a small metal box and placed it on the desk, then unlocked it.

Bill took all of the money, stuffing it into his jacket pocket. Dragging the man into the workshop, he asked, 'Which one is ready to go?'

Pointing, the man indicated a Ford Anglia.

'Keys?' demanded Bill.

'In it,' the man said.

Bill shoved him aside, telling him to open the shutter. Starting the engine, he noted the tank was half full; it should see him through the night. Putting the car in first gear, he pulled up next to the man and wound down the window.

'I expect the police will be visiting you soon. Remember what I said about your family.' And, tapping the side of his nose, he pulled away into the darkness.

A T THE SAME time Adie and her children were moving their meagre possessions into a self-contained wing of the farmhouse. Upstairs were two bedrooms with washstands; downstairs the living room had a wood burner, housing one hotplate. There was no kitchen. Two doors led off from the living room. One was locked; the other went outside where a bath hung on a hook. Under it was a log store, next to that a tap, and next to that a hut housing the outside toilet. It was small, the furniture was shabby, dust and cobwebs abounded, but the children were smiling, and Adie was thrilled to have a roof over their heads and employment.

In her gut she had a tentative feeling of safety, but she chased this foolish emotion away. Being married to Bill had taught her to encase herself in an impenetrable cage; it stopped him from breaking her. It would not be easy for her to release those locks that had kept her from being beaten into submission. Now she was free of him she could feel her spirit wanting to rise. She restrained it, locked it down – she must not weaken now. But was it possible that she had achieved her goal? Could it be that they were actually free?

Around mid afternoon Doris arrived with newspaper and matches to light the stove, a pot of stew to heat, a broom, a feather duster, and bedding. She stayed, and they chatted while they cleaned and made up the beds. When they had finished, she said, 'There's just one more thing to do, then I'll be on my way. I've got a small house-warming present for you.'

Disappearing outside, she was gone for a couple of minutes before returning with a basket covered by a blanket. Sitting the basket on the floor in front of the stove, she lifted the blanket and a blue-eyed, grey-and-white tabby kitten blinked at them. They called her Tinker; she came into their lives and lifted their spirits further. Fiercely naughty and incredibly clever, she ran up curtains, leaped on their heads and made them laugh.

Later that evening, when the children were in bed, Adie heard the bolts being drawn back from the locked door. There was a short burst of knocking. Her heart leaped in terror, and the door opened.

Farmer Thomas stepped into the room in his stocking feet. Water dripped from his chin and fingers, the hair on his head was smoothed against his skull, and Adie was baffled, but not afraid. Her heartbeat quickly receded. Offering no explanation for his wet condition, instead he looked around the room, and then once again looked her over, reassessing her, before he spoke. 'I should like to speak with you in the kitchen. You will find it through this door, at the end of the rear hall. Can you come now?'

'Of course.'

She followed him along the hall. When they reached the kitchen, he sat at a large table with papers strewn across it. He made no indication for her to sit down, so she stood at the other side of the table.

'I shall require no meal this evening as I will shortly be leaving on a business trip. I will return on Monday. This will give you ample opportunity to get to know the house without me looking over your shoulder. The only work you will be expected to do while I am away is breakfast for the staff, house cleaning, and making sure that the pantry and store cupboards are full. I do, however, expect you to be in full control of running things by the time I return. I will require a meal on the evening of my return. Does that all seem straightforward to you, and do you have any questions?'

'There is no kitchen in our accommodation – where should we take our meals?' she asked.

'You and the children are staff, like the rest of us. You will take your meals here, with us.'

'The door between our accommodations – will that remain unlocked?'

'Yes, unless you wish to go outside and walk the border of the house every time you need to be here.'

She did not like Lilly and Sam to be thought of as staff, and had mixed feelings about the door, but thought it too soon to confront her new employer. 'That all makes sense,' she said. 'I can't think of any more questions at the moment, but I'm sure some queries will arise in your absence.'

As she spoke, he began perusing the papers in front of him. Indignation at his rudeness rose quickly within her. A few seconds after she finished talking, he looked up at her and smiled, a gesture that did not reach his eyes.

'So, if that will be all, you may go.'

Leaving the kitchen, she marched back down the hallway, feeling like a chastised fourteen-year-old scullery maid who had been dismissed from the room.

The second she closed the connecting door, there was a tap on the other one. Making an effort to remove the scowl that must be on her face, she opened the door to find the man who had been driving the second tractor. He removed his cap and, with a broad smile, offered her his hand. It completely enveloped hers. Inviting him in, out of the cold, she saw him clearly for the first time. The scar that sliced through his left eyebrow to the centre of his forehead, and should have been unsightly, gave him a rakish air, despite his senior years.

'I thought I'd drop by and introduce myself, proper, like. My name is Jack and I am the farm manager. I see you've got the place warmed through.'

'Yes, with Doris's help.'

'You've probably got a lot of questions.'

'Yes. And the first one is how to deal with the very rude Thomas?' As soon as the words were out, she wished they weren't.

'Oh, been chatting already, have you?'

'I'd hardly call it that.'

'I've got a feeling you'll end up dealing with him better than the rest of us. Now, what I suggest is that you write a list of questions and we can discuss them in the morning. It's you, me, your little 'uns and Doris for breakfast at seven. See you in the morning, then.' With another of his smiles he donned his cap and was gone.

THE FOLLOWING DAY she was up at five. Outside she filled Doris's pot with freezing water, then placed it on the wood burner to warm. After washing and dressing she stood by the connecting door, hovering, feeling like a trespasser. Then, eventually putting her mind straight, she went to work.

In the kitchen she stoked up the range, before going through every drawer and cupboard. In the corner there was a large door which opened into a pantry, and here she found all she needed for breakfast. After preparing as much as she could, she went back to their rooms to wake the children, wanting them to be ready to meet their new colleagues.

Breakfast ran smoothly. Her questions were answered, and her children made her proud. When they'd finished, Doris departed to her office, the children went off to explore, and Jack offered to help clear the dishes.

'This evening, before it gets dark, we'll go for a walk. You'll need to get your bearings on where everything is,' he said.

———✦✦✦———

A T THE START of their walk they passed through the kitchen garden; all was harvested and winterised. There were fruit cages, as tall as a man, and a glasshouse full of pots and troughs. To Adie, this area alone looked like a farm. Further on, there were barns containing tractors and equipment, then stables, some with pigs in them and some empty. Horses in the fields, and sheep on the hills. Realising for the first time how little she knew, a stark awareness of what she had taken on began to sink in.

As if reading her thoughts, Jack laughed aloud. 'You'll be all right; you're plenty bright enough and you'll learn as you go along. And if he shouts at you, ignore it and let it pass straight over your head – don't let him fluster you. He's testing you.'

She gave him a nervous smile.

'Good. Now let's take one day at a time; he's away for three days and by the time he's back you'll have everything under control.'

She didn't believe him, but she could tell that he was going to be a friend, so she listened intently to everything he told her. On their way back to the house he explained some history of the farm.

'I've worked here man and boy,' he said. 'Thomas's father employed me when I was just thirteen, and Thomas barely out of nappies. His father was a great man who employed most of the village. But he died young and Thomas wasn't really old enough to take on the responsibility. Then he was smitten with his wife. A beautiful woman with a black heart, who tore him to pieces.'

'How sad.' Adie refrained from commenting further; she wanted him to continue.

'Thomas comes across as cold and without feeling, but you shouldn't let that bother you. He's a kind man, really. A good farmer who treats his animals well. This farm is his whole world.'

She began to realise that, although Thomas was difficult, he somehow managed to command loyalty.

'I've worked here for just over fifty years now,' said Jack. 'No one knows the place better than me.'

H E SAT ON the ground, knees bent, his back pushed upright against an old oak tree. The army fatigues he wore were too big for him. The smell of his own body odour escaped from the open-necked shirt, but did not bother him. Long rats' tails of dark hair fell about his face. His sunken eyes saw nothing; instead, he listened intently.

The sun had set, although it was not yet completely dark. A few birds still sang their goodnight songs, and, in the distance, the first owl call haunted the air.

The voices came to him, soft and filtered through the copse of trees. There were two: one he knew well and the other he did not. It was female. His lurcher heard them; she raised her head from the woodland floor, nose to the air, and drew in their scent.

In one fluid movement he gathered his rifle, rose to his feet and moved swiftly through the woods, bent low. At the edge of the tree cover he lay flat on the ground, face down, dog in sync at his side.

Their voices came to him again, clearer now; his low and steady, hers light, with laughter in it. It wrenched his guts and creased him into a ball. Slowly, he unfurled and raised his head just enough to see them striding up the hill. Silently, he lifted his rifle and aimed the sights at the centre of Jack's forehead. Beads of sweat escaped from his brow and trickled into his eyes; his hands shook.

Breathe, he said silently to himself. *In... count, out... count, in... count, out... count. Calm – take him again; quickly, before they get to the top of the hill.*

He aimed, held the gun steady and, on his out-breath, pulled the trigger.

His mind slipped and, moving fast, not caring about stealth, he fled. Beyond the woods he crossed a field of scrub, then hit the ground, rifle in hands, and dragged himself through the dirt on his elbows, dog low at his side. *A hedgerow; squeeze through the hole the badgers made; more elbow work. It's dark now, they won't be able to see me.* He stood up and began to run again.

Laughter – he heard children's laughter. Weakness engulfed him, and involuntarily he dropped his rifle to the ground and curled up like a foetus on the damp earth. Silently, his mouth screamed. His hands and feet turned numb. Violent shudders travelled the length of his body, his bowel loosed, and warmth seeped around his groin.

Peals of childish giggles reached his ears on wicked air. He opened his eyes. On the top floor of the house the lights were on, the windows open. He saw her shadow play against a curtain, and this time her laughter came to him.

On all fours he crawled towards the barn, his dog whining and nudging, encouraging. Another hedge, another badger hole and he was on home ground. Inside the barn, door still open, he collapsed face down. Like a dead man, he stared, blind and motionless, across the floor.

Willow the lurcher settled herself. Lying down in the open doorway, she crossed her front legs and laid her head on them. She would wait as long as it took for Rupert Fitzroy to come back to her.

THE FOLLOWING DAY Adie set about the house looking for work to be done. Even though Doris said she had taken over the running of the house, it had obviously not been cared for in a long time. There was both cleaning and mending. Starting in the boot room, she worked her way through to the kitchen. This large room was much more than a place to prepare food. Its hefty oak table and chairs stood centre stage. Against one wall a huge cooking range with several ovens gently dispersed heat. The scrubbed, scarred butcher's block and knife, its surface curved with age, stood next to it. Oak dressers adorned with crockery and china filled two more walls, and on the fourth side was a large, comfortable settee and two armchairs. They were threadbare but covered with blankets and strewn with odd cushions. Attached to the beam was an assortment of hooks and rails where pans and cooking equipment hung. It took the rest of the day to clean the kitchen, but Adie didn't mind; she enjoyed the feeling that it was alive, with its roaring, ticking ovens and creaking wood.

The next day, Sunday, she entered the main hall, and as she did so the grandfather clock struck the quarter-hour, announcing her arrival. Her previous look at these rooms had been perfunctory and now she noticed a thick covering of dust and cobwebs on the imposing front door suggesting it had not been used in a long time. Her eye followed the sweeping staircase upwards, and then at the top noted the vaulted ceiling with a window that looked out over the valley. From here on the house was dark, its drapes closed, its air stale, and she could hear the rustling of rodents who had made their homes in its musty corners.

In the formal dining room, she struggled to open heavy purple drapes that juddered on dust-clogged rails. The room was furnished in black ebony, dull with dirt. Against the wall a large, intricately carved dresser dominated the room; the head of a lion snarling out from each of its cupboard doors, and old photographs, where no one was smiling, did little to lift the gloom.

It was the same in the drawing room. The drapes were closed; no light penetrated. Damp, stale odours assaulted her nose. She tugged at the drapes, but they would not move. Using more force, she tugged again, and to her horror the curtain began to tear. She left it hanging, cursing herself, knowing she would have to repair it before Thomas's return. With the little light the torn curtain created she could see the inglenook fireplace, its brickwork decorated with tarnished brass and copper. Logs, coated in dust, were stacked either side, and in front of it stood a green velvet sofa, its material dull and threadbare, flanked by two button-backed leather chairs.

She assessed the rest of the house before setting about the task of cleaning and mending. The study was obviously used. Here the curtains were open. There was a roll-top desk and chair, and two more of the green button-backed chairs sat aside a small table. On it was a silver-framed photograph. Adie picked it up, and the face of a beautiful woman with dark, lustrous hair looked back at her. She replaced the picture on the table, for some unknown reason eager to leave its touch. This room was clean and aired.

Upstairs there were four bedrooms and a bathroom. Three of the bedrooms were closed, like the dining and drawing rooms downstairs. The other was Thomas's bedroom. Neat and functional, there was not a hint of personality in the room, except that exactly the same photograph as she had seen in the study sat on his bedside table.

She was torn, unsure what to do with the house. Should she clean and air the rooms? They had obviously been closed off for some considerable time. It was annoying that things were not straightforward, that she had been given no instruction. These rooms were dark and dead and the thought of them made her feel uneasy. Maybe she had made a mistake and brought them to a precarious place, to live with another dangerous man.

Suddenly, she knew she had to take control and rushed through the house tearing wide the curtains, not caring if they ripped, and flung open all the windows. Dust fell everywhere, dancing and twinkling in the sunlight. Cobwebs broke, and spiders and mice ran for cover. Standing in the drawing room, watching the dust move in the light, a gentle movement of air brushed over Adie's face. It was like the sweeping pass of an angel's wing. She chastised herself. She would never be a victim again, and she certainly would not be Thomas's victim. The grandfather clock in the hall struck its repetitive hourly chime and she began the work of cleaning and repairing the house, toiling for the rest of the day, the evening and long into the night.

On the morning of the day of Thomas's return, she moved through the newly aired and cleaned rooms and was pleased with the result. Their first days had gone well. Adie and her children had been conditioned to live in a state of fear and loneliness, starved of tranquillity. Now, they took pleasure in soaking up the friendly mealtime chatter of Jack and Doris.

——✳—✳—✳——

I T WAS BILL'S second day of driving north on the A6. Having slept in the car overnight, his body was aching, but it didn't bother him. He had stopped at every café and garage along the way. No one had seen them. Undeterred, he'd driven onwards, staring straight ahead, rarely checking his mirror. Adie may think he would have given up by now, but she would be mistaken – he would never give up. His mind was fixed on his subject, focused on the next place she could have pulled into. Dedicating his whole self to the task meant he was able to keep the voices behind bars in the deepest recesses of his mind.

He could see the next transport café ahead. He was hopeful; she must have stopped by now. Inside it was warm and busy, noisy with the sound of many voices. Waitresses called out their orders to the kitchen. The smell of fried food made his stomach growl, and saliva flooded his mouth. He had not eaten since he set out on this journey, more than twenty-four hours ago. But he was afraid to eat, afraid that the taste of food, so very much needed, would weaken him. It would surely decrease his urgency and open a door to the intruders in his mind. He looked about him for someone to show his photograph to.

'Take a seat, love, someone will be with you as soon as we can.'

Searching for a table, he saw one at the back, its occupants about to leave, and reached it at the same time as another man. Bill gave him a look making it clear he did not want to share. The man raised his hand in compliance and walked away, to look for another spare seat. Picking up the plastic menu, Bill pretended to read it. After he had been waiting about ten minutes he was tempted to leave and try somewhere else, but this place was so busy, she could have been here. In his mind he could see Adie, Sam and Lilly sitting at one of these tables, and he studied them.

'So, what's it to be, love?' The elbow of a peroxide-blonde waitress landed on the table in front of him, her breasts straining at her blouse.

Bill dug in his pocket and pulled out the picture of his family.

'Look, love, I haven't got time for other stuff now. My boss sees me looking at that and I'll be in the shit. How about I take your order and I'll have a look at it when I bring your food?'

Reluctantly, Bill ordered egg, chips, bread and butter, and tea.

On her return, the waitress slapped his food down on the table, slopping his tea over the rim of his mug. Turning quickly, she began to walk away, looking for the next customer. Bill grabbed her wrist and yanked her backwards.

'Ouch! What the bloody hell you up to?'

He slid his picture across the table.

'I ain't seen them,' she said, attempting to walk away. But he held on to her wrist. She looked at him then, and knew he wasn't the sort to upset. Taking a closer look, she said, 'I don't remember seeing them. They could have been in here, but you see how busy it is. I might not have noticed them.'

Bill let her go. He stared at the food and, although he felt hungry, he also felt sick. Shoving it aside, he left the café without paying.

Back in his car he tried to concentrate, but his sight kept blurring and dizziness plagued him. Slowing his speed, he carried on, fixing his gaze on the grass verge, trying to stay the right side of it, as if driving in thick fog. Cars were beginning to overtake him, their horns blaring, drivers' fists shaking.

The landscape had changed; he was in the North now. Maybe he should stop. Up ahead was another sign for a café, and he pulled into its parking area.

Inside it was quiet and he took the seat nearest the door. A man who thought he was Elvis came to take his order. Bill ordered the same as before and the food arrived quickly. Giving in to his basic need, he wolfed it down, and even though the voices rattled their bars and mocked his weakness, it made him feel better immediately. Approaching the counter to pay, he pulled out his photograph along with the money.

'Seen these?' he asked, not expecting a result.

Elvis picked the picture up to examine it more closely, thought for a moment, then looked up at Bill. 'They were in 'ere day before yesterday, in the morning. Wanted change for the phone.'

'Did she use that phone?' Bill asked, pointing through the glass to the red kiosk outside.

'Yeah,' Elvis replied. He gave the photo back to Bill and went back to splashing melted lard over frying eggs.

Outside, Bill entered the red phone box. Standing there, he inhaled deeply and imagined he could smell her. He flipped through the phone directory, looking for scribbles indicating who she might have called. Nothing. Deflated, he made to leave, then, on the floor of the booth, crushed to the corner, he noticed a *Farmers Weekly* magazine. Picking it up, he saw Adie's handwriting, and his skin tingled.

I T WAS LATE on Monday evening when Farmer Thomas returned from his travels.

Adie, expecting him earlier, had prepared food which had gone cold. A short while after his return she went to the kitchen to enquire if he needed anything.

He was sitting at the table glancing over a newspaper.

'Good evening, sir,' she said, not sure how to address him. Expecting him to reply with something like, 'Just Thomas will do', she waited, stood in front of him like a penitent, but he said nothing; didn't even look at her. Her composure began to crumble. 'I have prepared dinner for you, as you requested. It will not take long to heat up.' Her voice sounded a little too high.

'I require no food,' he said, without looking at her. Then, in a dismissive manner, 'And I do not need to see you until the morning, when we will talk immediately after breakfast.'

'Goodnight,' she said as she left the room. She received no reply.

Again, she felt like a dismissed, naughty child. Seething with anger at his ignorance and rudeness, she wanted to burst back into the kitchen and challenge him, but her instincts warned her against this. She had too much to lose. Like the rest of his staff, she found herself making excuses for him: *he must be tired after his journey*; *he doesn't mean it*; *his mind is occupied with other things*; *he's had a rough time*. Well, so had she, but she was not rude to people.

While he had been away, mostly, she'd felt as though she had made the right decision for herself and her family. It had only been upon discovering those dark and dead rooms that she'd had doubts. Now, once again, she was not so sure.

The children were happy. They had enjoyed their first day at their new school. Adie had not wanted them to go, she wanted them to stay hidden safely at the farm with her, but of course, that could not be. It was a little Victorian building with one classroom and a tiny bell tower to mark the beginning and end of each lesson and day. The children loved it, fascinated by the fact that all of the pupils, regardless of their age, were taught together. Their innocence allowed them to believe that their troubles were over, their future was rosy, their terror gone for good. They did not understand the complexities of their own minds, and how their horrors would come back to haunt them.

Neither did they understand the intricacies of their father, the way Adie did. She knew he would not give up.

She knew her eyes would never stop searching, checking if he was there, watching and waiting.

———✳✳✳———

T HE FOLLOWING MORNING, after delivering the children to school, she prepared the second breakfast of the day for Farmer Thomas and the staff. Once it had been served, she stood back and watched as everyone took their place at the table, not quite sure which seat was hers. Eventually she sat opposite Jack and they began to eat, but the atmosphere was quiet. The convivial conversation of the previous days was replaced with a cool, restrained mood. As soon as the food was finished the staff thanked Adie for their breakfast, got up from the table and headed for the boot room where they donned their outdoor clothing. She could hear their chatter lighten as they felt less inhibited. She wished she was going with them.

Thomas remained at the table. Adie was halfway across the kitchen with a tray of dirty dishes when he started talking. He did not ask her to sit down. Very quickly she realised they were not going to have a discussion, just another of his statements.

In a plain-speaking voice, he said, 'Last night I noticed that you had been into the other rooms of the house. I should have realised that you would do so, and I should have explained to you that I did not want those rooms touched. They have not been disturbed in many years and it was a shock to me to know that a stranger had desecrated their peace. You, of course, were not to know this and so you are not to blame.'

There was a pause, during which Adie, who was standing with her back to him and the tray still in her hands, did not know what to do.

'Now that you have started, I give you permission to clean and air the rooms as you have already begun to do so, but you are not to change anything about them. Do you understand?'

'Yes.' She turned to face him, willed him to look at her. But that was it; there was nothing more to be said as far as he was concerned. Rising from the table, he went to the boot room, put on his boots and hat and left the house.

'WHAT THE HELL do you mean, he's not there? I specifically requested that he be watched day and night, and that I be informed of any movements. Now you tell me he is gone. Have you been inside the house?'

'Yes, sir.' Jonesy was standing up straight, taking his punishment. 'We got in there this morning, sir, and he's not there.'

'Obviously.'

'By the looks of the dirty mug and plate in the sink, he's been gone for a couple of days.'

'How did this happen, Jonesy?' Lawrence was fuming, but restraining his anger, saving it for where it would count.

'He must have gone shortly after we left him on Friday. There was a small window of time before we got the men on the job. It wasn't until the Monday-morning shift that a neighbour tapped on the window of the surveillance car and told our boys he'd gone.'

Lawrence did not answer immediately. He was biting down on his fury. Jonesy waited, clearly aware that now was not the time to offer excuses.

'That woman and her kids are at risk – risk of losing their lives. That's why I wanted him watched.' More silence, during which Lawrence breathed deeply, containing himself. 'Get me the details of that garage, the one where she got her number plates done. That's where I'll be going this morning.'

'But it's out of our area. You'll have to get the chief to speak to them first, see if they'll let you have the case. You know what happened last time.'

Lawrence was entirely aware of his investigative history. For someone who was such a stickler for the rules, when it came to his bottom drawer cases, he lost all sense. 'It will take the chief two days at least to come back to us and tell us that the London boys will deal with it, a case they know nothing about. Get me the address and the owner's name. I'm leaving straight away.'

The pang of excitement that flashed through his belly when he got in his car lifted his spirits. It wasn't often he got time to drive his Austin Healey, a present to himself. Today, if he could get away with it, he didn't want to be a copper.

His raised spirits were quickly dashed by a journey fraught with hold-ups. First a lorry spilt its load, and then a minor accident that caused two men to stand shouting at each other brought him to a standstill. He shook his head and tried to practise patience. Now the men were raising their fists, their faces nose to nose. Getting out of the Austin Healey, Lawrence strode past the stream of waiting cars towards the scene, walked up to the men and showed them his identification. Instantly each man took up his own argument, simultaneously shouting into Lawrence's face. For a few seconds he stood and listened, then replaced his identification in his pocket. With one swift movement he took hold of each man's little finger and crunched them to almost breaking point. Shocked, they fell silent and bent awkwardly in pain.

'That's better,' said Lawrence. 'As you see, I am an officer of the law and you are holding me up with your overgrown egos. Are your cars drivable?'

The men nodded in unison.

'Then if I were you, I would drive them out of my way, otherwise I will charge you with obstructing a police officer in his duties. Do you understand?'

Another nod.

'I need to hear your answer.'

The answer was given, the men released, and the road cleared.

As the journey continued Lawrence found anger replacing his earlier joy. In his mind he was a boy again, watching his mother from a hiding place as she tried to free herself from the hands of his father. Once in their bedroom, where he could no longer see them, he would listen to her cries of pain and fear. Much later, he would find her, usually in the garden, frantically weeding as silent tears slid down her face. Bruised and shaking, she would tug angrily at the unwanted plants. When he became a teenager, and understood a little more of the world, he begged his mother to tell someone. But she swore him to secrecy; she could not live with the shame. Besides, his father, a doctor, had promised to have her committed to an asylum, should she speak out.

Shaking the memories from his mind, Lawrence focused on those he could protect now.

<hr />

W HEN HE ARRIVED at the garage, he parked in the lane a short distance away, remained in his car and watched. There were four men working: three adults and a youth. Industrious in their welding and panel beating, they did not notice him. One of them had a black eye and bruising to the side of his face.

Lawrence was hoping his car would earn him some conversation time. 'Who's the man to speak to for special work?' he asked as he approached, indicating his car.

Four pairs of eyes looked up and appraised the vehicle enviously.

'I'm the man you want, but we don't usually work on classy stuff like that.' The man with the bruises held out a congenial hand for Lawrence to shake.

'That's a shiner you've got there.'

'Yeah, took a tumble and whacked my head against a toolbox.'

'Can we talk in there for a minute?' Lawrence said, indicating the office and giving the man a look of collusion.

As they entered the small room, Lawrence shut the door behind him. 'I think you're the man who helped my girlfriend last week. Put a different number plate on her Morris Minor. Adie's her name, remember her?'

The man remained silent and studied Lawrence's face. Lawrence knew he didn't look like a copper, certainly not with his Austin Healey, and neither did he appear to be a violent man, but he wasn't sure if he would pass for Adie's boyfriend.

The man in front of him seemed to conclude his assessment. 'Look, I'm beginning to regret ever meeting Adie Lewis. Last Friday her husband comes here and beats the shit out of me, threatens my family, wanting to know where she and his kids have gone; then he steals a car to go after her. All I know is she's gone to Cumbria; that's where she said she was going anyway. That's it, that's all I know. Now I find out she's got a bloody boyfriend.'

'You did change her number plates, then?'

'Yeah, I changed her plates and repaired a leak in her radiator.'

'Did she pay you?'

'Yeah, she gave me cash. Not enough, mind you. Me and my missus, we put ourselves out for that woman, what with her husband terrorising her. I may be a bit of a rogue, but I don't go for that sort of thing.'

Lawrence reached into his pocket and produced his identification.

'Fuck, and I told myself you weren't a copper, looking a bit of a spiv and with a car like that.'

'How about you and I do a deal? You see, you're not on my patch, and in exchange for me not telling your local constabulary all I know about your dodgy car dealings, you tell me every detail you know about Adie Lewis, her kids, her car and, most important of all, her husband.'

L AWRENCE SPENT THE rest of the day in London. After questioning Steve, he spoke to Steve's wife, to Norman and to the doctor who had treated Lilly in Greenwich Hospital. Then he went to a pub. It was dark and smoky. The other customers, all male, eyed him with suspicion. Ordering a pint of beer and a pasty, not his usual fare, he took a seat on a stool at the end of the bar. The barmaid tried to flirt with him, but his look sent her back to her regulars. The Moody Blues, 'Go Now' belted out from the jukebox, and the futility of the song lowered his mood further.

He was angry, knowing that this was another case that would be lost to him. The details, no doubt distorted, would be passed on to the Cumbrian force, who would see it as just another domestic. Something between a husband and his wife; nothing for them to interfere with.

The pub was becoming crowded with men at the end of their working day. They were loud, foul-mouthed and made derogatory jokes about women. With fury rising, Lawrence hastily consumed his pasty, downed his pint and stood to leave. Threading his way between tables, chairs and men, the odour of male perspiration assaulted his nose and The Righteous Brothers, 'You've Lost That Lovin' Feelin'' followed him on to the street.

Driving home, he made a decision. He was not going to let this one go. He was too close. He'd take leave; he was owed a bit. He'd get himself up to Cumbria, hunt down Adie, her kids and Bill, get the evidence, then get the local constabulary to listen. Jonesy would help.

——————

DURING ADIE'S FIRST days of employment the pervading mood of her workplace was tense, a situation she found difficult to navigate. Thomas used no more than the bare words necessary for the day's instructions. Mostly, they were spoken without looking at her. If it hadn't been for the friendly companionship of Jack and Doris, Adie would have struggled to cope. It was Jack who told her not to call Thomas 'sir' – 'Just call him Thomas, that's what we all do.' She wondered if this would raise any reaction. It did not.

The daytime was difficult, and the night-time was no easier. Lilly often woke with night terrors. She didn't call out, but would toss and turn in sweat-soaked sheets. Adie, who slept in uneasy expectation of danger, would sense her daughter's distress, rise from her bed and see her child with eyes wide open, mouthing silent words. All she could do was soothe her until sleep came.

Sam was also a cause for concern. At first he'd seemed full of joy, but then silence smothered him like a blanket. Adie asked if he was all right, if he was happy at school, at the farm. 'Yes,' was the fullness of his reply. His every spare moment was spent assisting Jack with whatever task was at hand. Jack could not fathom the boy, and asked Adie about his quietness. Not sure how to reply, she told him that he'd always been that way.

For Adie, too, there were nightmares, panics and traumas. She tried not to let the others see, but often she would look into a dark corner, even in daylight, and see Bill there. She never spoke of their past. Fear was a part of her life and she doubted it would ever leave her. She didn't want her children to live that way.

Although not interested in idle gossip, she found sharing a house with someone who never smiled, said, 'Good morning', or proclaimed what a beautiful sunny day it was, very depressing. She watched Thomas speak to her children, and noticed that he looked at them, and spoke with care and attention. But she found it intolerable that he spoke to her as if she were a robot; something to be given orders.

At the beginning of the second week Jack suggested that she walk the dogs every morning. At that time of year, around 6.30, it was just light enough. Each day she would go in a different direction, enabling her to learn the lie of the land. Before the walk she and Jack would feed the dogs and talk. Thomas's lack of communication was often a problem, so their morning chat was useful for their working day.

One morning, when Adie decided to bring Thomas's attitude into the conversation, Jack rested his elbows on the fence, placed his chin in his powerful hands and remained silent for some moments before he spoke.

'His wife leaving ripped him apart. She had an affair with another man. Took his heart, his children and most of his money. He had to work hard to get out of debt. I haven't seen him smile since.'

'Is it since then that those rooms have been shut up?'

'Yep, until you came along, that is!' He raised his chin to look at her with a crinkly grin on his face.

'I wasn't to know the circumstances, and if no one takes it upon themselves to explain to me, I can hardly be blamed!'

'I know, he doesn't mean to be bad to you,' Jack explained. 'It's just that he's never been able to move on. There's never been even a hint of another woman. He treats all women the same, if that's any comfort to you.'

'He's so different with the children, though. I mean, he's not amazingly talkative or anything, but he has patience with their continual questions and explains thoroughly if they don't understand.'

'Yes, I know what you mean. I suppose he misses his own children; they were good kids until their mother ruined them. They've never once returned here since she ran off with Mr Rich. Now the only beings that receive friendship from Thomas have four legs.' Jack straightened up and turned to look at her. 'Until Sam and Lilly came along.'

Adie did have sympathy for Thomas, but ten years was a long time to be closed off to the world. Maybe her children would make a difference, but it was not their responsibility to be the route to Thomas's healing. They had their own healing to do.

DURING THIS PERIOD Lilly started to spend time with the ponies, and they seemed to chase away her troubles. Within a few days she was pestering her mother for a pony of her own.

'I'm sorry, sweetheart. I know it's your dream, but I'm afraid I cannot afford to buy you a pony, and besides, when would I find the time to help you to look after it? You couldn't do it all by yourself.'

After listening to her mother's words Lilly looked thoughtfully at the floor and then, with a sad face, climbed the stairs to her bedroom. Adie hoped it was the end of the matter.

At the end of the following day, Thomas entered the kitchen and gave Lilly a thick, heavy book entitled, *How to Care for Your Pony*.

'Now, young lady,' he said, looking down at her. She was sitting in one of the large armchairs, the book cradled to her chest. 'You have two weeks to read and absorb this book, and at the end of those two weeks I am going to ask you questions about it. If I am satisfied with your answers, then we'll see about you having a pony, but only if I'm satisfied that you've learnt all you can and will be willing to do all the work. Your mother will not be able to help you. Do you understand?'

Lilly looked back at him with serious eyes and nodded silently. Adie watched as her daughter's chest heaved with the weight of responsibility. Getting up from the chair, she gave her mother a little smile and then ran towards the back hall, heading for the room she shared with her brother.

Adie was boiling with anger. How dare Thomas make such a decision without asking her? Did he think everything and everyone was his to control? Had he considered the pressure this would put on her very young daughter? She wanted to confront him immediately, but Jack was in the kitchen. She would prepare her words and wait until the children were in bed.

At dinner that evening Thomas and Sam discussed tractors; types, sizes and their varying functions. It was good to hear her son talking enthusiastically, and this softened her attitude towards Thomas. But then she took a look at Lilly. Her daughter's mind was obviously miles away, no doubt already trotting around a field on her pony. How could he be so irresponsible to set Lilly up to something she was incapable of doing?

Later that evening Adie found herself tiptoeing back down the hall towards the kitchen. Stopping halfway, she asked herself, *Why are you skulking like a guilty teenager? You have every right to this conversation.* Tapping on the kitchen door, she inwardly bolstered her confidence.

'Come in,' Thomas's voice called. 'There is no need to knock.'

He was at the table reading a letter. She pulled out the chair opposite him and sat down, straight-backed, hands resting in her lap.

'I have come to talk to you about Lilly having a pony.'

'I thought you might,' he said, still perusing the letter in front of him.

'Firstly, I think it extremely irresponsible of you to raise my daughter's hopes of taking in all the information in that book. Secondly, that you think she could be capable of looking after a pony on her own. She is only seven years old, you know. I am her mother, in case you have forgotten, and no such conversation with her should have taken place without my prior knowledge and permission!' Adie stopped abruptly and placed her hands firmly on the table, her chin jutting forwards.

Thomas glanced at her, so briefly that it was almost imperceptible, and now that his eyes were back on his letter Adie wondered if she'd imagined it. The silence grew long, and she was about to speak when he raised a hand to stop her.

'First of all, I apologise to you. Of course I should have spoken to you first, but I knew you would take this stance and dismiss this opportunity for your daughter to prove herself.'

Still his eyes were on the letter. With her temper near the surface, Adie was once again about to speak when he looked directly at her and said, 'Hear me out. I know she is only seven, but she is a very bright girl and she has a natural way and patience with the horses which should be nurtured. It is my belief that she has every capability of caring for a pony on her own. When she does, she will benefit immensely, and it will give her great confidence in her own abilities.'

His eyes were making her feel uncomfortable, but she pushed on. 'I agree she is a very bright little girl, but I still do not see how she can care for a pony on her own at such a young age. Ponies are very strong animals, in case you hadn't realised. And it is my job to protect her.'

'Perhaps you have forgotten that I am a farmer and know very well the strength of a plough horse, let alone a pony. I believe that young Lilly has every ability to handle any situation with a pony. You do her a disservice by not having faith in her abilities.'

Adie's anger was about to overflow. He was turning the matter against her. When she spoke again her voice took on a new desperate pitch and she despised the fact that her emotions were so easily on display. 'Now that you have given her the book, and have said that if she passes your test you will consider giving her a pony, you leave me in a situation where I can do nothing about it. But promise me that if you give her a pony and she should fail to take care of it properly, you will provide some sort of assistance.'

Still looking directly into her eyes, he said, 'I will give you no such promise. Lilly has made this agreement with me and I believe she will carry it through. If you do not have faith in your daughter that is your affair.'

Adie was astounded. He had not raised his voice, and was so sanctimonious in his manner that she was lost for words. She stood up, scraping the chair across the floor. 'I pray for my daughter,' she said, scowling at him, then turned to leave the room.

'There is no need,' he called after her.

---*-*-*---

B ILL HAD FOUND Beckdale Farm, and rented a cheap room. The house, run by an old lady, was in the same village as the school his children attended. From his room it was a five-minute walk to the school and a twenty-minute walk, across fields, to the farmhouse. He had been watching his family for ten days.

From the highest point on the farm Bill could get almost a 360-degree view of the land beneath him. He had been coming here at sunrise, most mornings. From here, if he looked to his left, he could see the house and its garden; in front of that were the farm buildings, and spreading out down the hill, into the valley and the river beyond, was grazing land.

He had watched her walk along the riverside with those dogs. Even at this distance he recognised her movements; she stopped often, thinking, her hand touching her face. Now and again she'd squat down on her haunches and rest her chin on her arms. Bill liked to think that she knew he was coming for her, that she was deliberately teasing him. It would give him so much pleasure to disturb her rural idyll.

Waiting to get Adie back into his loving arms was like living in hell, he needed to have her under his control, but her surroundings gave him problems. When she went out walking, she was always with the dogs, and dogs frightened him. Then there was the farmer. He would have fun broaching that subject with her. It was his biggest shock to learn that Adie had another man. Bill wanted to know about them. What turned them on, where they had sex, how she had met him. It must have been recently. There was a lot to punish her for.

Occasionally, in the evenings, after the dogs had been put in their kennel, he sat in the rafters of the barn opposite the house. Bill liked this perch. From here, when it was dark and they had the lights on, he could see through the windows. He liked to watch Adie serving food and talking with her new lover. Through thin curtains he saw her body move. Their ignorance of his presence made him feel as if he had power over them.

Only the kitten knew he used this place. Strolling across the beam one evening, she'd seen him. Her fur raised and her lip curled back in a hissed alarm. He'd lunged for her, almost unseating himself. Next time he'd get her. He'd like to see their faces when they found her.

At the weekend, during the day, he hid behind hedgerows and stone walls and used binoculars to view his quarry. During the week, if the men were not close by, and if Adie had gone out, he liked to snoop close to the house. His plan was to get inside it; he wanted to know its layout. Usually when he did this the dogs were out with the farmers, but once, when they had been left in their kennel, they snarled and bared their teeth at him.

It was not going to be easy to get his family back. Adie and his children had a fortress around them.

—⊹—⊹—⊹—

I T WAS EARLY on a Saturday morning that Lilly took her test. Sam was at the kitchen table finishing his homework. Adie sat opposite, updating the household accounts. Lilly was in one of the armchairs, perched on its edge, her feet swinging nervously. The large chair framed her, accentuating her immaturity. Thomas was asking questions, speaking to her as if she were an adult. Adie listened intently to every word, proud of her daughter's confident voice. After an hour Thomas fell quiet and silence enveloped the kitchen. Sam and Adie glanced from Lilly to Thomas and back again. Thomas's eyes were cast downward. After a few moments he raised them, looking directly at Lilly.

'Well, do you want to come and see your pony?' he asked.

Lilly could be an adult no longer; she leapt to her feet and ran to her mother, dragged her off her chair and made her dance around in circles. Sam and Adie were infected with her happiness and laughed at her exuberance. They had not laughed like that for a very long time, and it felt strange.

Adie glanced at Thomas, who wasn't looking at her, but at Lilly. She saw something cross his face – it wasn't a smile, but a sort of softening of the hardened corners of his mouth.

As the four of them walked through the garden and out to the paddocks, Thomas explained that, of the six ponies in the field, five were at the farm on livery, and he owned the sixth. It was this pony that would be Lilly's.

Upon reaching the paddock they counted only five ponies. The field was surrounded by post-and-rail fencing and had two five-bar gates. They were standing by one of the gates; the other was on the opposite side of the paddock, and led to an adjacent field where winter wheat had recently pierced the soil. Their eyes searched for the missing pony.

Thomas saw him first. The stocky steed stood in the middle of his winter wheat, grazing on the young, delicate spears. 'If I have any more trouble from you, you will be dog meat!' he bellowed. The pony raised his head and looked in their direction. Knowing the owner of this angry voice, he flared his nostrils, snorted and swished his long tail. Adie saw that he was a large pony, with a proud, muscular carriage – far too big for Lilly.

Thomas entered the ponies' field and began striding across it to the wheat field, all the while grumbling and cursing. On the way he picked up a long stick and began waving it in time with the obscenities coming from his mouth. The pony gave a little rear and then cantered around the wheat field, sending great clods of mud and damaged wheat flying through the air. After completing two laps he gathered himself to a raised trot, gouging the soft ground. This enflamed Thomas further. Finally, turning at an angle, the pony lowered his head and lurched into a gallop towards the fence dividing the fields, clearing it effortlessly. Back in his own field, he set about grazing quietly with his muscular rump pointed towards Thomas.

Sam, Lilly and Adie smothered their giggles with their hands; it was the first time they had seen Thomas lose his composure. But, after the humour of the moment, Adie began to realise what a challenge this pony would be, and her anger at Thomas returned.

Knowing that further interaction with the animal was futile, Thomas headed for the tack room, signalling for Lilly to follow him. She dashed up to his heel, then looked down at his feet and attempted to keep pace with his stride. Adie watched her daughter swing her arms like a marching soldier and her heart leapt. Following on behind, she and Sam looked at each other, and read each other's worried thoughts. Lilly seemed wedded to Thomas's every word.

In the tack room they stood back, listening. Feeling unable to intervene, they did not want to dash Lilly's dream. Thomas explained all the equipment and the different types of feed, and Lilly seemed to understand everything. After a few minutes of this, he finally brought up the subject that was on everyone's mind, except Lilly's.

'The pony's show name,' he said, 'is Prince of Harlequin; Prince for short. His breed, a Section D Welsh Cob, and, as you saw, a spirited animal.'

'Spirited!' The word burst from Adie's lips.

Disregarding her, Thomas continued. 'He is both spirited and intelligent and it will take an intelligent person to get the best from him, which is why I think Lilly will do very well. This pony does not need someone who is going to use brawn, he needs someone who will use brain. Lilly knows what to do; she'll start work with him immediately.'

Back in the kitchen, Adie voiced her opinions to Thomas. The pony was too strong, too feisty and too big for a seven-year-old beginner. And, once again, Thomas got the better of the conversation, saying he could not believe her lack of confidence in her daughter, that all ponies are too strong for human beings if they want to be, and that this is where intelligence comes in.

Silence fell between them and Adie knew that further conversation was futile, so she made to leave the room.

'I've not been able to catch that beast for months. He's a talented pony and if Lilly can build a bond with him, they'll make a formidable twosome.'

'Can we make an agreement, then,' Adie said, turning to face her employer, 'that if she has not caught Prince by tomorrow evening, she may have a different pony, one of a more agreeable nature?'

Thomas inclined his head to one side in thought, and then nodded his agreement.

ALL OF SATURDAY and Sunday morning, Adie watched from the windows of the house, as her daughter attempted to catch the pony. Lilly tried every method: calling; approaching with a halter; tempting with apples; standing with her head down and her back to the pony, hoping curiosity would bring him to her; and once, even chasing the blessed animal around the field in sheer frustration. The pony stopped every now and again, waited for Lilly to catch up, and then trotted away as she came close. Unintentionally, she caught all the other ponies, but not her own. By the time they sat down to Sunday lunch Adie could see that her daughter's confidence had drained away. The only consolation was that soon it would be over, and they could set about finding a suitable pony.

That afternoon when Adie was alone in the house, Lilly came running into the kitchen and buried her face in her mother's apron. Her sobs tore at Adie's heart. She had been impressed by her daughter's fortitude and patience. And now a strange thing had happened: her anger had transferred from Thomas to the pony. The damn creature was so obstinate, and her child was trying so hard, she didn't deserve to fail. Adie hugged her until her tears dried, then held her daughter's tragic face in her hands.

'You're not beaten yet, you know.'

'But I thought you didn't want me to have a pony,' Lilly gulped through a fresh onset of tears.

'It's not that I don't want you to have a pony, I'm just not sure about *this* pony. He's so big and stubborn and strong. But I'll tell you what – why don't you try to catch him for just one more time, and if that doesn't work, I'll speak with Thomas about finding you another pony?'

'But I want Prince, he's the best.'

'Well get on out there; it's always when you think you've been beaten that you should try one more time. Then you'll know for sure that you gave it your best shot.'

Lilly left the house. Adie watched her daughter through the kitchen window with a sinking heart. The child walked slowly towards the field, head down and feet scuffing the ground. As she reached the gate Jack approached her from one of the nearby barns. They talked for a little while, then he opened the gate for her, and she walked towards the centre of the field, halter in her hand.

Turning from the window, Adie went about her chores. After a few minutes she glanced through the window again and saw that Lilly was sitting cross-legged in the middle of the paddock with her back to Prince. The pony stood some thirty yards away, staring at the child. Adie went back to her polishing. Then movement from the field attracted her attention, so she looked again. Lilly was still there, sitting in the middle of the field, cross-legged and looking down. The only difference was that now Prince stood behind her with his head lowered so that the soft underside of his muzzle rested on her shoulder. The motionless pair could have been a statue. Leaving the house, Adie ran towards the field wanting to congratulate her daughter, but Jack halted her, holding a finger to his lips.

'Don't disturb her yet; she's got some way to go before she's got it cracked.'

Thomas and Sam joined them and together the four of them watched as Lilly slowly got up and walked around the edge of the field. The pony followed; his head hung over her shoulder. She made her way back to the middle and, after stroking him from his ears to his haunches, very slowly put the halter over his head and led him towards the gate. Tethering him to the fence post, she calmly left the field and hugged her mother, a triumphant smile on her face.

Thomas broke the moment of joy. 'Now take him back into the field and let him go.'

Lilly, Sam and Adie threw him an incredulous look. Jack spoke, supporting Thomas's words.

'That's exactly what you have to do. From now until it gets too dark to see, you've got to practise catching him, letting him go and catching him again, until he knows exactly who is boss.'

— ✳✳✳ —

F ROM THAT DAY pony and child became inseparable. Every morning, before school, Lilly did her chores around the stable. Every afternoon, when school was finished, Prince trotted up and down the fence looking for her. With daily tutoring from Thomas her skills quickly improved, and Adie was persuaded to allow her to ride out alone, as long as she stayed on Beckdale Farm land.

Filled with pride for both her children, Adie reluctantly began to stand back and allow them to expand their lives. Lilly had her pony, and Sam had gained the male guidance and companionship he desperately needed. Jack, both gentle and strong, taught him about rural life and the working side of farming. The three of them had grown fond of this man; everything worked better when Jack was about.

Thomas continued to give his time to the children, but his approach was different. He tested and pushed them into achieving things they thought they could not do. They respected him, but he never changed; his face and feelings were always locked behind an impenetrable guard.

In her private moments, Adie was still full of anguish. She would stand by the window looking out at a black night, knowing she could not lock herself and her children in this sanctuary forever. But she knew Bill would be out there, hunting for them, and would eventually find them. They could be safe if they stayed here, but Lilly riding a pony alone, Sam out on a tractor, both of them at school; it was not safe. She had no choice but to let her children go, she knew it was good for them, but she was also frightened for them. Would they ever really escape from the prison Bill had built just for them?

—※—※—

RUPERT COULDN'T HELP it; he liked watching her. The first time he saw her he thought she was a ghost sent to haunt him, but somehow, the sight of her soothed him. He no longer carried his gun through the undergrowth, aiming his sights at men's heads. Instead he waited, the same time every afternoon, for the cat to appear first, then the pony with the little girl. She looked tiny on her sturdy steed, wayward hair escaping from her black riding hat. The pony's ears twitched as he listened to her talk to him. He knew Rupert was watching them, the cat did too, but not the little girl; she just rode on past him as he hid behind the hedgerow.

—※—※—

A T THE WEEKEND Lilly normally hacked in the afternoon and practised her gymkhana skills in the morning. But this morning it was misty, and the low sun shed a golden light across the landscape. She decided it was too pretty to work and chose to ride out; she would practise in the afternoon.

Sitting hunched in the saddle against the cold, she was beginning to regret her decision when a tall, skinny dog stepped out of the hedgerow in front of her. To her surprise, Prince did not shy but stopped and lowered his nose in greeting. The dog tilted its head to one side and disappeared into the hedgerow. There was a gap she had not noticed before. Looking beyond the gap and over the hedge, she saw the dog sitting in the middle of the field with the same tilt to its head. Bored with her usual route, she urged Prince through the gap. As soon as she was through the dog turned and made its way to the other side of the scrubby field.

Lilly felt sure this was not Beckdale Farm land, but was enjoying the tummy tingle of her little adventure and could not see how she could come to any harm. She pressed Prince forwards, and as soon as they moved the dog went through another hedge. She paused for a moment to look back and make a mental note of the way they had come, then, intrigued at what she might find, she pushed on. Here the hedges were overgrown and the grass long; it all felt mysterious.

Beyond the second hedge she saw the roof of a low barn, and was astonished to see Tinker sitting in the middle of the top ridge. Seeing her cat gave her the courage to go on. As she approached the unkempt hedge another gap appeared, and she realised this must be a path used regularly.

On the other side of this hedge she halted in astonishment. A man slumped in an old deckchair seemed to be fast asleep, or maybe he was dead. The skinny dog sat next to the man and stared at Lilly.

She dismounted Prince and crept up to the bedraggled figure. On close inspection she decided he was long and skinny, like his dog. He had long dark hair and an equally long beard, and he smelt. The only skin she could see was part of his face and one of his hands that clung to a sack; she had never seen skin ingrained so deep with dirt. She thought he needed a very hot bath. She also decided he was very old, probably older than Farmer Tom, or even Jack for that matter.

She wasn't afraid of him. She knew a man far scarier: her father, he scared her a lot.

The dog stood and trotted off, wagging her tail as if greeting a friend. Lilly looked to see who it was and was surprised to see that Tinker had come down from the roof and was now playing with the dog. This amused her because Tinker always snubbed the farm dogs.

The man groaned, a sad sound, and Lilly stroked his hand to soothe him. She pitied him living in this shabby place.

THE SCENT CAME to him first. Crisp and clean, it evoked memories of his childhood. An image of his mother floated into his vision. She was happy; he could hear her laughter. She wanted to speak to him, but there was something irritating his hand. He tried to shake it off and hold on to the dream so he could hear what his mother was saying, but as he did so, his dream and his mother faded. He woke with a start, aggravated.

The little girl stood in front of him holding her nose. 'You smell,' she giggled, sounding nasal. Her free hand picked up his and shook it. 'I'm Lilly and I'm training for the gymkhana. I could bring you a sandwich because you look very skinny. I don't think I can do anything about a bath, though.'

The little girl was looking at him, open-faced and smiling. He was staring and there was a strange sensation in his face – movement. He looked down at the hand she still held, and tears fell from his eyes. He could not remember the last time another person had touched him.

'Well, would you like a sandwich?'

He was finding it difficult to take his mind from the feeling of her hand touching his. 'Yes, I would like a sandwich.'

'OK, I'll bring it tomorrow afternoon.'

'I – I'll need to pay you,' he said, his mind churning desperately. 'I could teach you to be good at all the gymkhana games.'

'Can you? That would be brilliant. I'll see you tomorrow afternoon, then,' she said, as she clambered aboard her pony and turned to go. 'Cheese or ham?' she called back.

'Cheese, please.'

For a moment she was still, thinking, then she said, 'We'll have to keep our meeting a secret because I'm not allowed to ride off the farm. Do you agree?'

With a nod of his head he agreed, and she crossed the field and passed through the hedge, looking back with a smile and a wave.

Rupert sat in his chair thinking for a long time. Now that the girl and her pony had gone, part of him could not believe what had happened. Maybe she had been just another dream, like his mother. He touched his hand where she had held it and could still feel the smoothness of her delicate fingers, and he knew she was not a dream.

For the first time in more than two years he thought about his appearance and realised he had no idea what he looked like. It could not be good. In the barn he found his kitbag; it had not been moved since the day he came here. After wiping away the cobwebs he rummaged through the bag, convinced there was a small mirror in there somewhere. On finding it he viewed himself and then snatched it away from his face. That couldn't be him.

He stared out through the barn door into the distance and questioned how old he was. Was he thirty-eight? Or forty? No, he was thirty-eight; he had spent two winters here, and he was thirty-six when it happened.

With that thought his body began to shake and his heart tried to break free from its cage. There was the feeling he was going to vomit, and then, shamefully, but not for the first time, he urinated, and the warm liquid seeped down his legs into his already rotting boots. For many minutes he stood still, trying to regain control, to breathe slowly and bring himself back to the present. His dog nudged the hand the little girl had held, and he looked down into her deep brown eyes. They seemed to implore him.

Again, he looked in the mirror and this time he studied his appearance. His hair and beard covered most of his skin. His once-clear blue eyes were sunken, his nose beaklike and his mouth not visible. Sweeping his hair away from his face, he touched his skin and could feel the gritty dirt and oil that covered it.

He thought of the child touching him and a warmth ran through him. Maybe she was a dream and maybe she wasn't, but he was happy to live in the dream for as long as it lasted.

In a kind of madness, he ran to the back of the barn where there was a water butt. It was brimming with cold rainwater. Stripping off his clothes, the only ones he had, he dunked them into the liquid, including his boots. It was a cold late January morning, parts of him were turning blue and he was shivering, but it felt good to be naked.

Putting his hand in the water, he cupped some of it in his palm. For a few moments he watched its fascinating movement and shine as it drained through his fingers. Then he filled his palm again and splashed the cold liquid onto his stomach. His mouth let out an unexpected laugh. It was a strange sound. His dog barked encouragement, and he knew he was mad.

Dipping his arms deep into the barrel, he washed his clothes and boots as best he could and then strung them over the barn doors to dry, perching his boots upside down on the upper corners of the doors; they had no laces to hang them by. He went back to the barrel and for the third time that day caught his reflection. With his senses awakened, thoughts were coming quickly; he turned on his heel and sprinted back inside the barn to his kitbag, dog bouncing along at his side. Breathing heavily, he searched through the bag. Triumphantly, he held high his Swiss Army knife.

Washing his body and cutting his hair and beard seemed to clear a path in his mind, and for the first time he could think rationally about his past.

———✳——✳———

As a captain in the British Army, Rupert had been a good tactician and was instrumental in the planning of many successful missions. Loyalty and responsibility towards his men and the communities whose lives they were trying to protect and improve were uppermost in his thoughts. Therefore, he was held in high esteem not only by those who served under him but also by his commanding officers.

He spent time with the people, learning the idiosyncrasies of Northern Irish ways and the sensitivities that surrounded their religion, politics and lives. Therefore, he was trusted by much of the local community.

When the SAS singled him out for assistance in a covert operation to capture a number of IRA activists wanted for murder, he was eager to assist in removing these vermin from the streets. Initially his skills had been required for planning only. But, after the first few meetings and subsequent reconnaissance work, it became clear that the SAS would need Rupert's assistance on the ground, while the mission itself was being carried out.

The activists held monthly meetings, always in a different location. They used the houses of ordinary families, threatening their lives if they did not conform and keep the secret. It was the mother of one such family, whose home had been chosen for the next meeting, who had informed. She was already mourning the loss of her husband and eldest son; she did not want her two younger boys dragged into the same life of violence and hatred.

Rupert's part in the operation was to protect the family. They would be located in the kitchen at the back of the house. He was to ensure that they were quietly removed through the back door to waiting British Army vehicles and whisked away to a safe house. As soon as the family were safely away the SAS would silently enter the front of the house and dispose of the activists in their unnervingly noiseless way.

During the hours immediately prior to the operation, Rupert had run through the plan many times, looking for flaws. Although he was satisfied it was good and it was an easy, clean operation, he knew that if things went wrong, all could turn sour and unwanted deaths could ensue.

Dressed in plain clothes, Rupert had parked the Ford Cortina at the end of the alleyway. After checking his watch he'd made his way down the narrow pathway that ran between the backyards of the terraced houses. The yard gate was left unlocked as planned.

Through the kitchen window he could see the family sitting at the table, eating their tea. He opened the back door and signalled for them to leave. But no one moved; they stared at him, their plates of food untouched in front of them.

The door that led from the kitchen into the hall began to open very slowly. All eyes focused on it. A little girl, all freckles and curls, biting her bottom lip and carrying a tray of beer tankards, entered the room. Rupert's mind went into overdrive. Who was she? She was not meant to be here. He took in the face of the mother; it was petrified.

Behind the little girl followed a man wearing a balaclava; he was pointing a gun at her head. In deep Irish tones he said, 'Why don't you come in?', and gestured with a twitch of his gun.

As Rupert stepped into the kitchen a shot sounded in the front room. Seconds slowed into minutes. The man looked at the mother sitting with her boys at the dinner table. 'You fucking bitch,' he said. And with that he grabbed the little girl by her dress and picked her up, so her eyes were level with his. The tray crashed to the floor. At point-blank range he shot the top of her head off. Her blood and brains plastered the wall, her body slumped, what was left of her head hung. Somehow, her eyes were still intact, and they stared accusingly at Rupert.

The man dropped the girl and disappeared into the hall. Rupert rushed forward as if to catch and save her, yet he knew he could not. She had fallen like a rag doll. He scooped her body up, shouted at the shocked family, and shoved and pushed them out of the back door.

As they ran down the alleyway, he heard more shots from inside the house. He was at the back, carrying the little girl. Bullets started to chase them; he felt a searing pain through his left thigh, but adrenaline kept his legs pounding.

They made it to the Cortina. The boys in the back, the mother in the front. Rupert placed the little girl on her lap and drove away. Blood from his leg stained the seat and dripped onto the floor. The mother's mouth screamed silently. The boys sat, heads down, building their hatred. No one explained about the little girl.

At the meeting point Rupert was whisked away to a base he had not been to before. He never saw the family again. At the base they tended his wounds and he was told his debriefing would be in a couple of hours. While he waited, he wrote his list of questions.

The debrief didn't happen until the following day and all of his questions were answered with 'I'm sorry, that's classified information.' He was informed that he would be sent home to convalesce and would not serve in Northern Ireland again. He was reminded that he had signed the Official Secrets Act and the penalty for breaching it was prison.

He went home to heal, but the little girl would not leave him alone. Every night the nightmare was the same: she looked at him accusingly and then her brains splattered the wall behind her, blood poured down her dress and the sound of her body slumping to the ground woke him. He began to class himself as one of the bad men, guilty of her killing. Rupert went AWOL.

———✼·✼·✼———

CURIOSITY ABOUT ADIE'S new life occupied Bill's every thought. He watched her from close up and at a distance; he peered through windows, sat in trees and hid in hedgerows. From the rafters of barns, secreted behind the paraphernalia of farming equipment, he viewed her. It was almost impossible to find moments when she was vulnerable and alone. She was either surrounded by the pack of dogs or with one of the men. During the day, when she was in the house, was the only time she was unaccompanied. But even then, there were frequent visitors; one of the men or the fat lady could return at any moment.

One morning, at around 5.30, Bill waited, hidden in a hedgerow at the edge of the garden. He watched the usual routine of the household, as he had done many mornings. Lights appeared on the upper floor, and the dogs, housed overnight in their kennel, began to whine. Soon these lights extinguished, and the kitchen was illuminated. He saw Adie approach the sink to fill up the kettle. He wondered if they slept in separate rooms to hide their activities from his children. After several minutes they would both leave the house. He with a cup of tea in his hands, heading for the barns, and she to the kennel, where the dogs waited eagerly for her. Bill hoped that his children, left alone, would still be asleep.

Leaving his hiding place, Bill ran towards the house, back bent low, each footstep leaving a trail in the dew-covered grass. He entered by the unlocked boot-room door and passed through it to the kitchen. The heat of the room overwhelmed him, and he wanted to remove his jacket, but there was no time. Quickly, he took in the surroundings. Crumpled cushions on the sofa, a scrubbed table and a wood-burning stove brought to life from its overnight slumber. These things caused a hateful jealousy to rise in his gullet, and he yearned for Adie and all she had provided for him.

On the dresser was a freshly cut loaf of bread. Bill opened the drawer beneath it. Inside was a selection of kitchen knives. He ran his finger across them, stopping at the carving knife. With its bone handle and curved blade, it appealed to him. Predicting it would be razor-sharp, he picked it up and ran it gently across the tip of his forefinger. It sliced easily through his skin, causing a large drop of blood to appear. Bill wiped his finger on a tea towel, wrapped it around the knife and anchored it inside his trousers.

Relying on knowledge gained from his observations, he found his way to the stairs, listened for a moment, and then, treading softly, he climbed them. On the landing all the doors were closed except one. This, he guessed, was the room where the light had been; the room they had used. Bill wanted to smell the sheets and visualise them tangled in each other. He knew this would cause him bitter pain, but it was pain that would fuel his need to punish her.

Entering the room, he stood still, eyes closed, and strained to inhale Adie's bodily scent. It was not there. This was the place where he'd expected to find their mingled odours. When his eyes adjusted, he crossed the room to the bed and was disappointed that it was pristine. Like the window, it had been left open to air, its sheet stretched tight across the mattress, the pillows plumped. Angry, feeling cheated, he left the room.

With caution, he opened every door on the landing. Each revealed an unused space. Time was running out on him. Quickly, he mentally pictured the bearings of the house from the outside and walked towards a far wall. Placing his hand on it, he realised this was not the end of the building; there must be another staircase. Less concerned about noise, he took the stairs four at a time and headed towards the corresponding place on the ground floor; there was no way through. Back in the kitchen, there was only one more door to try. He opened it and saw a narrow hallway with a door at the end.

Finding himself standing in a small sitting room where his children's coats hung on pegs, he was confused. This was not what he had expected. Against a side wall he saw a primitive staircase, and climbed it. At the top were two doors; one was open.

As Bill entered Adie's room her odour enveloped him. No open window here. His body burned with arousal at her scent. Slowly, he moved around the room, touching her belongings. He knew no sex had taken place here; they must have a secret room somewhere else. He could not contemplate a man living in such close proximity to his wife and not wanting to have her. Reaching across the bed, Bill picked up Adie's nightdress and crushed it to his face. Its fabric still held the warmth of her, and his craving intensified. She was everywhere in the room, holding him there, making him lose time.

Some distant noise from outside snapped him back to the present. Dropping the nightdress on the floor, he stepped out of the room. He should have left then, but his children were probably sleeping behind the other door. It couldn't hurt just to glimpse them. Gingerly, Bill turned the handle and was thankful the door made no noise. A few feet away, facing him, his daughter slept. The first glimmers of dawn cast a faint light across her face. For a few seconds he studied her. He could have taken her before now, could take her now, but that was not his plan. Leaning a little further into the room, he was able to look around the door. Sam lay with his back to him and Bill wondered if he was asleep. Then something disturbed Lilly's slumber and her face creased as if in pain. Quickly, Bill closed the door and deftly made his way back down the stairs. When he was halfway down, he heard her scream. It was good to know she hadn't forgotten him.

———✳✳✳———

WHEN ADIE RETURNED from walking the dogs that morning, her children were still in their bedroom. Sam was on Lilly's bed, holding her hand while she cried.

'She says Dad was here. I said she was dreaming, but she insists he was here. She says she smelt him.' Sam raised an eyebrow at his mother. 'I explained it was just you she heard, looking in on us before you went out with the dogs. But she won't have it.'

Lilly seemed genuinely upset and disturbed. Adie, not registering her son's words, sat on the bed and cradled her daughter.

'Go and get the hot-water kettle, Sam; bring it up and let's see if we can wash these tears away.'

Coaxing and gentle persuasion finally calmed her child. Once down in the warm kitchen, and with porridge inside her, Lilly seemed prepared to accept her night terror and was happy to walk to school with her brother. The upset had put Adie behind with breakfast for Thomas and Jack, so she gave her children a quick wave and rushed back to the kitchen.

When breakfast was finished and cleared away, Adie went back to her children's bedroom, needing to tidy after their rushed start to the day. As she climbed the stairs her heart began to pound; she stopped, placed her hand on her chest and felt its hammering beat. The hair on the backs of her arms stood upright. With unsteady legs, she sat on the steps. *It's just panic*, she told herself, *caused by Lilly's nightmare raising old fears*. Adie had suffered this before and she knew it would soon pass. She tried to relax and counted her breathing in and out, but her body refused to shake off its heightened state, so she decided to ignore it. It took only a few minutes to tidy the room. When it was done, she picked up the kettle and headed for the stairs.

On the threshold of the door she dropped the kettle, and it clanged and bounced its way down the steps.

She was sure she had left her nightdress on her bed. She was most particular to be tidy in her new environment. But now, it was on the floor, lying in a crumpled heap. Knowing her children would not have done this, she picked it up between her thumb and forefinger, as if handling an infectious disease. Feeling a sudden need to burn it, she half-slid down the stairs in haste and shoved it in the wood burner. Grabbing the poker, she stabbed at it in violent rage until every last shred was gone. Smoke poured into the room. Shutting the wood burner's door, she opened the window wide and let the cold air wash over her.

Stunned, she sat motionless for an immeasurable amount of time, trying to put her incoherent thoughts in order. Panic had not left her, but now it was tempered with anger. Eventually, she quietened her breathing and raised the steel guard that had protected her so many times in the past. At last, finally able to think straight, she burst into hysterical laughter at herself for burning her nightdress to a cinder for no good reason. Bill had not been here. Lilly had just been dreaming. Echoes of the past were bound to affect them. He could not have found them so quickly. This whole episode was a fluke. She must have dropped her nightdress on the floor. But these considerations came from her head and were not the same as those in her gut. In her gut, the thought that he had found them, was waiting in the wings until she was strong enough for it to be heard.

—⋆⋆⋆—

THE FOLLOWING DAY promised to be bright even though it was February.

As Adie crossed the garden, heading for the kennel, a fresh breeze blew away any leftover gloomy thoughts. She could hear the dogs yip and whine with excitement. They seemed to have bonded with her. Jack said it was because she was female, like them, and therefore one of their pack. Adie thought this comment amusing. For her, their morning walk was a kind of remedy; a gentle, ongoing cure for her troubled soul.

Passing the barn, she caught sight of the owls who nested there. They swooped in on ghostly wings, returning from their night's hunting. One of them landed on a fence post and observed Adie and the dogs with that strange, dislocated movement of its head.

She decided to climb the hill to the top of the farm and open country. It was her spot to watch the sunrise. As she traipsed up the uneven pathway, her breathing a little laboured, she smiled at her anxiety of the previous day, dismissing it as foolish. When she reached the top, she sat on the old tree stump, her usual resting place. Here she would take a few moments to absorb nature's ever-changing view and then begin the descent, ready for the day. With hands shielding her eyes, she scanned the horizon. Something caught her attention, way down in the valley on the farm road. It was a fox, sitting still, sniffing the air. She guessed they must be downwind from him, otherwise he would have caught their scent by now. Then, in a flash of red, he disappeared into the grassy bank.

Adie brought her focus back to the immediate surroundings. Normally, at this point, the dogs would have wandered away, sniffing the ground. But today, except for Patch, the Jack Russell, they had not moved. She shivered against the chill air and wrapped her arms about herself. The pointers sat around her, as if on guard, and Fern, the collie, stood a few feet out in front. All the dogs looked in the same direction, towards the woods. Fern's eyes were narrowed to slits and a low growl began to emit through her bared teeth.

Standing on shaky legs, Adie looked around. At first she wondered if a bull or a boar had got loose, but then she knew, by the sound the dogs were making, that this was not the case. The pointers moved closer to her, grumbling under their breath, curling their lips. And still Fern stood bravely out in front, guarding them. From what, Adie did not know.

It seemed like an eternity that she was frozen to the spot, feeling naked and vulnerable, as if eyes were watching her. Then, unexpectedly, Patch dashed across in front of them, chasing a rabbit. The pointers and Fern did not move.

Adie called the dogs to heel and began to make her way down towards the valley. Glancing back, she saw that the pointers were with her, but not Fern. The dog had not moved, but whined and fidgeted. Adie turned back up the hill and the pointers followed her. When she reached the collie, she noticed a large stone at the dog's feet, pinning an envelope to the ground. Picking it up, she saw Bill's handwriting. A wave of revulsion ran from her head to her feet, her fingers opened involuntarily, and the letter fell to the ground. It lay there, pretending to be innocuous, but Adie knew it contained danger. She picked it up, stuffed it into her pocket and resumed her walk home.

That evening she sat by the window in her tiny living room, with Tinker, the kitten, on her lap. Stroking her silken fur, she listened to the cat purring and tried to soothe her nerves. The envelope was on the sill; she had been staring at it for a long time. At first, she thought she wouldn't open it, just burn it; then she was cross with herself for picking it up.

If she had left it where it was, it would have shown him that he no longer had control over her. But she had picked it up, and so she decided to open it.

———※※※———

My darling Adie, my wife,

It amazes me how stupid you are. Did you think you would be rid of me? Silly girl, you'll never be rid of me. You know you don't really want to be without me; you've never had more excitement than when you were with me.

I miss our children; they were getting to such an interesting age. I could be having so much fun with them. You took them away from me. You know you are going to have to pay for your crime. You have been so cruel.

You think you are safe with your dogs and your farmer. I can't wait to find out what it is you do with your farmer. And maybe you are safe, but are the children? Think about it – aren't they alone sometimes?

When you meet me again, which you will, you will tell me all about your new life. Then we will discuss how delighted you are that your husband has returned to your loving arms and we can all live happily, here on the farm. You see, your life doesn't have to change; as long as you follow my rules, you can have the best of both worlds. What a lucky girl you are, that I love and adore you so much that I am prepared to share you, as long as you remember you are mine.

You know I am obsessed with you, that I am hooked on you. But now I know that you are cunning as well as clever and beautiful, I am even more excited by you. I will not, cannot, go back to life without you.

I will be at the derelict cottage near the top of the farm, at 8.30 on Friday evening. If you are not there someone else will have to pay for your crime.

Love always and forever,
Bill

————————

WEAVING LIKE A drunk, she staggered outside to the toilet, the letter screwed up in her hand. After retching until there was nothing more to leave her body, she collapsed on the floor. For a long time, she sat, dumbfounded, her mind unable to contemplate any action. She could not move or think; every part of her was frozen. Then, without warning, Bill's ugly words sliced through her brain like a vicious dagger and her hands whipped to her head to crush it, to dispel the evil within.

Now that movement had returned to her, and she was slowly coming back to life, she began to shiver. It came first in judders, then her whole body shook uncontrollably. The February night was cold. She stood up on quaking legs and felt for the light switch, flooding the space with cruel brightness. With shaking hands, she tried to smooth her skirt, but quickly removed them as they slid across the slime of some of her vomit.

Bent crooked, she felt her way inside, where she collected a bucket, scrubbing brush and cloth. Back outside she filled the bucket with freezing water from the external tap, cleaned the toilet and the surrounding floor, threw away the dirty water, then rinsed and refilled the bucket. Once inside again, she removed her skirt and left it to soak. Finally, she climbed the stairs to her bed where she lay curled up in a tight ball, eyes wide open, and listened to her heart beating.

Trying to keep her thoughts logical was impossible. They migrated to parts of her mind where secrets were kept locked away. She wanted to stop them; strained to keep the gates shut. But they creaked open and she could not hold back the tide. Words and visions flooded her brain and she tightened her grip on her knees lest madness break free. For many minutes she stayed that way, locked in. Then her fingers began to hurt, and her nails dug into her knees. She released her hands and massaged the pain away.

Next, a numbness paralysed her heart and soul, and cold calculation started to replace instinct. It would be a useless exercise to take this letter to the police. She would not waste her time with them. This time she would be ready for him. She would not allow him to destroy their new life. Her children should not have to live with fear again and she would do whatever it took to finally be rid of him. She did not know what to do except take one step at a time, and the first step was to ignore his letter.

———✴✴✴———

F RIDAY ARRIVED AND she had been thinking hard, covering the problem from every angle. Her head hurt and her body ached from multiple sleepless nights, but her mind was made up: she would not meet him; she would call his bluff. He could not do bad things here on the farm and get away with it. In any case, she had to pull herself together; everyone thought she was acting strangely. If she did not behave normally soon, Bill would have succeeded in destroying her new life.

———✴✴✴———

L AWRENCE HAD HAD to wait three days before he'd been able to speak to his boss about leave. The conversation had not gone well. The chief inspector, who had recently returned from a seminar where the main topic had been increasing conviction rates, was not keen to hear holiday requests. Lawrence was told to wrap up the case he was working on and then reapply. If things were quiet, it might be granted. It had taken many weeks, but now it was looking as if the case would be solved in the next couple of days.

During that time, he hadn't forgotten about Adie Lewis and her children; they had plagued him every night. Thoughts about how they were surviving, and whether Bill had managed to track them down, would not vacate his mind.

Now, sitting at his desk with his office door open, Lawrence called for Jonesy's attention. Leaving a WPC in charge of his counter, Jonesy went to see what his DI needed.

'I'm pretty sure, Jonesy, that this Mark Taylor is our guy. Here's the charge.'

Lawrence handed Jonesy some paperwork. The sergeant looked at it; it was not the charge, but details of the Lewis case that had previously been sent to Cumbria.

'Get a couple of the boys out to the docks and arrest him, will you? I should be able to get a confession with the evidence we have, and then we can wrap this up.'

'Er, yes, sir. Already on to it, sir.' Jonesy remained at the desk, knowing by the tone of Lawrence's voice that there was more to come.

Lowering his voice, Lawrence added, 'And get on to the Cumbria schools board, find out if they've had a brother and sister by the name of Lewis move into the area. Ask them to tell you which school they're attending.'

'Come on, boss, you know that case isn't ours any more.'

'The trouble, Jonesy, is that it isn't anyone's now. The Cumbria Constabulary dropped it like a stone, and no one has any idea whether that woman and her kids are alive and well, or dead. So, I'm taking a holiday in Cumbria, Jonesy. And I want to visit some friends who have recently moved there; only trouble is, I've lost their new address, and you, Jonesy, marvellous detective that you are, are going to find it for me.'

'Promise me you won't do any police work; you won't get involved.'

Lawrence raised his eyes and smiled at his sergeant. 'You're sounding like a wife. I didn't know you cared so much.'

Jonesy turned on his heel and slouched away, mumbling under his breath.

———※※※———

AFTER ADIE DID not turn up for their meeting, Bill left another letter under the stone. He watched her the following morning as she picked it up and, without a glance at the words he'd written, shredded the paper into little pieces, throwing them to the wind. She would have to pay for that defiance.

That evening, on the opposite side of the valley, the sun had just slipped away below the horizon. It gave a final display for the day, sending streams of gold, purple and pink across the evening sky. Bill took in none of these things. Right now, after a day of thinking about Adie's actions, he was devastated to know that she did not love him as he loved her, that she thought she was safe and that he couldn't get to her. Didn't she realise that he deserved to be loved by her? He didn't want it to be over; he was enjoying watching her battle against his control; loved watching her fear and, most of all, relished the idea of playing with her like a puppet.

He picked up the sack that had been writhing around at his feet, thrust his gloved hand into it and drew out the kitten, holding it tightly around its neck. In his other hand he held the carving knife he had stolen from their kitchen.

———※—※—

A COUPLE OF days after Adie had torn up Bill's letter Doris stopped by the house. Having collected the post from the box at the entrance to the farm she expected a coffee and a chat. Adie was not in the mood.

'Oh! I must tell you about the postmistress,' Doris said, the words spilling from her mouth as soon as she entered the kitchen.

'Really?' said Adie, frantically polishing a side table that already had a high shine. She carried on buffing the table, unable to stop, and wondered what stories Doris told others.

'She's only carrying on with that postman,' Doris continued, placing the palms of her hands on Adie's polished table. 'You know, the young, good-looking one, always flirting with everyone! You know who I mean.'

'I do not know who you mean, and I have far more important things to do than stand here with you, gossiping about innocent people.'

'Are you all right, love? You look pale and tired.'

'I'm fine. Just a bit… time of the month,' Adie said, hoping this would satisfy her.

Although Adie continued to speak brave words to herself, inside she was falling apart.

Doris left, crestfallen at being rebuked for delivering her news. Adie felt bad about the way she'd spoken to her, but right now, she could not cope with such banal topics. As the day wore on anxiety attacked her, pounding her heart against her ribs and constricting her lungs. At times, she was not able to breathe at all and thought she might faint. Later, at dinner, she served food to the others, then feigned a stomach ache and retired to her room.

But being alone did not help – her thoughts went back to the beatings, rapes and mental torment. The praying that it would all be over soon and wondering how many blows she could take before one killed her. Then, in the middle of it all, thoughts of her children would enter her mind and she would promise herself she would stay alive. Afterwards, he would turn into Prince Charming and praise her, saying that now she had received her punishment, she would know not to make those errors again; that now he loved her again. He would tell her that it was for her own good that these punishments took place; that they were all to make her a better person. But, of course, there was always a new crime she would commit, something that would require further retribution.

Adie wondered now how she had managed to live through it all. She knew he had dehumanised her to the extent that she was used to living in hell, receiving daily cruelty. Since being on the farm, with these warm, down-to-earth people, she had begun to lower her guard; maybe even started to trust, to build relationships and dare to think she might be a worthwhile person. Even with Thomas she knew what to expect. She was becoming human; no longer did she have to live like a trapped animal with a cruel owner. She could not risk losing it all by allowing this parasite to invade their lives again.

She was standing clutching the windowsill, as if for support, when she heard her son's voice.

'Can you help me with my spellings before I go to bed, please?'

Adie glanced at her watch; it was 8.40.

'Are you OK, Mum? Do you still have a stomach ache?'

'My stomach is fine now.' She smiled at her son and caressed his face to wipe away the concerned frown. 'Come on, let's go and sit on the sofa and see if we can get these spellings right.'

Together, they curled up in comfort. Lilly was already in bed and fast asleep, tired from her pony work. The spelling practice began. Later, Adie returned to the kitchen to clear away the dinner things. At first it was a pleasant surprise to find it clean and tidied, but then she wondered who had done this? Would Thomas have cleared away or was it Bill?

———※———※———

THE MUSCLES IN Jack's back groaned; he needed a break. Now that he was in his sixth decade, the time when he could swing a sledgehammer for an entire day had passed. He straightened up and placed his hands in the small of his lean back, arching backwards and forwards to relieve the ache. He looked over their handiwork for that morning. It was the weekend, and Jack and Sam were erecting new fencing strong enough to contain the farm's pig family. He looked forward to the days when Sam worked with him. The boy listened to his stories, asked questions and paid attention to the answers. He was a serious, intelligent boy and enthusiastic about the work.

But this morning things were different. Thomas wanted Jack to ask Sam about his mother and try to find out what was troubling her. It was almost lunchtime, and still he hadn't found the right way to broach the subject.

He took his time relieving his back, thinking about the boy, his mother and his sister. For some reason, their behaviour wasn't normal. They never left the farm, except to go to school or to pick up supplies. Neither Adie nor the children had any friends. Sam was always willing to learn, always respectful and polite, but never just a boy. Not once had Jack seen him kicking a football around, or just skiving off doing his own thing. The boy had an old head on his shoulders. Jack wanted to see him be mischievous or cheeky, but instead he was obedient and correct, doing everything that was asked of him without a word of complaint. It didn't seem natural.

Sam watched his old friend in his baggy trousers and cotton shirt, worn thin from washing. 'Why do you do that moving about with your back every so often?' he asked.

'Because it aches if I don't, and it helps me to carry on working.' Jack sounded tense without meaning to.

Sam wanted to ask more questions about his age – he thought Jack must be very old, judging by the wrinkles on his face. But he noticed that Jack seemed to be a bit quiet this morning, so he concentrated on his work instead.

'Is your mum all right?' Jack said. 'Only she seems a bit off colour; she's not ill or anything, is she?'

'No, Mum's not ill.' At the mention of his mum, Sam

looked down and began scraping mud off one boot with the sole of the other.

'Is she unhappy, then? Because she isn't her usual self, is she now?' Jack watched the boy's reactions closely as he probed a little deeper.

To avoid Jack's gaze, Sam went to collect the next fence post from the trailer. 'Yes, she is unhappy,' he said over his shoulder, feeling as if he had betrayed her. He took time selecting the post. Heaving it over his shoulder, he paced heavily back towards Jack and looked him straight in the eye. In a voice far older than his years, he said, 'But I don't know why, so don't ask me.'

'We'll have to see if there's a way to cheer her up, then, won't we?' Jack said, smiling as he took the post from Sam. But Sam was not looking at him; his face was pinched closed, studying the ground.

At midday they were back in the tractor shed. The fence was finished and they were planning their work for the small window of afternoon daylight, when Thomas appeared and drew Jack aside.

'Any luck with the boy?'

'No, he didn't say much at all; just that she is unhappy, and he doesn't know why. But the thing is, it's the way he said it – he was really dismissive, as if to say, *Don't pry again.*'

Thomas thought for a moment. 'Maybe I'll have a chat with young Lilly; she's more likely to let something slip.'

He was trying to find her about the yard, when he bumped into Doris.

'Have you seen Lilly about?'

'Saw her a few moments ago, riding Prince in the far field,' she said.

Thomas noted what a keen rider Lilly had become, and began walking in that direction.

She had finished her practice and was returning Prince to his paddock. She pulled his halter over his ears and gave him a slap on the rump. He cantered off, bucking twice, to celebrate his freedom.

Lilly was striding out towards the tack room, lost in her thoughts. Their paths almost crossed before she saw Thomas, and she jumped and giggled.

'How's the riding going?'

She had been having lessons with Rupert for a number of weeks and her skills had greatly improved. She wanted to show her mother and everyone else all the new things she had learnt, but was afraid of getting into trouble for lying about where she had been, and for stealing food from the kitchen.

'Good,' she said, not able to meet his gaze.

'I should get some time next weekend to help you with the gymkhana games, if you like.'

'Oh, don't worry if you're busy, I... I'm getting on fine.'

'So how do you know if you've got the rules right?'

A slight pause, then, 'I've got a book.' Finally she was looking at him.

It crossed his mind that it was just like her to take matters into her own hands.

'Is your mum all right?' he asked. 'Only she seems a bit unhappy.'

Lilly was relieved that the conversation had turned away from riding practice. 'I think so.'

'Oh, that's good, then.' He let her go by.

She was on her way to the house when he called after her. 'Have you got a father?'

He didn't know what made him ask that question; it left his mouth before he realised it. Lilly stopped in her tracks. As she slowly turned round, her neck sank into her shoulders, her hands clenched at her chest and her skin drained of colour. She looked at him with fear and distrust.

'Not any more,' she said, then ran to the house.

Thomas instantly regretted delving into her private world. It would take him ages to regain her trust. But that look of fear had given him insight into the lives of his resident family. As he strolled slowly towards the house, he wondered about his housekeeper. He knew she'd run away from a bad marriage, Doris had told him. He'd understood that the man didn't know where she was. Was he giving Adie trouble now? It would account for why she never went anywhere.

Thomas's respect for Adie had grown during the short time they had known each other. She was hard-working, intelligent, a lioness of a mother, and deserved a better life than the one she had.

A DIE WAS CUTTING thick slices of freshly baked bread, when she glanced through the window and saw Thomas approaching.

From the boot room he called, 'Adie, is there anything I can help you with?' These last few days he had been kinder, more considerate. Adie had not noticed until now, when his question took her by surprise.

'No, thank you,' she said.

She did not want to be alone with people. It was difficult to cover her fears, to make herself appear normal. But now he was standing at the kitchen door, hands in his pockets, watching her. An involuntary frown creased her forehead. Why didn't he go away, do his own work and come back at the correct time? She had enough to cope with, without having to put on a happy face for him.

'Look, I don't want to pry,' he said, a little awkwardly, rubbing the back of his neck, 'but you're part of our community now and it's obvious that something is making you unhappy. So, if there's anything we can do to help, please tell us; we don't like to see you like this.'

'There's nothing,' she said, without looking at him. Then, realising she was going to have to try harder to convince him, she faced him, showing him a sunny smile. 'Really, I'm OK.'

'Shall I come back shortly, then, for lunch?'

'Yes.'

'You're sure there's nothing—'

'Nothing,' she said, cutting off his words.

Over lunch, the five of them tucked into bread, butter, cheese and pickles. Their conversation was more animated than usual, each person, in their own way, trying to lift the mood. Except Adie, who remained silent. She was incapable of sharing her problems with the people who had come to care for her. She would not allow the dirt of her previous life to sully her new-found sanctuary.

T HE FOLLOWING DAY, over dinner, Lilly asked, 'Has anyone seen Tinker? Only she wasn't in her usual spot in the stable this morning.'

The cat had not been seen by anyone for four days. None of them were particularly worried; Tinker had gone missing before.

'I wouldn't worry, my lovely. She's probably found some well-populated rodent patch to keep her busy,' Adie said.

'Yuck! That means she will be lining up dead bodies outside the boot-room door again.' Lilly screwed up her face in disgust. The worst bit about Tinker's war on rodents was being the first unsuspecting person to go out of the door in the morning. It was usually Thomas who stepped into the bloody detritus, but he didn't mind.

'That cat's a good ratter and has saved me time and money that could've been spent on the vermin control man. And as I've said before, there is room enough for everyone as long as everyone understands, children included...' And with this comment he wagged a finger at Lilly and Sam, until he realised that they were holding down giggles in response to his speech; the one they had heard so many times before. 'Well, you all know what I mean,' he said, still unable to smile at himself.

Jack winked at them. Lately, Thomas, used to being alone, was beginning to realise that his new team were pulling together, and he was enjoying their company. The situation unsettled him.

O N THE FOLLOWING day, at the height of the noonday sun, Jack went up to the ruined cottage to collect some straw bales stored under tarpaulin. He turned off the tractor engine and walked towards the ruins, then, hearing a droning sound, turned back to check that he had silenced the engine. Realising that the engine was still, he stood and listened. It was then that the telling smell of a dead animal reached his nostrils. He followed the buzzing sound that came from inside the tumbledown cottage walls.

Hanging from a beam were four seething balls of blue flies and maggots. So numerous were the maggots that they dropped to the ground in clumps. As he approached, the agitated flies lifted momentarily, and Jack's heart sank as he recognised the grey-and-white markings of Tinker. The cat had been cruelly quartered. Her head was hanging grotesquely from one section, her pink tongue swollen and distorted. Writhing maggots filled every orifice. Each delicate paw had been tied to the beam with string.

Using his knife, Jack cut the strings one at a time. Holding each piece in turn in one hand, he brushed away the flies and maggots with the other. Gently he wrapped the pieces of the body in some sacking he found nearby.

He wished that whoever had done this cowardly act was here now; he would show them how to cut properly.

A DIE WAS UPSTAIRS putting clean linen on the beds, when she heard Jack calling. She entered the kitchen to find both Thomas and Jack waiting for her with serious looks on their faces.

'I found Tinker,' Jack said, his voice flat.

'Oh, where is she?' Adie asked, looking from one man to the other.

'Jack found her up at the ruined cottage,' Thomas said.

'Ah, been holed up there killing mice, I suspect.' Her voice sounded hollow, she knew their faces were revealing bad news, but she didn't want to hear it.

'No, Adie. I'm sorry to tell you, but Tinker's dead,' Jack said.

'But how? There are no roads here. Did the foxes get her? I thought she was too clever for that…'

She was about to ramble on, but Thomas held up a hand to silence her. Jack was looking at her with a pained face when Thomas said, 'Adie, Jack found her hung, quartered and strung up on a beam in the most horrific way. I know everyone in this area and there is no one who would do such a thing. Adie, would someone *you* know do something like this?'

A sob wrenched itself from a place deep inside Adie, and she clasped her guts as if in pain. The two men were startled by her reaction. Then they watched her battle with her emotions, pulling them in, locking them down. Her body straightened, her chin lifted, and then she levelled them with her eyes.

In a voice of steel, she said, 'The children are not to be told what happened to Tinker.'

The men indicated their agreement.

'It is to be left that she has gone missing and that is that. Jack, will you bury the remaining pieces of her down by the river? That was her favourite hunting ground. And of course I know no one who would do such a thing.' Looking as if she was about to say more, she frowned for a moment, then simply said, 'I have to get on,' and left the room.

O N T H E I R W A Y to the barns, the two men tried to understand Adie's response.

'What did you make of that, then?' Jack said.

'It feels like we told her about a whole lot more than the awful death of her cat. But I don't know what,' Thomas replied.

'That sob was primal. The way she pulled herself together and applied that shield of steel made the hair raise on the back of my neck. I've seen that sort of thing before, back in the war years. I tell you, that girl has been through something.'

'Maybe she's still going through it.'

The two men parted company to go about their individual chores, but neither found he had the concentration for work.

VISIONS OF THE control he'd once had over Adie ran through Bill's mind. At the same time the voices in his head scorned him, told him he had failed, that she was never coming back. He would not believe them. He tried to shove them out of his head, but they stayed in a corner where he could not reach them and continued to mock him.

There were no thoughts in his head for Adie's needs.

He watched her all the time, but he couldn't get to her; always he was hindered by those dogs, or the men. Going to the house again was too risky; he could not take a chance of getting caught. He had asked her nicely in his letters. He had killed her cat to show her how much she had upset him. Didn't she realise yet that he deserved her love?

Angry and frustrated, he began to look at other women, knowing he could still attract them. But they were not Adie; they would not satisfy him like she did.

When Adie had first left him, he'd been sure of her return, but now his confidence was dwindling. His love for her was extreme, necessary; he needed her to survive. But instead of her coming back to him, doubts were creeping in that she did not love him.

For days his temper raged, bringing on headaches and palpitations, and with little sleep the voices grew stronger and his frustrations needed to be vent.

His money was beginning to run out. Getting a job meant someone getting to know him, and he didn't want that. Instead he studied the plethora of corner shops in the nearby town of Kendal. Choosing one run by an old man, he waited until closing time, donned a balaclava and punched the frail gentleman senseless. Shoving the coins into his pockets and the notes into a paper bag, he strode away down the high street, and was gratified by the weight of his return.

Instead of releasing his pent-up madness, beating the old man had only succeeded in raising his blood heat. Late in the evening he went looking for tougher prey to fight; someone who would kick back. But there were no young men to challenge; the town was quiet.

THE FOLLOWING EVENING, he was in the Rose & Crown, in the village of Rosthwaite, some ten miles from Beckdale Farm. The previous day's crime had supplied him with rich pickings. There was enough money not only for rent and food, but also new clothes. When Bill looked at his changed reflection in the tailor's mirror his ego was bolstered. He decided he didn't need Adie; he would get a new woman. He told this to the mockers in his head. That softened their voices.

With his victim of the previous day long forgotten, he sat on a stool at the end of the bar with his back against the wall and a pint of beer in front of him. Having taken extra care with his appearance, he was full of confidence. The checked jacket, polo-neck sweater and corduroy trousers gave him the air of a country gentleman.

He stared out at the men who shared the bar with him. Their faces were animated, flushed by the beer and the warm glow of the fire. Friendly chatter filled the air. Occasionally, they called across the room to greet a friend or deliver some well-worn repartee, causing laughter to ripple through them all. Many played cards or dominoes, but none of them talked to Bill. Every so often, one of them would glance at him and then say a few quiet words to his pal. Bill was not concerned by their lack of friendliness; he did not want to contend with their nosiness. If needed, he could be the charming country man they would like, but it was not needed, and he remained indifferent. He knew that this was their Friday night out with the boys. Soon, they would go home to their wives and families.

Later in the evening the pretty young things would arrive. They would play the jukebox, and the girls would gyrate their hips to the latest sounds in a kind of stationary dance. It was these naive youngsters he was interested in. He would be looking for one whose senses were not yet mature or streetwise enough to smell a threat.

Just after eight a group of young friends entered the pub. They stood back from the bar while one of the more mature-looking lads got the drinks.

It took Bill only seconds to hone in on a teenage girl wearing white knee-length boots and a baker-boy cap. The girl could not take her disapproving eyes off the barmaid. Bill guessed that she found the woman's tight, low-cut dress and red lipstick offensive. Eventually, she drew her eyes away from the woman's jostling cleavage and began to study the other customers. The older boy returned with their drinks and they sipped in silence.

Being pretty, the girl attracted a lot of attention. Bill noticed how she held her head high and tried to appear aloof. He liked her pride. He waited for her eyes to land on him, for he was sure she knew he was looking at her. Finally, their eyes met, and he did not look away. He'd been right about her. She locked eyes with him and held his gaze. After a few seconds he pulled a funny face and winked at her. This was so unexpected that her face opened up into a smile. Bill had chosen his prey.

He introduced himself to the youngsters as Rod (it was a name he used frequently), and told them he was up from the South looking to buy land. The girls were clearly intrigued by his self-assurance, his charm and his good looks. The boys were taken in by his appearance of wealth and power. They told him their names, but Amanda, the girl with white boots, was the only one he remembered.

They were going on to a house party and the older lad said, 'Why don't you come with us? I'm sure they won't mind.'

'Er... well, if you're sure?'

'I'm sure it will be OK – anyway, there's always too many girls at these things.'

Bill decided to join them. When they had finished their drinks, the youngsters left the pub and piled into an old Ford Zodiac. The girls had to sit on the boys' laps for them all to fit in. Bill did not offer any of them a lift. He followed their car along narrow country lanes in his stolen Ford Anglia.

Even though the house was not yet in view, he could hear the throb of music coming at him in waves through gaps in the trees. Soon he could see lights through the woodland, and shortly after this they turned into a driveway. Cars were parked everywhere at haphazard angles. Bill watched as the Zodiac parked up and the youngsters clambered out and made their way towards the open front door. When they had entered the house, he did a three-point turn, left the driveway and parked a short distance up the lane.

Walking down the drive, he saw that the house was large, with many windows facing the front. Through each, the shadow of bodies could be seen against strobing lights, drinking, dancing, smoking or loving. Inside the house, verbal communication was impossible as the music pounded through his body, at odds with his heartbeat. Inhibitions were laid bare. The sweet smell of marijuana was so strong he didn't need a joint to get high. Getting the feeling that this was not the sort of party at which his white-booted young lady would feel comfortable, he spotted the bright light of the kitchen and made his way there, hoping to find her. Disappointed, he poured himself a beer from a giant party can and went in search.

He found her in a darkened room and watched her. Alone, leaning against a wall, she sipped her drink and tried to appear cool. A young man came and stood next to her, shouted something in her ear and offered her a spliff. She shook her head, and he closed his eyes and slid down the wall until he was seated on the floor, leaning against her leg.

In this setting, where joints and little packets of pills were freely passed, where couples were having sex against the wall amongst the noise and smoke, where the sickly smells of drugs, alcohol and sweat all mingled, Bill watched the girl's nerves begin to fray. And then, while she was distracted, he saw another girl spike her drink.

Leaving the safety of the wall, letting the boy slump to the floor, Amanda went deeper into the house. Bill followed her down a long hallway, where she opened several doors, eventually finding what she was looking for. But a girl was kneeling on the floor with her arms wrapped around the toilet, her hair hiding her face, and her knickers at her ankles. 'Fuck off!' she said, as she began to retch into the pan.

Amanda closed the door and turned back the way she came, uneasiness showing on her face. Bill ducked out of sight. She was heading for the front door. As she passed a youth, he closed his hand tightly around her wrist and yanked her backwards. 'Not so fast, my lovely,' he said, pressing her against the wall with the length of his body.

Bill backed off further into the shadow underneath the stairs and watched with rising excitement as the boy covered Amanda's mouth with his. His hand was pushing up her skirt, reaching for the waistband of her tights, pulling them down. She tried to turn her face, but he was pressing his mouth hard against hers. She pushed her fists into his chest and struggled to heave him away, but her efforts were futile. Now he had his hand in her knickers and she stepped up the fight, attempting to bite him.

Bill decided it was time to intervene. Suddenly the youth cried out in pain and collapsed to the floor.

The instant the boy disappeared from Amanda's view, Bill was there, his hand held out to her, a grin on his face.

'This isn't the sort of party a high-class girl like you should be taken to. Come on, let's get you out of here.'

With a crooked smile she grabbed his hand gratefully, stepped over the groaning figure of the boy and trotted after Bill as he strode out of the house.

Outside, he led her up the driveway and along the lane to his car. They climbed in, and Amanda began to cry. Gently, he pulled her into his strong arms and hugged her until the sobs receded. Holding her away from him, he wiped the mascara from underneath her eyes and winked at her again. As she attempted to smile back, he noticed that her pupils were dilated, the drugs were working.

'I suspect you're all done with partying tonight, aren't you?'

She nodded her reply.

'So, which way is home?' he asked, flashing her his handsome smile.

'I'm not sure,' she replied. Then, in a voice that was beginning to float away, she said, 'I think you turn left; I know the way from the pub.'

'Right, back to the pub it is, and then straight home for you, young lady.'

Amanda relaxed into the seat, her head leaning back and a smile on her face. Bill kissed her hand, replaced it on her thigh and stroked her knee. She didn't shrink away.

The left turn would take them up into the hills, away from the main roads, prying eyes and the pub. It was exactly what Bill wanted.

When he had been driving for about ten minutes, he pulled off the road and cut the engine. Without the car lights the moon cast tree-shadows over them.

'I don't think this is the way to the pub,' she said.

'I think you're right, but now I'm completely confused about where the pub is.'

A fox screeched, causing Amanda to jump and grab Bill's arm. Taking his opportunity, he swept her into his arms, kissing her hard and deep. His arousal was instant, and his stifled frustrations began to unfurl. Gripping the back of her neck, he explored her body in a grasping rush. There was flesh missing. Her breasts were small, childlike. This body was hard and inflexible. He needed relief and he was not prepared to give up now. His hands searched for the usual curves and crevices, but the skin felt wrong. The eyes would do it; he always had to see her eyes. He pushed her away from him, clutching her face by the jaw. Her eyes, wide with terror, stared unblinkingly at him.

She was not Adie.

The bitch was trying to fool him. He hit her head against the window of the car door. Twice more, he smashed her head into the glass, trying to dispel his anger. Blood smeared the window.

Opening the passenger door, he pushed her out of the vehicle, throwing her handbag after her. Firing the engine, he manoeuvred the car to turn around, and drove away, leaving a cloud of exhaust.

L ILLY HAD BECOME an accomplished rider. Thomas had never seen a child gain such skill in such a short space of time, and, after consultation with Adie, had decided to enrol her with the local Pony Club. It was a particularly frosty day when Lilly attended her first meeting. After the introduction of new members and then covering a small amount of business with regards to future meetings, the organisers decided to keep things fun and arranged a Chase Me Charlie competition to be held in a large open sided barn. Thomas, Jack and his wife Vera, Adie and Sam were all watching.

After many eliminations the final two competitors were Lilly, riding Prince, and a seventeen-hand hunter with his experienced adult rider who did not want to be beaten by a child. All were intrigued by the stocky pony and the little girl who rode him; no one was going home.

As the jump got higher, the tension grew. When Prince and Lilly landed safely a cheer went up from the small assembled crowd. Adie was barely able to watch. Long after the rider of the hunter thought the hardy pony should have been beaten, Prince was still going strong. Eventually the jump was so high it looked impossible for him to clear it. Adie wanted Lilly to concede, but she had a determined look on her face; they would not give up.

Every time the jump was made higher, the hunter went first and sailed over gracefully; then the plucky pony would trot round in a circle as if mentally preparing, gather himself and lurch forwards. Lilly was no longer in charge. As Prince reached the jump, he looked as if he was going to duck under it, but in fact he had to get close enough to launch himself over it. Rising almost vertically from the ground, Lilly hung on to the saddle and stood in the stirrups as Prince's powerful rump released its coiled strength and they sailed over, Lilly's bottom too high in the air.

In the end the hunter and his rider made an error and down came the pole. The crowd cheered and groaned all at once, pleased that Lilly and Prince had won, but disappointed that the competition was over. Prince became the hero of the day, with Lilly admitting she'd had nothing to do with their victory.

During the competition a man standing at the back of the crowd had caught Adie's eye. He was tall and lean, with unkempt hair and scruffy clothes. She didn't like the way he was staring at Lilly with a broad smile on his face; to her he looked unhinged.

'Who is that man over there?' she asked Thomas as they were getting ready to leave.

'Oh, that's just the old squaddie who lives in the barn off the west side of the farm. He's looking better than the last time I saw him.'

'He must have looked awful; he looks pretty bad now. Is he all right?'

Tom could see that Adie was disturbed by him.

'You don't have to worry about him; he wouldn't hurt a fly. They say he's on the run from the army; whether that's true I don't know. But I do know that one night he threw stones at my window to wake me. I followed him out to the pasture. One of my cows was having trouble trying to birth her calf. I'd have lost the pair of them if he hadn't told me. He's just a harmless, damaged soul who walks around at night. The dogs don't bark at him so he must be all right.'

Adie watched the man as he lowered his face, as if not wanting to be seen, and left the ground. It had been a few days since the knowledge of Tinker's death and Adie felt as if she was on borrowed time, like someone with an incurable disease. She had trained herself to show the world that all was right with her, but inside she felt their time was limited. Bill would find them.

———※※※———

A S RUPERT MADE his way back to the barn, with his dog at his side, he realised he was enjoying the sun on his face. He thought about Lilly and all she had achieved; it made him feel good to have helped her. Was he beginning to heal? He still had to check his surroundings every night, he still had panic attacks and nightmares, but at least now he could smile.

Once, Lilly had asked him why he lived in the barn all alone, and he'd told her that he had done something terrible and didn't deserve to live with other people. Strangely, she'd said she knew someone who was far worse than he could ever be. He didn't believe her.

She was a curious child and asked many questions about his life. He answered nearly all of them, telling her about his privileged childhood full of ponies, good schools and good parents. He would not answer questions about how he'd come to be where he was now; he steered her away from the subject and she was too polite to insist.

——✦✦✦——

THE NEXT TIME Rupert saw Lilly she was not quite her usual self. Unable to concentrate on the jumping poles he had set out for her, she eventually lost her seat and nearly fell. She reined Prince in sharply. Rupert could see she was close to tears.

'Want to tell me what's wrong?' he said.

She raised her chin and looked at him. He'd expected tears, but instead he saw fear, and it stabbed through his heart.

'Last night Mummy was screaming in her sleep. It woke me up. I went to her room and tapped her arm. She sat up and stared at me, then roared at me like a lion. I was frightened, so I ran back to our room and slept at the bottom of Sam's bed.'

Lilly began scraping her boots with her riding crop.

'I'm sure it was just a very bad dream,' said Rupert.

'She has lots of bad dreams.' Lilly's voice was sharp with anger. 'They did go away, but now they've come back again.' Each word was punctuated with a stab at her boots.

'You sound very angry,' said Rupert.

She burst into tears and, between sobs, told him, 'Daddy must be coming, because the only time Mummy has bad dreams is when Daddy is around.'

'Are you frightened of Daddy?'

'He hurts Mummy,' she said in the faintest of whispers.

Rupert lifted her chin with his fingers and looked into her eyes. 'When was the last time you saw Daddy?'

'The day before we left.'

'When was that?'

'Just after Christmas. Mum's not been dreaming until now, so I know he must be here. I don't want him to hurt her again.'

'So, you haven't seen him?'

'I don't think so.'

Rupert decided that she must be confused and thought it better not to ask more questions.

'Then your mum is probably having bad dreams about things in the past; I do that all the time.' He tried to reassure her.

'But you don't understand. You think you're bad. You're nowhere near as bad as my dad. He killed a little girl.'

Rupert gripped his deckchair as a wave of dizziness and nausea swept over him.

'He told me how he did it when he used to come and get in my bed in the night. He said if I didn't keep quiet, he'd kill me.'

Rupert had no words. Her statement had stunned him.

She mistook his silence for annoyance with her. 'I'm sorry, I didn't mean to tell you that. Can it be our secret, like the riding lessons?'

He nodded his reply.

'See you next week?' she asked in a slow voice.

'Yes,' he said.

She urged Prince on and was gone, through the hedge and out of sight.

He sat, motionless, thinking for a long time. Visions of the Irish girl swam in and out of his head. Rupert thought about the man who could treat his own family so badly. Lilly was right; he wasn't as bad as that. He tried to think logically about the things she had told him. Lilly's mother was probably just dreaming about her past, but he felt a duty to protect Lilly, and made a decision to be more vigilant.

———✳✳✳———

I T WAS NEARLY March, and winter's grip had not left them. Overnight the wind turned and came directly from the north, blowing in a blizzard that rattled the windows and blasted an icy draught through every tiny gap. The temperature plummeted, and in the morning, although the wind was gone, snow was still falling in earnest. It covered the hills and the valley in a thick coat of virgin white, wiped clean the barren ground and turned the countryside into a winter wonderland. Drifts had built themselves high against trees and buildings, and sounds became muffled, so that a hush settled over the land.

As Adie waved her excited children off to school, she saw Thomas striding across the garden towards her. His ankle-length riding coat swept across the snow, giving him the appearance of a highwayman. She guessed he probably needed her help. Recently, she had been more involved with actual farm work.

'Jack just telephoned to say he's snowed in and he'll be late. I need your help with the ewes.'

'OK, let me get some suitable clothes on and I'll be with you.'

'I'll be in the Land Rover,' Thomas called over his shoulder.

Two minutes later Adie emerged into the glare of the winter's day fully clad for the cold. Climbing into the vehicle, she noticed that the dogs had been confined to their kennel and that the hay bales were already loaded in the back. Thomas was concerned for his pregnant ewes. They needed to check the water supply wasn't frozen and provide additional food.

'They're probably in the daisy meadow. There's a crag where they shelter when the weather turns. We'll try there first.' He was negotiating a bumpy track, slipping from side to side.

Adie nodded, knowing a spoken reply was not required.

As they climbed higher, the snow fell thicker.

'When we find them, I need you to climb in the back and spread the feed while I drive the length of the crag. I don't want them to have to look too hard for their food.'

When they reached the meadow and Adie had climbed into the bed of the vehicle, Thomas tracked slowly backwards and forwards in a zigzag motion, heading downhill. Adie trailed the feed across the land, so that all of the sheep would be able to reach some food.

The snow was about a foot deep and the vehicle slewed and slid. Many a time Adie had to grab hold of the side to prevent herself from losing her balance, and this, along with splitting the bales and throwing out the hay, was strenuous work.

They had gone about half the length of the crag and were traversing at quite a steep angle when there was an almighty jolt and the Land Rover lurched violently, throwing Adie high into the air. Her shoulder hit the ground first and crumpled beneath her in a sickeningly unnatural manner. For a few moments she lay still, disorientated, not understanding what had happened. Sheep ran past her, and for some reason she thought there must be a dog chasing them. Then there was a strange, continuous grinding sound of metal upon metal. Looking in the direction of the noise, she saw, to her horror, that the Land Rover was on its side and sliding down the hill at a rapid pace. Thomas was desperately trying to get himself out of the vehicle by the driver's door. It was open to the sky, but for some reason he seemed to be stuck.

At the bottom of the hill, where the crag gave way, the usually fast-flowing stream was now frozen to a halt. Over the years the stream, which often carried floodwater off the hills, had gouged out a deep and wide gully, so that now there was a drop of several feet from the edge of the meadow into its depths. It was to this edge that the vehicle was sliding, gathering speed as it went.

Picking herself up from the snow, Adie was acutely aware of severe pain in her left shoulder and arm, but the scene that was unfolding before her eyes demanded all of her attention. There was nothing she could do, except run, slip and slide after the vehicle and attempt to hold her arm steady. As she chased it, her mind racing, it glided downhill, rapidly gaining speed. There was no doubt that it was going to fall into the gully, and possibly land on its roof. Thomas was still desperately trying to free himself. She could see he was battling frantically with something inside the cab. At the very last moment he launched himself from the open door, but it was too late: the vehicle plunged over the edge, taking him with it.

There was a long, unearthly sound of screeching and crushing metal, followed by a loud bang, a few moments of silence, and then a rhythmic rocking that slowed and eventually stopped.

A flock of crows squawked into the air, panicked by the desecration of their once-silent day. They made their way back to the woodland and safety, complained to each other for a few seconds, and then silence returned.

As Adie continued to run, she fell heavily. Something in her shoulder gave, and the pain increased. She allowed her feet to slide out in front of her so that she was lying on her back, sliding down the hill, gaining speed. In the last few feet before she reached the drop, she attempted to grab, with her good hand, at snow-covered shrubbery to slow her speed. After five or six attempts, she managed to get a good enough grip to stop, but at the sudden jolt an involuntary cry of agony erupted from her mouth.

Clutching her left arm, she rose onto her knees and, fighting pain and vomit, slowly made her way to the edge. The silence was sinister. She was hoping to hear Thomas's clipped tones shouting orders from inside the truck, but there was nothing; he was not even groaning. As she peered over the edge, all she could see was the underside of the vehicle. It had landed on its roof, as she had predicted.

Grunting at the pain, she gingerly climbed down into the ravine.

'I'm nearly with you, Thomas,' she said, her voice shaking. Making her way towards the stricken truck, she lost her footing and hit her injured shoulder against an icy edge. 'Shit!' Gasping, she stopped momentarily and hoped for some sort of curt rebuke for her swearing, but there was none. 'I've hurt my bloody shoulder, Thomas. I hope you're all right in there because I'm in a heck of a lot of pain out here!' But there was nothing but silence from Thomas in this eerie, frozen trench.

Her already pounding heart began to race, so she closed down the frightening thoughts that were invading her mind. From now on she talked to him continually, although she didn't know why. She told him what she was doing, that she would be with him in a moment and that everything would be all right. Her words were interspersed with profanities as each movement caused her nauseating pain. Still, there was nothing from Thomas; no groan, no word and no movement.

Stepping over the bull bars that had detached from the vehicle along with the twisted metal of the bumper, Adie made her way to the other side of the wreckage. It took a few long moments to decipher the tangled mess of metal and man that confronted her. Thomas was trapped upside down, his torso wedged between the vehicle and the opposite bank of the stream. This was the side that he had been trying to climb out of. His legs bent at the knees and hung at a bizarre angle. Stooping, she could see that his hair was a mass of blood. She couldn't see his face;

it was turned away from her. Believing he was dead, she gently placed her hand on him.

'Thomas?' she whispered, but there was no response.

Her hand trembling, she touched his neck, hoping it would be the right place to feel a pulse. To her relief and amazement, she felt a faint, regular beat, and it galvanised her into action. In the weeks to come she would often wonder whether it had, in fact, been Thomas's pulse, or just her own heart pounding in dread.

Grateful now that she had borrowed a man-sized jacket from the boot room, she shrugged her good shoulder and arm out of its warm protection and gradually slid it off her injured side.

'Everything's going to be all right, Thomas,' she said, wrapping the jacket around him as best she could. 'I'm going to get help; I'll be back as quickly as possible.'

The climb up the stream's bank was excruciating, and as she reached the summit her stomach heaved out that morning's breakfast. For a few moments she was light-headed and shaky, but the sight of Thomas's legs at that weird angle brought her swiftly back to the present.

Following the stream back down the hill, she turned right to go over the fields that would cross the valley and eventually take her up to the house. As she climbed the hill the wind rose; it bit into her flesh and stole the air from her mouth. At the top she stopped to take two deep breaths. From here she could hear a cacophony of howls and barks coming from the kennel. Her shoulder was sending fresh pain through her back and arm with every step and she was freezing, but she had to press on.

In the house she stood looking blindly out of the kitchen window while she gave the 999 operator instructions. Outside the dogs were still howling in a desperate bid to be free. Somehow, they seemed to know their master was in trouble. She replaced the handset and made for the boot room, grabbing the first two coats she could lay her hands on. Tentatively, she slid a coat over her damaged arm and put it on. The pain in her shoulder burned, but she could not think about that now, she had to get back to Thomas.

Moving as quickly as she could, she dragged her feet through the snow in a kind of loping walk-cum-jog and prayed that Thomas would still be alive when she got to him.

It was snowing harder now, blowing into her face, blinding her and filling her mouth as she gasped for breath. Needing to check her direction, she looked about her – everything was white and so she could only guess at the correct route. Now and again she had a floating sensation and could not always feel her feet coming into contact with the ground; the feeling was both wonderful and frightening in equal measure. She wondered what time of day it was. Was it morning or afternoon? When would the children be coming home from school? Who would be at home for them? Jack and Doris were snowed in. Then it occurred to her that Bill would do it and she did not like that thought, but she was not sure why. Looking ahead, she could not see. Thinking she had gone the wrong way, she turned around, but still she could not make out where she was. Somewhere out there, through the wind and snow, she could hear the sound of a tractor, or was she imagining things? Who would be driving it? And a dog, barking.

She could not think about these things now. Thomas was suffering, and she had to get back to him. Then she recognised the lower end of the stream and began to scramble up it on her one good hand and knees. The skin of her palms stuck to the brittle, crystalline ice with each movement forward. The sound of the dog came to her again, and there was another sound, that of metal against metal; a distant, high-pitched screeching. She looked forward to see how far she had to go, but the snow was driving hard into her face and she had to bow her head against it and battle on.

Then she felt something warm and soft against her hand. Looking at it, she saw a skinny dog she did not know nuzzling and gently mouthing at her, as if to lead and encourage her up the stream. Was she dreaming? Adie decided not to believe in the dog's existence, and battled on, crawling through the blizzard. Still the creature bounced along in front of her, its face turned towards her.

She couldn't feel the ground any more. The pain was subsiding and warmth, delightful warmth, was spreading through her body. She was talking to her father now, telling him not to worry, that she'd be all right; as soon as she'd had a little sleep, she'd be all right…

'AHA! YOU'RE WARMING up, then.' The blur of a smiling face appeared before Adie's eyes, and a finger removed the tendril of hair that was pestering her mouth. 'How's your shoulder? I injected it for the pain so you should feel more comfortable now.'

Although she heard these words, it took some time for her mind and vision to clear. The smiling face had turned away from her, not waiting for a reply. Instead he was tending to his more urgent patient. Finally, the motion of the vehicle and sound of the ambulance siren brought Adie back to full alertness.

'What about Thomas? Is he alive?'

'He's alive, but he is in a serious way. I suspect he'll be in intensive care for a while.' The man did not take his eyes from his comatose patient. 'In the meantime, you, with your dislocated shoulder and hypothermia, need to look after yourself. I understand you've got children to go home to. You're lucky to have such a good friend who can not only rescue your husband, but collect your children from school as well.'

'Who? Who was here? He's not my husband. Who was here? Was his name Bill?'

'Calm yourself. The man said his name was Rupert and that he is your friend. Made a good job of your husband – er, I mean Thomas.

'Bill mustn't pick up the children – what is the time? I have to be there to pick up the children.'

'Try to stay calm; it's just the hypothermia making you feel disorientated. Rupert seemed such a kind man; he even helped us to get the two of you to the ambulance, we'd had to park it way back on the road. Must have been in the military, the way he fixed Thomas up. I don't think he'd have made it at all without the good work your friend did.'

Adie laid her head back on the stretcher and felt more at ease. She knew that Bill had no medical knowledge, and that even if he had, he would not have used it; he would have taken pleasure in watching Thomas die.

At the hospital, Thomas was whisked away and Adie was sent for an X-ray. After informing her that nothing was broken, her shoulder was put back in place and then in a sling.

Adie assumed she'd had all the treatment she needed, but the doctor told her that because of possible side effects from the hypothermia she would have to stay in overnight. At this news Adie protested, telling him she had children at home with no one to look after them. In the end the medical staff agreed that if she showed no ill effects within the next four hours she could go home. Later that afternoon, after a final round of checks she was discharged.

Adie was eager to be under way, but not without checking on Thomas first. From Accident & Emergency they directed her to Intensive Care. Once there, she had to wait some time before anyone was free to talk with her. Then she was told only that he was stable and to phone the following day when they would have further knowledge of his injuries. Like the ambulance man, the staff at the hospital assumed that Adie was Thomas's wife. She saw no reason to correct them; it would make life easier while he was in their care.

Impatient to be home, and worried about the children, she left the hospital. With no money for a taxi, she made her way to the bus stop, praying that when she told the driver of her day and predicament, he would let her travel for free. It was still snowing and bitterly cold. Moving from one foot to the other, cradling her newly repaired shoulder, she tried to maintain some warmth and hoped the bus was not too delayed by the weather. Darkness fell quickly, and there was still no sign of the bus. Feeling the cold sinking into her body she was frightened of becoming disorientated again and made the decision to return to the hospital to telephone for a taxi. Somehow, she would sort the fare when she got home.

A short distance from the bus stop a white Hillman Imp pulled up next to her. A hand stretched across the car and wound down the window, then the face of the ambulance man smiled up at her.

'Can I give you a lift home? I'm going off duty now, so won't be around to save you from hypothermia for a second time.'

When she was persuaded that the journey would not take him out of his way, she accepted and climbed into the warm car. It was a long and hazardous ride to reach the entrance of the farm, and, since the morning, the road to the house had become snowbound. The little Hillman Imp could not manage it. Adie tried to assure him that she would be fine taking a shortcut across the fields. He would not hear of her making the last piece of her journey alone. After taking a torch from his glove compartment they set out towards the house.

Light from the windows shone out through the skeletal trees and cast golden rectangular shapes onto the snow. She could smell woodsmoke on the crisp air; the fires must have been lit. As they reached the kennels and the dogs whined, the paramedic felt it was safe to leave her. Adie wanted to thank him, with money, a hot drink, or a meal, but he would have none of it and went, quickly, on his way. Adie hurried on towards the house.

As she turned the corner to enter by the boot room, she noticed the small kitchen window was open. Steam escaped from it, along with the aromas of cooking and the sound of animated voices. In the boot room she was struggling to remove her jacket when the door from the kitchen opened.

'Mummy! It's Mummy!' Lilly squealed in excitement, hugging her mother and not letting go. Adie winced in pain.

Sam appeared and kissed her on the cheek, then looked into her eyes, wanting to know if she was all right. The message passed wordlessly between them: *I'm OK.* Sam relaxed, removed his sister, and helped Adie take off her jacket while asking a stream of questions.

'What have you done? Why do you need the sling? Are Thomas's injuries bad? Is he going to be all right?'

'Let me come in first. You have to tell me all about what you've been up to and who has been so kind to have cooked your dinner. When you've told me your news, I'll tell you mine.'

On entering the kitchen, she came face to face with Rupert, who had a plate of hot food in each hand. Lilly stood in front of him, her arms outstretched as if trying to protect him. The skinny dog Adie had encountered earlier in the day was lying contentedly on the rug.

'I know he's dirty,' Lilly said. 'But he did wash his hands. And he phoned the hospital and they said you were on your way. And he cooked dinner too. And he said I have to tell you all about the riding lessons, but it's all my fault.'

Sam stood back, arms folded, with an amused look on his face.

'Lilly, please stop gabbling and introduce me to your friend.'

Lilly stopped talking and stepped aside. Rupert put the plates down and, even though he didn't need to, wiped his hands on a towel before presenting one for Adie to shake.

'Mummy, this is Rupert who lives in the barn – you know, the one in the flower meadow.'

They shook hands, but Rupert struggled to meet Adie's gaze.

'Was it you who helped Thomas today? They say that without your help he would have bled to death.'

'I did what I was trained to do. I've cooked you some dinner. I hope you don't mind; I cooked the sausages I found in the fridge.'

'Thank you. What would we all have done without you today? You are going to stay and have some dinner with us.' Adie was aware that her voice sounded strange, and wished it did not. She wanted to see the man's eyes, but he was unable to face her. Close to, she realised he was not much older than herself.

'No,' he replied, almost jumping. Then, more softly, 'I'm sorry, I have things to do.'

Promptly, he called his dog and she came instantly to his side. On bare feet he strode to the boot room. Adie followed him and watched as he pushed his feet into boots without laces. In a hurry, he threw on a heavy knitted sweater, nodded at her, opened the door, allowing snow to blow in, then closed the door behind him. Adie stood and watched the flakes of snow melt on the floor. It had been a strange day.

AFTER RUPERT HAD trudged a short way, his pace began to slow, until he became stationary. Like a stray dog he looked back at the house, hungry for the affection contained within its walls.

THE FOLLOWING MORNING, Adie rose earlier than usual. Determined not to be a burden, she headed for the kitchen, hoping the wood burner would still be alight. The house was silent without Thomas making his tea, banging things about in his usual blustery manner, or barking orders for the day.

Adie made her tea, then, in a trance, stood by the window, cradling the cup in her good hand. Staring out at the desolate winter landscape, visions of Thomas upside down, his head smothered in blood and his legs at that crazy angle, kept filling her mind.

In the short space of time she had known him, he had become a stalwart in her life, a trustworthy rock she could rely on. Used to his bark, knowing he didn't mean it, she would have given almost anything to have him there with her in the kitchen, instead of lying in a hospital bed, fighting for his life.

The quiet of the morning weighed heavily on her, and feelings of despair began to seep through her veins. Just when life was getting better, Bill had turned up, and now Thomas had been struck down. Would she ever climb out of the pit? Putting down her tea, Adie placed her good hand on the sill for support as tears fell freely from her eyes. She sat in the armchair and tried to hug her knees, but her shoulder gave a painful reminder that her body, too, had taken some punishment.

It didn't take long for Adie's silent crying to stop. She began to lecture herself, telling herself to get up and get on with it. With a resolute sigh she was about to stand, when a hand stroked her hair. Looking up, she saw Sam standing in front of her with her sling in his hand. She had no idea how long he'd been there.

'You should be wearing this, Mum; it's too soon to take it off.'

'I know, sweetheart,' she said, taking the sling from him. 'I'll put it back on when the jobs are done.'

Later, when the children had gone to school, Adie telephoned the hospital and requested to speak with the ward sister.

'Good morning, Sister Mason speaking, how may I help you?'

'Good morning, this is Adie... mmm... Lambton speaking. I—'

Adie was cut off from saying anything further by the sister's commanding voice.

'Yes, dear, your husband is a very lucky man; he lost a lot of blood. Obviously, someone at the scene knew what they were doing. He has suffered severe concussion, massive bruising and many lacerations. His legs are fractured in several places, but it seems that all his wounds will heal. He will be removed from intensive care later today. If you would like to telephone the switchboard after luncheon, they will be able to give you the details of his new ward. His broken legs will keep him with us for a while and he will be using crutches for some time to come. Do you have any questions, dear?'

'Erm, no, that all seems clear.'

'Good, then I'll bid you good day.' And with that Sister Mason replaced the handset.

The news that Thomas would heal and was not fighting for his life sent Adie into a little involuntary dance of glee around the kitchen, while holding on to her damaged shoulder.

With her earlier gloom lifted, she decided to walk the dogs to Jack's cottage. She needed to tell him about the accident and Thomas being in hospital, and to discuss the running of the farm.

Outside, the morning was eerily quiet. Low, lingering clouds hung heavy in the still air. When they passed the barns all was silent; no noise of tractor engines, no working on repairs as would be usual on a day like this. After tucking her scarf more closely inside her coat, she patted the head of the dog nearest her; it was good to reassure herself of their company.

At the top of the hill she looked down into the valley. The world as she knew it had changed: a white, frozen mist filled the basin and, between this and the grey sky, snowy fields slept. Adie didn't want to enter this blinding fog, but it was the only way to reach Jack's cottage. Both the snow and her shoulder made it impossible for her to drive.

As she made her way down the hill, the mist gradually closed around her until she could see only a few feet in front. She called the dogs in close, knowing they would find their way to the river's edge and follow it in the correct direction. Walking slowly, watching her footing, ice crystals formed on wisps of hair protruding from her hat. The cold bit into her and she was, once again, afraid of becoming confused. A spike of fear rose up from her belly. Feeling vulnerable, she wondered if Bill was watching, and her stomach turned. Then, the shadow of Jack's cottage started to reveal itself through the mist, and she laughed nervously at herself.

Vera, Jack's wife, opened the door, letting out a waft of warm air. 'Oh, my dear, what are you doing out in this cold? Come in, come in. What have you done to yourself?'

Adie instructed the dogs to wait.

'Oh, they can come in; no living creature should be made to wait outside in this weather.'

Vera was not of the farming community and had a more tender outlook towards animals, especially dogs.

With a nod from Adie, the dogs barged their way into the little cottage, nearly knocking Vera over. With her good hand, Adie steadied her.

Once Adie had delivered the news, the three of them discussed how they were going to manage the farm with Thomas incapacitated.

It was Vera who had the solution. 'I can do Adie's job, and Adie can help you as best she can with that shoulder.' She looked at her husband. 'It'll just be temporary. We can start tomorrow.'

With the problem solved, Adie left the cottage. She was relieved to find that a breeze had got up, and the sun, peeping through broken clouds, had begun to disperse the mist. The dogs were in need of exercise and the brighter weather felt good, so she decided to take a longer route home, giving her time to reflect on the previous day. Realising she was needed, useful, and even liked, fed her ailing soul. She had friends. Since yesterday, she had overcome so much that was fearful, that now, the threat of Bill didn't seem so great.

With positive thoughts driving her on, she strode up the hill. Nearing the top, the sound of bleating sheep caused her to stop and listen. Worried about their safety, she lengthened her stride further. As she crested the hill, she saw Rupert splitting hay bales and spreading them for the sheep to feed.

'Morning, Rupert,' she called.

He did not acknowledge her. Twice more she called, all the while getting closer, before he waved at her and then continued, head down, with his work. When she was next to him, she called the dogs to heel.

'Morning. It is very kind of you to feed the sheep. By tomorrow Jack and I will be back on duty.'

Rupert had stooped low and was stroking Fern, the collie. Adie noticed that he was not wearing gloves.

'There is no need for you to do farm work; I can take care of it until Thomas is better,' he said.

'Thank you, that would make our lives easier. You must let us pay you. I presume you know what you are doing?'

'I was brought up on a farm. There is no need to pay me.' He was looking at the dogs, directing his answers to them.

'But you must let me pay you.' Adie was finding the conversation difficult – why wouldn't he look at her?

'There is no need.'

'At least let me give you your meals each day; you cannot work outside in this weather without hot food in your stomach.'

This time he did not answer straight away. 'OK,' was all he said, before he turned away to continue feeding the sheep.

Adie wondered if the reason he had agreed was to be able to see Lilly. She had been banned from going to him for riding lessons due to her telling lies and stealing food. Since then she had done nothing but carry on about what a good friend he was.

'Lunch is at one,' she said, as she turned to leave.

———*＊*———

A T FIVE PAST one Adie peered out of the window, looking for Rupert. She saw him at a water butt that was sheltered enough not to be frozen; he was washing his hands and splashing his face. He continued, vigorously, for a couple of minutes, then made his way to the house.

When he knocked on the boot-room door Adie called to him to come in, but he did not. She opened the door and gestured for him to enter, but instead he handed her a bag.

'Would you be kind enough to put the food in here? There is a lot to do.'

'But the soup will be ruined if I have to prepare a hot flask for it now,' she said.

An aroma of beef broth and herbs reached Rupert's nose, and saliva filled his mouth. He was afraid he would dribble if he spoke again, so he stepped inside and sat on the bench to remove his boots.

Adie led the way to the kitchen. When he was seated, she placed the soup, bread and butter in front of him, then quickly turned away. Putting her own food in the oven to keep warm, she excused herself, telling him she would return in a few minutes.

Without Adie in the room he was able to savour the food properly. He concentrated on eating slowly, relishing every mouthful. When he had finished, he wiped the bowl with his penultimate piece of bread; the final piece was reserved to be smothered in butter before its consumption.

Adie had still not returned to the kitchen. Rupert cleared his dishes from the table and was just thinking about whether it would be rude to leave, when she appeared with a pair of socks in her hand.

'Please have these; I hope they will make you more comfortable.'

Slowly, he took the socks and turned them over in his hands, inspecting them, feeling the softness of the wool on his fingers. For the first time he looked directly at her.

'I apologise for my awkwardness. Thank you for these, and for the food.' And with that he turned and left.

'Please borrow a coat if you would like,' she called after him.

The next day, Jack and Vera moved into the farmhouse. Apparently, this had happened before, in similar situations. Together, Vera and Adie made up the bedrooms in the main house where they all stayed, except Rupert, who declined.

Over the next few days Rupert began to relax in their company. Sometimes, when supper was finished and the plates cleared, he stayed a little longer into the evening, but always retired to his barn.

———✳—✳———

E VERY DAY ADIE phoned the hospital, feeling guilty; as far as she was aware, Thomas had received no visitors. One morning when she telephoned, she was told his progress had been good and he was being discharged into the care of his doctor and the district nurse. But, she was warned by the nursing sister, he was to have complete rest. His body had received a tremendous shock and there could still be some underlying problems that had not yet revealed themselves.

Thomas arrived home by taxi. Jack and Vera were at Adie's side to greet him. In the kitchen he brushed aside sentiments of gladness at his homecoming, preferring to be updated on farm news. Vera explained the new living arrangements and the reasons why. Adie expected him to resist, but he did not. She presumed he was lacking in his usual energy for a battle. In the end, Jack and Vera only stayed for three more nights before they went home, although Vera would still be on hand to help if necessary. Adie and the children, however, were never to move back to their wing of the house.

Late one evening, when the children had gone to bed, Thomas said, 'I owe you and the old squaddie my life, and now, here you are, running the farm for me. I am very grateful.' He was staring into some distant place, somewhere not in the room, and Adie was unsure how to reply.

'His name is Rupert,' she said. 'And he's not that old.'

She could see Thomas was struggling with some inner turmoil, and his lost face touched her heart, so she reached across to rest her hand on his. Her touch brought him back to the present. He looked at her, patted her hand, and then placed her hand back with her.

'I thought maybe you could offer him a job, at least while you're recovering. What do you think?'

'Yes, of course,' he said emphatically. 'Least I can do.'

Over the short time they had known each other, Thomas and Adie had become close. Often, they argued and vehemently disagreed, but somehow, both of them knew it would not disturb the friendship they had built. She wanted to tell him about her past and about the fears she lived with every day, but she believed that if she did, it would destroy the picture he had of her as a strong and capable woman.

Each morning Thomas declared that he felt fine, it was just his legs holding him back. Always, he tried to dress himself without asking for assistance, but then, awkwardly, he had to call for Adie to help him with his trousers, socks or boots. She noticed how pale he looked, and believed him to be in more pain than he was saying.

After breakfast Thomas would use his crutches to ably swing himself across the yard towards the barns. Once there, he tried to make himself useful. At lunchtime he would return to the house looking weak and hardly able to stay awake, but he refused to rest.

After lunch he went to his study and dealt with paperwork until the fire in the inglenook was lit. It was the aroma and warmth of the burning logs that would finally entice him to relax. Easing his pain-ridden body down onto the settee, he would gratefully accept the sweet tea Adie brought to him. After a few minutes his eyes would close in slumber and she'd cover him with a blanket, knowing that he would not wake until supper time.

O N A SUNDAY morning, when Thomas had been home less than two weeks, he made his slow journey across the yard to the barns. The dogs milled around him, barking encouragement. He wanted to check that the farm equipment had been properly cared for during the freezing weather, that the antifreeze had been topped up and the engines greased.

Having become skilled with his crutches, he leant one against a tractor, keeping the other with him while he checked an oil level. He was more than pleased with the work that Jack and Adie had done, but it made him feel redundant. He found it difficult to believe that Adie, a slight woman with no farming experience, had achieved so much. She was talented, intelligent and a diligent worker.

He screwed the oil cap back on and reached out for the crutch he had left leaning. Misjudging the distance, he accidentally knocked it to the ground so that it fell out of his reach. Cursing, he used the tractor for balance and stretched out with his supporting crutch to hook the fallen one to him. Managing to draw it close enough to pick up, he now had to bend to do so. Clinging on to the tractor, he mustered what strength he had and, ignoring the pain, reached down. Grasping the wayward crutch, Thomas stood it vertically and then began to walk his hands up its unstable length. It took all of his control to maintain his balance but finally, after what seemed a very long time, he was standing upright and supported again.

Feeling weak, he remained still, waiting for his heartbeat to settle, but then a powerful heat travelled through his back, followed by searing pain that almost knocked him off his feet. Outside he could hear Adie and Jack returning for lunch, so he remained hidden in the shadowy depths of the barn until they had passed by. The pain was diminishing and, although his heart was still pounding, he gathered his decorum and swore silently at his weakness.

By the time he reached the kitchen, Jack was carving the Sunday roast and Vera was putting vegetables on the table. When Thomas entered the room, everyone noticed his ashen face. Adie rushed to his side to help him sit down.

'I'm all right,' he snapped, waving her away. 'I just pulled a muscle.'

Thomas sat, holding a crutch with both hands, upright between his legs, his head resting against it. Jack continued to carve, and all exchanged worried glances.

Catching a glimpse of their faces, Thomas barked, 'I'm not dead yet; in fact, I'm very much on the mend.'

And to show them, he attempted to stand in a hurry, but his crutch slipped away from him and he crashed to the floor. They all rushed to his aid, except Lilly, who stood to one side, frowning at him. Again, his temper flared, only this time it came out in a growl of anger and pain. Everyone stepped back, not quite sure what to do. They knew he could not get up unaided, and they watched with embarrassment as he flailed ineffectively on the floor.

Lilly stepped forward and stood at his feet, her hands on her hips. 'Stop having a tantrum like a two-year-old,' she ordered, punctuating each word with a nod of her head. 'And I think you should know that you've split your trousers and I can see your underpants!'

She walked, with head held high and ladylike decorum, towards the range. 'Would you like the roast potatoes on the table, Auntie Vera?' she asked in angelic tones.

Sam could not contain his laughter, and it burst through his lips in splutters. Adie threw him a look of disdain, but then all of them, Thomas included, were overtaken with relief and glee.

After being helped to the table, Thomas ate his dinner, but Adie could see he was in severe pain. Eventually he gave in and explained what had happened in the barn. Her heart went out to him; he had been made redundant in the centre of his own universe. Bored and frustrated with his broken body, he spent time doing paperwork instead of working on his much-loved land.

After dinner Thomas was persuaded to ring his doctor. He made a house call that afternoon and immediately phoned for an ambulance, suspecting an undiagnosed fractured vertebra. Thomas was instructed not to move from his chair without the assistance of the paramedics.

'They will surely find nothing and then I can return home and get on with my work,' he declared.

None of them believed him. He sat in his chair in the kitchen, with the small suitcase that Adie packed for him at his feet, and five worried faces staring at him.

'Come on, chaps, I'm fine. In no time at all I'll be back to give you hell.'

When the ambulance arrived, Thomas tapped his case and indicated for Sam to carry it. After being placed in a wheelchair, he was pushed from the house, a humiliated look on his face. With everyone following, they headed for the ambulance, no one was speaking. Even the dogs hung their heads low.

As was becoming usual, it was Lilly who dispersed the atmosphere. 'You won't go to heaven without telling me first, will you? Only I've spoken to God many times, praying for things, but nothing ever turns out as I want it.'

A sort of spluttered, stunted laugh escaped Thomas's lips, followed by a full-bellied hoot that sent him into guffaws, causing him to experience both pleasure and pain as tears fell from his eyes. Jack gave him a steadying hand. This time everyone else did not laugh at Lilly's comments.

Adie seized her wayward daughter's arm and said, 'Apologise now, Lilly. That is extremely rude. I do not know what has got into you lately.'

'Sorry, Thomas,' Lilly said quietly, chin dipped, her eyes looking up at him.

'I promise you, Lilly,' said Thomas, his composure regained, 'that I will not go to heaven without first consulting you. Although, even if I am able to convey a message to God for you, I'm not sure how I'll give you his response!'

As he was pushed up the ramp into the vehicle, he looked back at them and said, 'I don't want visitors. If you're there seeing me, you're not here working.'

Thomas would not be able to work his land again until the following year. It transpired that he had several previously undiscovered fractured vertebrae and would need to wear a brace for some time to come.

———✴✴✴———

THE COLD WEATHER lasted for most of March, then in early April it turned again, and rain fell in saturating sheets. Gullies and streams filled with melting snow; water courses sprang up where they had never flowed before and flooded every valley. Above the noise of the rain the fast-moving liquid could be heard rushing as it sped towards already swamped destinations. Everyone wanted the snow to return; at least then the days had been bright and often beautiful. Now it was dark and dank, with heavy clouds that hung low in the sky.

Jack and Rupert had a constant battle to keep streams and ditches clear of the natural debris that washed down from the hills. On the fifth day of rain the swollen river broke its banks and flooded the lower fields. The ewes, not due to lamb just yet, were at risk of their health deteriorating. Jack decided to bring them down to the barns until the weather improved. The torrential water had washed away many of the usual routes and he, Rupert and Adie spent some time discussing the best way to bring the sheep home.

On the morning the sheep were to be gathered in, Fern was sitting by Jack's foot looking up at his face, every one of her senses eagerly awaiting a command. Adie marvelled at the dog's intelligence; she seemed to understand every word that was spoken, and at times read a man's thoughts before he had uttered them. But she would only work for Thomas or Jack, treating Adie as if she were an apprentice. Meanwhile, the other dogs, including Rupert's lurcher, were milling around, as fed up with the rain as the rest of God's creatures. Willingly, they returned to their dry kennel, to stay there until the droving work was done.

Wind and rain buffeted the Land Rover in waves as it slipped and slid its way across the land. In the back, Fern seemed oblivious to the weather that plastered her coat to her skin. She blinked away the rain and stood braced against the rocking and rolling of the vehicle.

Occasionally, they stopped to close gates to help channel the sheep in the correct direction. Adie's job was to stand at any gap left in the path, using the vehicle and herself to block an opening. On the way, Jack pointed out these places and left her at the one nearest the sheep while he, Rupert and Fern continued on foot. Once the flock passed the first opening, Adie would have to drive to the next, reaching it before the trotting animals. There were four such places, the last one being the most difficult. It was the entrance to one of the river fields, where the sheep frequently grazed.

Previously, Jack had explained that often, at the front of the flock would be older ewes who knew their way about the farm and could be relied on to lead the others in the correct direction. Today, however, he told Adie, those ewes could try to head into the river field, and she must stop them.

Since the river had burst its banks the field and waterway had become one great force of powerful, continuous motion; the gate had been swept away and in places the water was shoulder-deep.

She arrived at the spot with plenty of time to get organised. Parking the pickup sideways to the gap, she tried to fill the space, but the opening was too wide. She manoeuvred the vehicle twice more to get it in the best position, but it still left a gap. She looked back up the farm road and saw the flock approaching. They filled the width of the trail from wall to wall, compressed together and surging towards her like a mass of boiling white froth. The sea of sheep snaked back up the lane as far as the eye could see. Having built up some speed, they trotted down the hill at a fast pace.

The rain was blown vertical by the wind, and in the place where Adie was standing, she had no option but to face its full force. It blurred her vision, found its way down the neck of her coat and began to soak her jumper. For a few seconds she turned her head away from its onslaught and looked at the body of water behind her. From her vantage point, on a small rise, her eyes took in the swirling, speeding mass of the swollen river.

Hearing the bleating of the sheep, she turned her face back into the weather and prepared to do her job. On the horizon, Jack and Rupert came into view, and, on the wind, she could hear Jack's whistles and shouted commands to Fern.

Out in front was a large, powerful ewe, heading straight for Adie. She waved her arms and a spare coat she had found in the cab, shouted and jumped up and down, but the ewe was not put off; instead she seemed to gather her speed. Adie doubled her efforts, but to no avail, and the ewe leapt at her, knocking her over. Springing back to her feet in an instant, Adie took up her stance again and continued her manic waving, not wanting to let any more sheep pass. Thankfully, the rest of the flock carried on up the track.

Glancing behind her, she could see the large ewe, her nose high, being swept down the distended river at breakneck speed. By this time about a third of the flock had passed. Adie knew the rest would follow and continue safely towards the yard.

Leaping into the pickup, she fired the engine. Hand on the horn to scare away any sheep in front of her, she carefully steered a path along the side of the track, as she overtook the flock. Hoping that the stray ewe would get caught up at the bridge where the water was high, she made her way towards the road. If she could get there in time, maybe she could hang on to the ewe until help arrived.

At the top of the hill, she drove across the flooded cattle grid and out onto the lane. It was only then, as she pressed the accelerator pedal to the floor with a juddering foot, that she looked in the rear-view mirror and noticed Fern was with her. The dog was struggling to keep her balance, due to Adie's erratic driving. Heading downhill, approaching the bridge, the road in front of them was flooded by deep water. Slowing down, they crept through the constantly moving liquid as it rushed past in its perpetual need to reach the sea. Hanging her head out of the window, Adie checked its level, not wanting the engine to be swamped. The top of the humpbacked bridge was still out of the water, and she chose to stop there.

Looking up the river, at first she could not see the animal; then she spotted her nose above the water. Over the bridge, there was a swirling eddy, and she hoped the ewe would be dragged towards it. Getting out of the vehicle, she leant her hands against the wall, watching the movement and speed of the water. Fern was next to her, standing on her back legs, her paws beside Adie's hands.

Now that she was close to the river, Adie saw how powerful it was. It moved like a gigantic monster sweeping away everything in its path; even the bridge she stood on was vibrating in its attempt to withstand the force.

Adie hesitated – it was foolish of her to think she could save this creature. But when she looked again, she knew that if she did not act now, any chance she had would be gone. Hesitation went out of her head. Wading into the water, holding on to the top of the wall to withstand the fearsome flow, she made her way to the other side of the bridge. Once there, she headed towards the riverbank and found herself on a small mound where, thankfully, the water was below her knees.

She saw that the ewe was being drawn directly towards the eddy, which was just in front of her. Kneeling down, Adie reckoned that, if she could lean forward enough and grab hold of the animal, she might scramble out of the water. Fern barked just once; she was still on the bridge, her paws on the wall. The ewe's nose was now hurtling towards Adie and the animal crashed into the side of the bridge, placing her front feet on the higher bank. Adie grabbed its fleece and flesh at the shoulders but had not reckoned on the creature's sodden weight. The ewe began to struggle, and Adie knew she could not hold on to her.

Behind them, on the bridge, Fern began to bark and did not stop. With a choice of water, dog or human, the ewe headed for the human. With Adie's help, and continuous barking from Fern, the ewe hauled herself out of the water. Adie hung on to her fleece and the sheep dragged both of them onto dry land.

The wind and rain still battered them, but Adie could no longer feel any of it. She was completely drenched from head to foot, and the cold, seeping into her body, was causing her to feel light-headed. The fear of it worried at her mind.

The ewe had not given up trying to escape and made a last attempt to run, but Adie shook the fears from her head and threw herself across the struggling creature, forcing the animal to the ground. Finally, she gave up and lay on the sodden earth, her strength gone.

Rupert came to her rescue. Riding Prince bareback with only a halter, he crossed the bridge. When he reached dry land, he tethered the pony to a tree and relieved Adie of the errant ewe. Picking up the soaked animal, he waded through the water back to the pickup and placed her exhausted body in the back. Fern looked about her for a place to go, knowing instinctively that she could not ride in the now-occupied rear of the vehicle. Opening the door to the cab, Rupert instructed her to sit in the footwell. Shutting the door, for a moment he leant against it. So far, he had not spoken to or looked at Adie. She stood, shivering uncontrollably, unable to see his face.

'Will you be all right riding Prince back, or would you prefer to drive?' he shouted over the noise of rushing water.

She chose to ride, knowing Prince would take her home. Using the bridge wall to climb onto Prince's back, Adie lay forward, circling her arms about the pony's neck, and absorbed the warmth he generated.

By the time she reached the yard, Rupert had the sheep penned and was waiting for her.

'Don't you ever do anything that stupid again – you could have drowned! Not only that; Fern and the pickup could have been swept away. One sheep was not worth it.' Taking hold of Prince's halter, he told her he was going to give the pony a rub-down and that she should go to the house and get herself warm and dry.

Adie was utterly deflated.

That evening, after the children had gone to bed, she checked the doors were locked and retired early. Sitting in the darkness on the window seat in her new room, she stared out at the black sky. Occasionally, a new moon tried to appear, but was quickly extinguished by speeding clouds. Reflecting on her actions, she realised they had been foolish and thoughtless, and she wondered if the ewe would even survive her adventure. Adie's mood was strange: sombre one moment, ecstatic the next. Rupert's telling-off had been proof of how much she was cared for.

—⁂—

A T LAST, LAWRENCE had a chance to sort through his thoughts. It was Saturday, and it was just him and his car on the long drive to Cumbria. He'd completed the case, they'd got the conviction, his boss was happy, and now he had two weeks' leave. On the seat next to him was the Lewis file, containing all the groundwork, surreptitiously compiled by Jonesy.

He should feel better now that he was finally going to make sure that Adie Lewis and her children were all right. And she probably would be, let's face it; she'd managed to get to Cumbria, get her kids in school and a job with accommodation. Surely that was enough to set them up.

But still, there was a fire in Lawrence's belly and an itch in his brain that had pestered him for too long. Many times, he had pushed his thoughts aside. Now, away from the constraints of his job, he felt free to give rein to his feelings. He could not live with the restrictions of the force for much longer. The failures were driving him insane. He needed to be able to do more for the victims, and maybe the time had come for him to leave. Knowing he would be giving up a good career did not deter him; he knew that the higher he rose, the greater the constraints would be.

There was no personal life for him; no wife, no children. His own upbringing had sent him on this mission. Many times, as a small boy, he'd covered his ears, trying to block out the sound of his mother's pleading and occasionally her screams. The feelings that had arisen in him then had frightened him. He wanted to beat his father with his fists until he was bruised and bloody, until the man begged him to stop, but Lawrence was a child and his father a brute.

It was this childhood that instigated his study of ju-jitsu. He worked diligently at it, becoming a first dan when he was still a young man. But he learnt more from his teacher's spirit of peace and grace.

The last time he saw his parents, he threatened his father, by then an old man, and was disgusted with the cruel thoughts that filled his mind. As he had many times before, he suggested to his mother that she leave, but she was so conditioned and trained that this idea was beyond her comprehension. He left them to their life, hoping never to return.

As a young man he'd thought the police force would be a way to exorcise these childhood demons, but now he saw it was a falsehood, a trap, a lie to keep the public calm.

After several hours of driving and thinking, he came to the conclusion that he would not find all the answers now, but maybe over the next two weeks he could find an alternative life, another way forward.

By early afternoon his stomach was growling. Stopping at a large truckers' café, he was pleased to find that the lunchtime rush was over and the place was fairly empty. Taking a seat by the window to make the most of the weak April sun, he ordered liver, onions and potatoes, and a mug of tea. While waiting for his food he set about studying the file Jonesy had put together for him. This was the first time he'd been able to give the case his full attention.

As he carefully digested the contents of the file, Lawrence realised what a gem Jonesy was. The man was completely against what Lawrence was doing, but once you set him a task, he couldn't help but do it well.

In the file were three photographs. Jonesy must have gone back to the house, without a warrant, to get them. Two of the photos were school snaps of the children; the other was a family picture taken on what looked like a day out at the seaside. The children were holding a little monkey, and they and their mother were smiling broadly. Bill stared into the lens of the camera, and there was no smile upon his face. Lawrence wondered if it was because the photographer had flirted with his wife.

Once his food was in front of him it took him no time at all to empty his plate; he was eager to be back on the road. When the waitress came to clear the table and take his money, he showed her the photographs.

'No, I haven't seen them, but I am part-time. I'll go and get Bridget, if you like; she lives and dies in this place, so if anyone's seen them it'll be her.'

Lawrence watched the sprightly woman take fast steps across the café and disappear through the swing door to the kitchen. Moments later she reappeared with a tall peroxide blonde and pointed towards Lawrence.

'All right, love?' the blonde said as she approached Lawrence. 'Got a photo, have you?'

Lawrence showed her the picture. She frowned and stared at it for a long time, then put it on the table and placed her hand over Adie and the children.

'I recognise that geezer; horrible bloke. Ordered food, then grabbed hold of me, and left without paying for it.'

Lawrence could see she was still thinking, so he said nothing. Eventually she lifted her hand from the photograph.

'Now I remember – he wanted to know whether I had seen her and the kids.'

'Had you?'

'No, I hadn't, not that I remembered. So, what are you, then, a copper?'

'No, I'm just a friend.'

'Well, if that's her husband, she needs a good friend.'

IT WAS DARK when Lawrence picked up the keys to the self-catering cottage he'd hired. The landlady told him there was no parking space, so he'd better leave his car where it was; the premises were only a short walk away. It took a few minutes to get there, but on the way, the peace and fragrant air fed a need in him. Placing the key in the door, he felt, more than ever, that he needed this break. That Bill was on his wife's trail had not been the news he'd wanted to hear.

Telling the necessary lies to visit the farm where Mrs Lewis worked, and the school attended by her children, was a part of his work that did not sit easy on his conscience. Lawrence made up his mind: he would do it on Monday. He'd pretend to be a social worker, contacted by the caring people at the hospital they'd visited.

He hoped he would find them well and not disturbed by anyone.

———✳✳———

ON THAT SAME Saturday, Bill watched her, from his hiding place in a hedgerow. He took pleasure in studying the way her body moved as she carried out her physical labour.

The weather was mild after the snow and rain, and the exertions of her work had led her to remove her sweater so that she was wearing only a T-shirt above her jeans. Bill imagined her naked. Her hair was in a plait, and he could see the delicate curve of her neck. She bent low and stretched high, reaching up with both hands. He thought about tying her up like that, by her hands, so that they were high above her head.

Lilly stopped grooming her pony and called out to her mother, who was working nearby. Although Bill could not hear them, he watched them laugh and lay hands upon each other in gestures of affection.

Jealousy flooded his veins. Doubt crept through his mind. The voices sniggered. He had tried to leave Adie, even tried out another female, but it was no good; he was shackled to her, and he could not give up on her.

Unless the cold weather had prevented him from doing so, he'd been observing her since he'd butchered their cat, trying to get his hands on her, but it was impossible. And now his wife was growing in confidence, refusing to be intimidated by him, and he didn't like it.

He hadn't seen the farmer for a long time. Was he in hospital? He had certainly looked as if he should be. Maybe he was dead. If it was just the old fella and the hippy to handle, things were looking up. The old fella went home at night. Bill knew this, because he had followed him to his cottage, even spied on his rat of a wife a couple of times. He didn't know where the hippy went, but he was not concerned about him. That would mean Adie and his children were alone through the night. If so, there was no need to bide his time any longer; his opportunity had arisen. Leaning his head against the bark of the tree, he tuned his senses and felt his blood pulse at the thought that he would soon have his Adie back.

L ATER THAT DAY, Bill saw his wife and daughter head off up the farm road and follow a footpath that ran parallel with the lane. Lilly was riding her pony, with saddlebags attached to the tack.

Bill followed, travelling on foot through the fields, using the hedgerows and stone walls for cover.

After they had covered a little under a mile, they turned off the footpath and headed down a track. The track meandered on for longer than the footpath, but Bill was still able to keep up with his quarry.

Eventually, they came to a stable yard with a dozen stalls. The pony was led into one of them, and his tack and saddlebags were removed. Carrying the bags, mother and daughter continued a little further down the track until they came to a gate. Through the gate was a rambling farmhouse, fronted by an unkempt garden.

B EFORE THEY HAD a chance to knock on the front door, it was flung open, and Sara, all red hair and freckles, came rushing out with her arms wide open and a smile on her face. She greeted Lilly with a hug and then, holding hands, the two girls rushed off in the direction of the stables. For a moment Adie was left staring after them, until an upstairs window was thrown wide open and a voice yelled out.

'Sara! How dare you be so rude as to run straight past Mrs Lewis without even a "good morning"?'

'Sorry, Mum. Good morning, Mrs Lewis.'

Adie waved at the children as they disappeared out of sight.

'Got time for a cup of tea and a bit of a chat?' the voice from the window asked.

'That would be lovely,' Adie replied, keen to get to know Sara's mum.

Sara and Lilly were in the same class at school and had recently discovered that they both had ponies. Yesterday, Adie had received a phone call from Sara's mum. She hadn't realised that Thomas had been in hospital for so long and offered to have Lilly stay with them for a few days, thinking it would make life easier.

It made no difference to Adie's workload whether Lilly was at home or not. It was the thought of leaving her in the company of a strange man that worried her. Somehow, in her mind, Sara's father had become a sinister figure she could not trust. Adie had not met the man, and knew she was being unreasonable. But after all Lilly had been through, she could not help but be overprotective of her daughter. In the end, she'd asked Jack for his opinion.

'Of course you should let her go,' he'd said. 'You cannot keep her by your side forever.'

'Do you know the family?'

Having lived in the community for so long, Jack knew every person, animal and inch of land for miles around. 'Jim and Jenny Sutcliffe? Yes, I do. And what's their girl's name? Proper cheeky little thing, she is, covered in freckles.'

'Sara.'

'That's it. Yeah, Jim's a good fella, lets the Cubs and Scouts camp on his land. I think he was decorated in the war. Mind you, he won't say much about it, but that's what I heard down at the Black Horse. Is your Lilly friends with young Sara, then?'

'Yes, Jenny invited her over to stay for a few days and I don't know the family very well. I just wondered if you'd had any contact with them.'

Jack had glanced at her then, not for the first time, with a questioning look in his eye. He thought she kept too tight a rein on her children, but of course, he didn't know what they had been through. 'She'll have a fine time with them. That Jenny is a bit scatty but her heart's in the right place. Jim offered to help when Thomas first had his accident. The girls have both got ponies to ride; you should let her go. It'll do her good.'

In the end, Adie had said Lilly could stay for one night.

So now she was sitting in Jenny's kitchen, her teacup set down on the ironing board because there was no room on the table. Jenny had her sewing machine out; it looked as if she was midway through several projects. A pot simmered on the stove, a *Woman's Realm* magazine lay open at the fashion page, and vegetables remained half-peeled in the sink, but somehow it was a comfortable chaos and Adie was enjoying Jenny's company.

'Right, thanks for the tea. I'll see you tomorrow afternoon, then, but if she's any trouble before that, you just send her home. She's quite capable of riding home by herself.' Adie stood up to go.

'She'll be no trouble at all; I don't expect I shall even know they're here,' said Jenny.

WHILE ADIE WAS in the house, Bill had been watching the girls. Then he heard his wife's voice calling out, 'Cheerio. See you Sunday.'

Through the hedge he watched her walk down the track on her way home. He could have taken her then, but he didn't. He had a feeling that, after the long weeks of waiting, fate was turning his way.

AS ADIE LEFT the footpath behind and began to cross Beckdale Farm, she spotted Jack and Sam working down in the valley. They were replacing a gate that had been swept away during the flood.

She diverted down the hill to talk with them and take a look at how the land was drying out. Sam was squatting down, positioning the lower hinge. As he stood up to greet his mother, she noticed how bright his face was. Recently he had become more animated, as if looking forward to life. She hoped his newfound spirit would not be swept away.

'I'm going to get the tractor while you talk with your mum,' Jack said.

He strode off up the lane and Adie's face questioned Sam.

'Can I stay at Jack's place tonight? He's got some *Farm Journal* magazines I'd like to have a look at. Plus, we're going to start work at first light in the far fields, and that's nearer to Jack's than ours.'

Adie was so surprised by Sam's request that for a moment she stood open-mouthed. It was the first time he'd asked to stay away from home for the night. She had not envisaged both her children suddenly expanding their lives at the same time. 'Y-yes, of course you can. Are you sure that's OK with Vera?'

'Jack says it is. It means he doesn't have to drive here to pick me up in the morning and we can get on at first light.'

Sam was learning so many new skills from Jack that he was sounding more like a farmer every day. The special bond that had grown between old man and boy was a pleasure to see.

Jack arrived and brought the tractor to a halt next to Adie. 'That all right, then, if the boy stays over?' he asked.

'As long as it's OK with Vera.'

'It's her who's been nagging me to have your children over to stay; wants them to get to know our grandchildren, thinks they'll be a good influence. I told her I know Sam and he's no good influence!' Jack smiled, leaning out of the tractor to ruffle Sam's hair.

'Well, if you're sure it's OK, then that's fine. I'll see you later tomorrow.'

Approaching the house, the knowledge that she would be on her own all night sank in. Unable to remember the last time she had been completely alone, her stomach turned over and she felt vulnerable.

⸺✳✳✳⸺

F ROM HIS POSITION behind the hedge, Bill could not decipher the conversation between his wife and son and the old man, so he decided to take up his old sentry post at the top of the farm. From there he could monitor everyone's movements.

⸺✳✳✳⸺

A T THE END of the day Adie decided to take the dogs for a long walk before returning them to their kennel for the night. Crossing the main farm road and entering the river fields, she strode out along the bank, but the dogs looked back and began to yip, bark, and wag their tails. Adie turned around, and, after shielding her eyes from the setting sun, saw Jack striding through the grass towards her.

'Do you mind if I walk with you?' he said, falling in beside her.

Subconsciously, they lengthened their stride and, walking in silence, soaked up the golden end to the day. It wasn't until they began to make their way back that Adie remembered she had news about Thomas.

'I telephoned the hospital today and they said he has made good progress. He should be home in a few days. He'll have to wear a brace for a bit longer, but there should be no long-term problems.'

'That is good news; we'll all be glad to have him back in one piece,' said Jack. 'Actually, I wanted to double-check that it is not a problem for Sam to stay over tonight. When I asked him, I didn't realise that it's this evening that Lilly is staying with the Sutcliffes.'

'That's fine, not a problem at all. It'll be good to get some peace.'

As they approached the kennels, Jack placed a hand on her shoulder, and said, 'If you're worried about anything at all, you phone us. We'll be here in a minute.'

'Stop worrying Jack, I'm a grown woman.'

'Well, if you're sure, I'll bid you goodnight and see you tomorrow.'

For a few seconds, she watched Jack's back with affection, as he strode off to his pick-up. Then, with an inward smile, she opened the door to the kennel and the dogs obediently filed into their night-time lodgings.

Having prepared a simple supper of soup and bread, and dispersed her feelings of vulnerability by giving herself a good talking-to, Adie was looking forward to some peaceful reading. This evening the choices would be all hers and she'd have to do no one's bidding. The light was fast disappearing, and she noticed that the air had turned chilly. Opening the vents of the wood burner, she added more logs to the flames. Curling up on the sofa, with her food on a tray and a book in her hand, she settled down to an indulgent evening.

IT WAS DARK now, and Bill had seen all he needed to see. His observations over these last few days told him that his time had come. The farmer had not returned. He had observed Sam and the labourer preparing their work for the morning and then heading off to the old man's cottage. His daughter was away for the night. Then he'd heard the dogs barking and seen his wife take a walk with the old man. He'd watched as, at the end of their walk, they'd separated, each going their own way. Sam had not come home. Bill had watched Adie put the dogs in their kennel and make her way, alone, to the house. Now he just had to sit and wait under the dark, silent skies for the light to go out.

B Y NINE O'CLOCK Adie found that her eyes kept closing, so that she was having to reread every sentence at least three times. She cleared away the supper things, shut the draught down on the wood burner and carried her book upstairs. After her ablutions, she changed into a long, candy-striped nightshirt, folded her clothes, placed them on a chair and climbed into bed, hoping to read a few more pages before sleep overtook her. It was gone 9.30, but not yet ten o'clock, when she finally placed the book on her bedside table, turned out the light and curled up to fall almost immediately into a deep sleep.

I T HAD BEEN a simple job to release the locks on the boot-room door and make his entrance to the house.

On soundless feet he'd made his way up the stairs and along the hall to her bedroom – the door was open. Now, he was looking at her, lying on her back, one hand resting by her ear, peaceful in her sleep. She breathed out the gentlest of sighs and he was jealous of her quiet slumber. He thought of the life she had led, the things she had done since she left his side; the men, the lies, the betrayal. And the demons came dancing, performing Satan's ugly jig across the black ice of his soul.

THE COLDNESS CAME to her first. It was odd; only across her throat. Not fully awake, eyes still closed, she moved her hand to her neck, expecting to feel her own warm flesh, but instead there was a hardness. She tapped her nails on it and tried to flick it away, but it would not move. Grabbing hold of it, she attempted to throw it. Searing hot pain shot through her hand and her eyes opened wide in alarm.

She sat up. Someone there. A shaft of ice sprinted down her spine and her gut told her, without a single murmur of doubt, that Bill was in the room. He didn't speak, and her eyes searched the gloom, trying to speed their adjustment to the darkness. Long seconds passed, with the only sound being that of her heartbeat pounding in her ears.

Then she saw his silhouette, black against the moonlit curtain, a knife in his hand, and the shock of it chilled her innards. His free hand swooped down and grabbed her nightshirt, pulling her from the bed; it ripped apart at the shoulders. She tried to prevent it falling from her body, but he hauled her in close to him, bunching the shirt under her chin, pushing her face to one side. His mouth was twisted at a peculiar angle and exuded trails of saliva that fell onto her cheek.

In the few seconds she had been awake her mind had entered battle mode, sprinting ahead. She looked at his eyes – they were no more than a couple of inches from hers – and saw them shining with insanity, even in the gloom. Seeing the malevolence there, she thanked God the children were not in the house. Still he didn't speak; just pressed the knife against her face, and then placed it on the bed. Would he finally cut out her heart and soul so he could crush them?

Without warning she was hurled, spinning, across the room. Hitting the wall face on, splayed like Jesus on the cross, her teeth cut through her lips. In a slump she sank to the floor, leaving the wall smeared with a trail of her blood. Feeling herself being dragged up off the floorboards, the thought crossed her mind: how long would this beating last, and would he use the knife at the end of it?

A fist to the side of her face sent her crashing into the dressing-table mirror. The glass shattered, slitting her skin in several places. Blood was everywhere. Then a blow to the stomach left her in the foetal position. Air forced from her lungs, they rasped as she fought for breath.

Once again, she was pulled to her feet, stood in front of him and balanced, like a target, ready to receive more punishment. His hand snapped out and whacked her across the face using his full force, then immediately a returning blow struck, and everything turned white. Her knees went loose, and she could no longer stand.

Losing any sense of how many times she had been hit or crashed into the furniture, her mind retreated to a safe place and she pondered whether this was the beating she would not survive. The world around her blurred, blackness came, and stars sparked in her head. But at some level she was still conscious.

Somewhere nearby, the raw flesh of her body was being beaten like a steak on a butcher's block. Knowing she was going mad, she saw her flesh splitting open, a knife slicing through it sliver by sliver. Then, in her head, her children were there, and they were about to receive the same punishment.

Something wild and dangerous roared through her body, charging her with a new power. Pain no longer existed. A basic instinct surged and, with a beast's rage, she growled, rose from the floor and managed to slip free from his grasping hands.

Bill was taken by surprise; he had thought she was almost at her end and was about to halt his punishment so as to prolong his enjoyment.

She made a dash for the bedroom door, got to it before him and slammed it shut behind her. Wearing only tatters of her nightshirt and streaked with blood, she reached the top of the stairs. The door behind her flew open and Bill charged like a bull, shouting obscenities. There was no choice but to leap down the stairs from the top. Landing a few steps from the bottom, she collapsed and fell to the hall floor. Hearing his pounding feet on the stairs above her drove her forward, sometimes crawling, sometimes running through the hall. The heavy oak door was not an option. She headed for the kitchen. Once there, she flew through it, aiming for the boot room.

Suddenly her feet betrayed her, and she fell sideways, crashing to the floor. Pain seared through her ankle, but her mind dismissed it; only survival counted. On her feet again, he was almost upon her. She reached the boot-room door; the door to freedom. If she could get outside, she knew she could lose him in the darkness. Grasping the handle, she turned it and opened the door six inches, but a hand from above her head reached over and slammed it shut. Using the full force of his body, Bill trapped her against the door. The side of her face, her breasts and her abdomen were all crushed into the hard moulding of the wood.

'Darling, I haven't finished with you yet – it's been such a long time.'

She felt the length of his arousal. The sweat of his exertions and the sour odour of his breath rolled in waves over her face and her stomach began to convulse, pumping bile into her mouth.

The preceding minutes of violence were foreplay to Bill, the type he liked the best, and he could wait no longer. With one hand he grasped her neck, his fingers digging viciously into her throat. Using his other hand, he unfettered his swollen member. Adie managed to turn her head just enough to look into his eyes, and there she saw the black, glinting depths of his empty soul.

The rape that followed was as unnatural as it could be. She ground her teeth in pain as she was brutally buggered, and her unreceptive body began to tear apart. Not believing that he would leave her alive, her fear climbed to another level. She tried to move, to escape from him once again. She managed to twist her shoulders round and lashed out at him with her nails, leaving bloody streaks down his face. He hit her hard, his fist crashing into her cheek, slamming her face against the door.

There was nowhere to go. When the stars inside her head faded and full consciousness returned, she began to scream like a frantic harpy. She wanted the angels in heaven and the demons in hell to hear her. Nothing would stop her.

Bill, believing no one would hear, made no attempt to quell her stricken shrieks; the sound only added to his enjoyment. But in the kennel the dogs raised their noses skyward and howled like a pack of wolves. They scratched and clawed at the door and it began to rattle on its hinges as they attempted to break through it. Their long, doleful sounds travelled for miles through the still night air.

Unnerved, Bill stopped his brutal cruelty, his body not yet spent. 'It's not over yet, but thank you for the romantic time we've had this evening. Did you notice your carving knife is missing? Let's not forget there are three of you for me to have fun with. My patience has worn thin, and maybe it is time for our little love song to come to an end.'

He slung her aside, she dropped to the ground like a tattered rag doll, and he left, disappearing into the black night.

She lay motionless, eyes closed, unable to believe that he had really gone. After a time that was not measurable, the unceasing howling of the dogs began to reach her and, without moving, she opened her eyes. Slowly, agonisingly, she rose to her feet and stumbled outside, towards the noise. She felt a small piece of nightshirt fall from her beaten body and stopped her progress to stare at it in bewilderment. In the darkness she could not see ahead, and her hearing faded in and out as she staggered on towards the crying dogs. Each step became slower, shorter, until finally she closed her eyes and felt herself falling.

WILLOW LICKED RUPERT'S face one more time and then sat on her haunches, raised her chin and let out a deep, mournful howl. When the howl was finished, she sat still, listening, waiting for a reply.

'Go out, damn dog, if you want to,' Rupert grumbled. He turned over and buried his head under the jacket he used for a pillow. She followed with her snout, searching out his face. Finding his nose, she began to nibble it, but her action was cut short by the need to answer the achingly, desolate cries that came from her neighbours. Once again, she sat on her haunches and this time the howl came from deep in her chest, its sound rising in pitch until her head was vertical and she was in full cry.

The haunting response from the distant kennel reached Rupert's ears. He sat up, the hairs on his neck and arms tingling. Willow threw back her head and howled again.

On bare feet, Rupert began running before his thoughts had a chance to adjust. Ahead of him, Willow's paws ate up the ground as she flew over it. He followed her rump, unable to see anything else. Stones sliced at his feet and tall grasses attempted to entangle his legs as he crossed the fields and clambered through hedges, but he felt none of it. After passing through the second hedge, the cries from the dogs became clearer. He could hear them frantically throwing themselves around their kennel. Ahead of him, Willow was nearly out of sight.

On reaching the garden he came to a stop, needing to make a decision: house or kennel first? The dogs knew he was there and began to whine and claw at the door of their kennel. There were a few stars and only a thin slice of moon; the night was almost pitch black.

He began to make his way to the kennel, but then something about the house struck him as odd. Sweeping his eyes over the rear of the property, he realised that the boot-room door was open, and raced to its threshold.

'Adie?' he called as he stepped inside. There was no reply. Sliding his hand along the wall, he found a switch and light flooded the scene. Something tacky beneath his feet – was that blood?

The house was deathly still. The only sounds were the whining of the dogs and his heart battering against his ribs as he moved forwards through the kitchen. The hall door was smeared with blood. His gut constricted. He climbed the stairs. On the landing he picked up, then dropped, what looked like shreds of nightwear.

Ahead of him was an open door. He went to it and tried to peer into the darkness, but the gloom would not relent. He flicked the light switch. The shock of what he saw overwhelmed him, and he had to grab the door jamb until his dizziness receded.

Trailing from the bedstead was a tangled mess of bloodstained sheets. A chair and a bedside lamp were tipped over. On the wall, a handprint of red trailed to the floor. The mirror over the dressing table was smashed, its shards reflecting the gory details many times over.

For a few moments Rupert was stunned, unable to move; then suddenly his mind switched to another plane. He searched the debris in case Adie was hidden somewhere under it. She was not.

Deciding to check the rest of the house, he turned on his heel and almost fell over Willow. She trotted to the top of the stairs, looked back at him and whined. Rupert began looking in the other bedrooms. At the bottom of the stairs Willow checked to see if her master was following, then let out a sharp bark.

Rupert took the stairs four at a time, and dashed through the kitchen and boot room to exit the house. As soon as he stepped outside the dogs in the kennel raised their calls to the highest level.

After the light of the house, in the darkness outside he could see nothing, and he stood still, fearing some kind of trap. But Willow was at his side, mouthing his hand, egging him on. He made a decision to let the dogs out. As he approached, their whines began to quieten, until they were reduced to a gentle moaning. He was one step away from the kennel when he put his foot on something soft.

Adie's whisper reached his ears and relief swept over him. Kneeling down, he laid his hands on her and realised she was naked. Still he could barely see, but he could smell blood. He checked for broken bones, then, as if lifting a priceless treasure from its hiding place, he picked her up and carried her to the house.

Once inside the boot room he kicked the door shut with his heel, and it slammed in the face of his loyal dog, who lay by the step to wait. Softly, he placed Adie on the settee, opened the vents of the wood burner and threw on more logs. Draped over a hanging airer were clean sheets; he covered her nakedness with one of these and then placed a blanket over that.

After sweeping some hair away from her face and tucking her dangling arm under the covers, he tried to talk to her. There was no response except for a continuous whispering he could not understand. He was heading for the telephone, unsure who to call first, when he saw headlights approaching the house.

———⁕—⁕———

J ACK HAD BEEN having a poor night's sleep. He'd got out of bed to open the window, needing a breath of air, and heard the howling. After shaking his wife awake, he'd dialled the number for Beckdale Farm, but there had been no answer. Telling Vera to keep Sam with her, and praying the boy hadn't heard the dogs, he drove at reckless speed to the farmhouse. Leaping from his vehicle almost before he brought it to a stop, he ran the last few yards. Inside the house, disbelief stopped him dead.

'I heard the dogs and ran here. I found her on the

ground next to the kennel,' Rupert was saying. 'Maybe she was trying to let them out. She's not fully conscious and she's been murmuring like that since I found her. Her bones seem to be all right but she's bleeding heavily in places, and horribly bruised. The children aren't here.'

'Thank God. Sam stayed with us last night and Lilly is over at Jim's place. She's friends with young Sara,' said Jack.

'I was just about to call the doctor.' Rupert lifted the handset and was about to dial when Jack took it from him.

'No, I'll phone Vera; she'll be better for this. We don't want the local man seeing Adie in this state; he could even declare her disturbed and commit her. No, let Vera deal with this.'

Vera was the local healer and many people preferred her remedies to those offered by the doctor. She answered the telephone immediately.

'We need you here at the farmhouse. It's Adie; get all your stuff together and I'll come and pick you up. She's been savagely attacked by some lowlife. We need you here, Vera. Best wake the boy; he'll have to know sooner or later.'

'How bad is she?'

'We think her bones are OK, but there is lots of blood and she's not really conscious.'

'She needs a doctor as well as me; ring old Dr Andrew, not his son. If this attack is what we think it might be, he'll be best.'

'Maybe she needs an ambulance?'

'No!' Vera came back at him sharply. 'The hospital might make all sorts of assumptions, what with her living in Thomas's house.'

'What about the police?'

This time Vera didn't snap at her husband, but he heard the sigh in her answer. 'The same as the hospital. We know that if it's her husband they'll do nothing. Dr Andrew will know if anyone else in the area has been attacked – why don't we wait and see what he has to say?'

While Jack went to fetch his wife and Sam, Rupert could do nothing more than wait by Adie's side. Studying his lovely friend made him shed silent tears, and he cuffed his wet eyes and nose. He'd had reason to suspect all along that she'd suffered this sort of trouble, but he had not anticipated this level of wickedness.

It was a long thirty minutes before he saw the headlights. Both appeared at the same time, but the doctor entered the house first. Rupert saw him in and then waited at the door for the others. When they came, Vera went straight into the house. She and the doctor respected each other's knowledge, and they'd worked together before. Jack grabbed Sam by the arm, stopping him from dashing to his mother.

'Let me go.' Sam tried to shake his arm free.

'Your mum needs looking after right now; let them do it. You can see her when they've finished; meantime, we'll wait in here.'

The three of them shut themselves in the dining room.

'Will she be all right? How badly has he hurt her?'

'She looks pretty bad at the moment, but I'm sure she'll heal.' Jack wished he was as certain as his voice sounded. Seeing the pain on Sam's young face made him reach out and hug the boy to him. 'Sam, do you know who did this to your mother?'

Rupert looked on, wishing he had believed Lilly when she told him about their father.

'I've got a pretty good idea. Except I can't understand how he found us.' Sam stepped back from Jack and they sat face to face at the table.

'Is this your dad we're talking about?'

The boy nodded his answer and turned his head away in shame. It felt terrible to admit his father's barbarism to such a good man as Jack.

THE DOCTOR AND Vera had managed to get Adie upstairs to a bed. They worked in silence, both of them holding inside the anger they were feeling. Bathing, removing shards of glass, and stitching where necessary. When the physical work was done the doctor tidied away his paraphernalia, gave Vera a nod and told her he would see her in the kitchen when she was ready.

Vera had a way about her, a calm aura. She never formed an opinion without full knowledge. When Adie was fully conscious and a little more composed, she told Vera things she had never revealed before. The older woman remained quiet and listened with a breaking heart.

AFTER THE TRAUMA of the night, the dawning of Sunday morning was a blessing to Jack as he drove back to his cottage. He and Vera would, once again, be staying at the farmhouse, so he needed to get their belongings. A list of things to do ran through his head, and two items in particular stood out: he had to tell Thomas, and, on this occasion he disagreed with his wife, he would talk to Adie about reporting the attack to the police.

On his return, Rupert was waiting for him in the yard. 'How is she this morning?'

'It's painful for her to move, but she's clearer in the head.'

'Good. That's good.'

'Listen, Rupert, I don't know exactly what your situation is,' said Jack, 'but I think Adie should report this to the police. Do you want us to leave you out of it? We could say it was me who found her by the kennel.'

'It's probably for the best; I don't want to complicate things. Mind you, I want to know what's going on; I owe this family.'

'I'm not suggesting you should disappear; there's enough work needs doing around here. Just, if the police are about, maybe for your sake you should make yourself scarce.'

'I will, but keep me informed.'

The noise of a car approaching caught their attention.

'I'll catch up with you later, Jack,' said Rupert, as he headed towards the barns.

Dr Andrew pulled up next to Jack and wound his window down. 'Morning, Jack.'

'Morning, Dr Andrew. Did you find out if there have been any other attacks in the area?'

'Nothing similar. I spoke to my friend at the hospital and she said the only violence they've seen was about six weeks ago. One was an old man, a shopkeeper, robbed and beaten, so that doesn't seem connected. The other was an attack on a young woman, but not sexual, and the police seem to know who they're looking for in that case. Apparently it was drug related; the girl, a bit naive, I understand, had been to one of those parties.'

'Do you think Adie should report the attack to the police?'

'Normally I would say it's not worth it, but this was such a vicious attack that I think she should. Even so, they will probably resist, but I am prepared to stand up in court in this case. Shall we go in and see her, see what she thinks about it this morning?'

Jack and the doctor found Vera, Adie and Sam in the kitchen. Adie had been made as comfortable as possible on the sofa.

'How are you feeling this morning?' Dr Andrew asked.

'I'm fine, just aching a bit.'

The doctor gave her a doubtful look.

'Honestly, I know my own body; I will heal. I'll be fine.'

'I've got some personal questions I need to ask, Adie.' Dr Andrew addressed the room. 'So if we could have some privacy…?'

'There's no need for anyone to leave unless they want to. Every person here has been through this with me, one way or another. They know what happened.' Adie placed her arm around Sam, drawing him in close.

'We want to help,' said Vera. 'Why don't we stay, and if the doctor asks something you would rather not discuss in front of us, we can leave?'

Adie agreed, and the doctor asked his questions, phrasing one or two carefully, and culminating with, 'Shall I call the police, or would you rather go to the station?'

At the mention of the police, Adie's face fell. 'If we contact them at all I think we should go to the station. Having reported my husband's violence before, I have no faith in them. Mostly, they have set opinions about a woman who wants to leave her husband and they are not prepared to go against the man.'

Jack could hear the bitterness in her voice, but disagreed with her. He could not understand how any man could look at a woman so badly beaten and blame her for it. 'I know the sergeant down at Haybeck; he's a decent fellow. I'm sure he'll do all he can.'

Adie looked down at her hands resting in her lap. It was all pointless. She had come so far, and yet she had failed again. Silent tears fell from her eyes and Sam, knowing her pain, wanted to hold her tight, but her wounds prevented him from doing so.

Vera knelt in front of her, placed her hand under Adie's chin and looked into her eyes. 'I can see that you think it is all futile, but it is not. Look at us; we are not going away. No matter what happens, we are going to support you and your children.'

'But what about Thomas? He won't want all this shame I've brought on him. Surely we'll have to leave?'

Jack almost laughed then. 'My dear girl, if Thomas came out of hospital and found you and your children gone, he'd be hunting you down as well. Don't you realise how much he respects you and relies on you?'

Adie looked at her palms again. Was Jack right? It didn't seem possible that Thomas could respect her after causing this mess. But she knew that Jack and Vera were true friends and would not let her down. She had no more strength or will to run; she had to face Bill, win or lose.

THE POLICE STATION was a large, detached Victorian house, where the sergeant lived on the upper floor with his family. At the back of the building, on the outside, was an iron staircase so that his wife and children could leave the property without disturbing the daily running of the station. The ground floor consisted of a reception area, an office, an interview room and a single cell. The sergeant and his three constables managed the surrounding villages with the aid of one police car, two motorbikes and a dog that was not a trained police dog, but the pet of one of the constables.

Jack and Adie were standing in front of a high counter in the reception area. They were waiting to speak with the constable. He had his back to them and was whispering into the telephone. It was obvious that the conversation was not official, and so Jack cleared his throat to draw the man's attention. Briefly, he glanced over his shoulder, then turned back to the telephone. Then he turned his head again and looked at Adie.

'I have to go now, love – business to attend to.' His whispering gone, he regained his policeman's voice.

The constable approached the counter. Jack, who knew most people in the area, did not know this man. He asked Adie if she needed to sit. She shook her head. In a few moments they gave him the rudimentary details of what had taken place the previous night. When they tried to give more information, he indicated for them to stop talking. He didn't need to hear more; he just needed their names.

Then he directed a question at Jack. 'And what is the nature of your relationship with this woman?'

'We are friends and work colleagues. I found her.'

'In the middle of the night? Is that correct?' His voice was derisive, insinuating.

'Yes.'

'And you are not related to her – husband, brother, etc.?'

'No – as I said, we are friends,' Jack repeated, a little defensively.

'I see. And you say it is this woman's husband who has caused these injuries to her?'

'Yes, that's right.'

The constable directed no questions at Adie, but took a long look at her, as if assessing more than just her wounds. When satisfied with his visual examination, he said, 'Sergeant Wilson is supposed to be off duty today and now I'm going to have to disturb his Sunday morning with his family so he can come and have a word with you. You can sit over there while you wait.'

Behind them was a bench covered in dark blue plastic, running the length of the reception area. They sat. Jack leant in close to Adie, and whispered, 'I know the sergeant. He'll look at things differently.'

Adie looked up and, seeing the constable's expression, moved a few inches away from Jack.

The room had a damp, stale odour about it and her skin felt clammy. She tried to lean her aching back against the wall, but its blue tiles were cold, so she leant forward, resting her elbows on her knees, and stared at the mosaic tiles on the floor. Jack took off his jacket and draped it over her shivering shoulders. Looking towards the desk, they realised that the policeman had noted this action as well.

It was a long fifteen minutes before the sergeant appeared. During this time Jack and Adie had not spoken, just glanced at each other now and again, exchanging the odd wry smile. It had not been the reception that Jack had expected, but he was hoping his friend the sergeant would be more approachable.

'Right, then. If you'd both like to come into the interview room?' the sergeant said, holding the door open.

The small, square room, with pale green tiles on its walls and floor, was colder than the reception. They sat, Jack and Adie on one side of a square table; the constable and the sergeant on the other.

'Have you been to the hospital?' the sergeant asked Adie.

'No.'

'So, your injuries are superficial – just cuts and bruises, no broken bones?'

'That's right,' Adie replied.

At this point Jack interrupted. 'That's not quite true. He viciously raped her. This is a letter from Dr Andrew.'

The sergeant took the letter and placed it, unopened, in front of him. Then, speaking to his constable, he said, 'I thought Dr Andrew's son had taken over from him – didn't know the old codger was still working.' And then to Jack he said, 'We are not interested in the private lives of a husband and his wife.'

'But Adie did not consent to this.' Jack's anger was beginning to rise as he reluctantly saw where the interview was heading.

'A wife does not need to consent; the law says that rape between husband and wife does not exist.'

The sergeant turned his attention to Adie. 'Does your husband reside with you at Beckdale Farm?'

'No.'

'Do your children live with you there?'

'Yes.'

'So, you chose to take your children away from their father and live at Beckdale Farm in the house of a divorced farmer?'

'I have to protest.' Jack broke in. 'Your insinuation is unjust. Mrs Lewis works for Thomas – as I said, we are colleagues.'

'Jack, you and I, we know each other, right?'

Jack nodded and smiled, hoping this would be the start of a greater understanding between them.

'But I can't admit I know you in this situation. If I do, I'll have to get someone else to talk to Mrs Lewis, and believe me, they won't be as nice as I'm being. What I'm doing is letting you know how it will be seen in court, and I can tell you, Mrs Lewis, that you won't be in a good position there. And, Jack, I would prefer it if you did not interrupt again when I am speaking with her. If you do, I will have to insist that you wait outside the station until I have finished. Is that clear?' said the sergeant.

Jack did not answer but sat back in his chair, arms folded, his eyes fired with fury.

'As I was saying, Mrs Lewis, if you insist that you do not wish to live with your husband, then that is your wish. But I find it totally understandable that a broken-hearted man may go in search of his wife and, when he finds her living with another man, is bound to be overcome with grief and anger. In this case that anger has overflowed, but you will heal. And I'm sure that, should you realise the error of your ways, your husband will be delighted to take you back and even look at some of his own errant behaviour in the past. Even now you could still make a go of your marriage. Alternatively, should you wish to stay in your current residence, then I am sure that your husband has now vented his frustration and will not bother you again. My advice to you, Mrs Lewis, is to go home to your husband. Either way, the courts will not look lightly on their time being wasted on domestic matters.'

Jack was almost losing his composure but decided to make one final attempt to talk to the sergeant. 'Look, this man is dangerous, not just to Adie, but to his children as well. Adie's young son Sam—'

'No!' Adie said, grabbing Jack's arm. 'I will not have my children dragged into this; they have been through enough. I'm sorry, Jack, but I will not allow you to go down that route.'

She had remained calm and silent throughout the sergeant's speech, not once taking her eyes from his, or flinching at his improper comments loaded with implication. His words were everything she had expected; in fact, she would have been truly surprised if they had been different.

She was damaged, tainted by evil and violence; everything that was once pure had been ripped out of her and thrown to the wind. But there was a little part locked away, out of Bill's reach, and it belonged to her children.

She scraped her chair back and rose to her feet. Touching Jack's shoulder, she said, 'Come on, my dear friend, let's go home and not waste their time.'

———✳✳✳———

O N THE SAME morning, Lilly and Sara were riding their ponies. Lilly was wearing new gloves, but she was not used to them, and had dropped a rein. Luckily, Prince knew what to do; he turned the bend into the final set of jumps with a confident stride even though she was still fumbling with the rein. Just in time, she managed to get back in control before taking off for the final three jumps. He cleared the first one with copious amounts of air beneath. The second was equally easy. It was the third that was difficult: the triple bars stood together, high and deep. In the final approach Lilly concentrated hard and applied all of the skills Rupert had taught her. They flew over the jump in graceful union and Lilly hugged Prince's neck.

The girls had spent the morning building the course from show jumps that Sara's father stored for the local pony club. The atmosphere between them had been cool. It had started the day before, not long after Adie had left. As soon as they began riding it had been obvious that Prince was a more talented pony than Sara's Bonny. Both girls were competitive, and together they designed races and games for their entertainment, but by lunchtime Lilly and Prince had won almost every time. Sara was not taking well to losing. She wanted Lilly to be the underdog; after all, she didn't have a dad and her mother had to work as a skivvy.

After lunch Sara suggested they go on a hack. Lilly readily agreed, hoping it would lift her friend's mood. But unfortunately, that was not the case, and by the time they were back in the stables Sara was making comments about Lilly, her brother and her mother.

'Just because you beat me at riding doesn't mean you're better than me. Anyway, everyone at school says you and your brother are bastards because you haven't got a dad,' she sneered.

'We have got a dad, it's just he doesn't live with us.' Lilly fought back.

'That must be why your mum sleeps with Farmer Thomas.'

'She does not! She's got her own room.'

'I bet he sneaks into her bedroom when you're asleep.'

At that moment Jenny had called them in for tea. Lilly was fighting back tears of anger and shame as they made their way to the house. Once indoors, Sara had become sweet and amiable. Lilly liked Sara's parents; they were kind and funny and she didn't want to upset them by saying that she wanted to go home early, so she'd swallowed her tears, smiled politely and watched her manners, like her mum had said she should.

This morning's final triple completed Lilly's three rounds of the showjumping competition, and overall, she had two jumps down. Sara had completed two clear rounds and was starting her third with an expectant look of triumph on her face. Lilly watched from the edge of the ring, hoping that Sara would get another clear round; at least then she might be nice to her.

The little piebald had been lucky to go clear to this point; he was not well schooled in jumping and needed robust control from his rider. So far, she was clear, and, like Lilly, was determined for it to remain that way as she turned into the last bend. Even though she took the first jump with ease, she misjudged the paces for the second and only just scrambled over it, leaving her in the wrong place to be successful with the third. Pony and rider crashed into the triple bars and became a tangled heap of struggling hooves and poles.

Lilly feared that Sara was hurt. She leapt from Prince, threw his reins over the fencing and ran to help her friend. But as she got nearer, both pony and rider were able to free themselves from the mess. Bonny trotted off a distance and then stared back at the errant pile of poles in disgust.

By the time Lilly reached Sara the girl was red-faced and in tears, examining her scraped elbow.

'I hate you, you're horrible!' she yelled at Lilly, then ran off in the direction of the tack room.

Even though Jenny had made them a packed lunch with Victoria sponge in it, Lilly didn't want to stay near Sara any more. Head down, she turned and made her way back across the paddock towards Prince. On the way she collected the piebald and checked him for injuries; he seemed to be walking all right. After looping his reins over the fence, she mounted Prince and headed off down the track in the direction of the road. She let Prince take the lead; he knew the way home.

Slumped in the saddle with her feet and reins dangling, she bowed her head and allowed herself to cry. She had no idea why Sara was being so horrible, and could not see what she had done to cause it. In the end she did not think about it any more. It would be good to get home.

B ILL'S BLOOD WAS up, his frustrations running riot. The previous night with Adie had fuelled every lust in him and he was manic for more; so much that it filled him with pain. He still had the knife, wrapped in a cloth, anchored to his waist by his belt. It irritated him, not having used it properly. He'd had to shout down the voices in his head, so that now they were cowering in the recesses of his mind, but still they taunted him with their whispers. *Why would she come back when she can have her choice of men here?* His own voice joined in. *Why won't she come back? Why can't she see how cruel she's being, and how passionate I am about her?* He could take no more. She would have to suffer.

As he watched his little girl, she seemed very unhappy riding her pony home, legs dangling and tears falling. Obviously, it was time for her to come to the loving arms of her daddy.

It was easy taking his daughter off her pony's back, but getting rid of the pony was a problem. Bill ran, with Lilly thrown over his shoulder, across the fields towards the woodland that nestled between the Sutcliffes' land and that of Beckdale Farm. The stupid animal followed them all the way to the woods. Of course, he had to keep Lilly quiet as she kicked and fought like the plucky fighter she was, but that was not a problem. He shooed the beast away several times, but it just trotted off a few yards and then returned. In the end he let it follow them.

When he reached the woodland and stepped inside it by a few feet, a feeling of elation came over him. It was dank, dark and silent, brambles grew everywhere, and it was difficult to walk. Feeling safer now that they were out of sight, he began to pick his way through the vegetation. After a few minutes of this he could not contain his exhilaration and he ran, blind and wild, crashing through the undergrowth. Brambles clawed at his trousers and fallen branches attempted to trip him up, but he would not stop until lack of breath made him do so. Then he walked for a long time until he was deep into the woods.

There was no plan. He didn't know where he was taking Lilly, or what he was going to do with her. But he did know that he had to hurt Adie; she had to pay for everything she had done to him. And now that he had their daughter, he was back in control.

One of the whispering voices told him that his daughter was very quiet now; he chose to ignore it. Although, thinking about it, she was hanging limp, her arms floppy. Still, he needed to pay attention to his own instincts, not the babblers in his head.

Even though he had been running, he'd been unable to lose the pony. The animal was still plodding behind them, trailing brambles. Bill's eyes and ears were sharp, seeing everything in fine detail, hearing the breaking of every twig. It occurred to him that there were no trodden pathways in this wood; there was the occasional animal trail, but no pathway made by humans. *This is a good place*, he thought.

Then he stood still, staring at the ground, Lilly lying silent across his shoulder. He spent a few minutes in deep contemplation, letting the surroundings soak into him. When he finally looked up, he turned very slowly in a complete circle. In the distance was a small clearing that allowed a little light to penetrate; it attracted him, so he began walking towards it.

When he reached the place, he saw that it was a small, overgrown paddock encircled by dense forest. To the side of the clearing stood a primitive hut almost completely covered in ivy. He approached the hut, and then, lowering Lilly from his shoulder, laid her on the grass. She groaned and her eyes flickered. Blood came from above her hairline; he put his hand where he thought the gash might be and she flinched. The silly girl must have hit her head on something when he was running – still, if she was quiet it made his job easier.

It took him several minutes of ripping and tearing with his bare hands to get the door of the hut open. Thick dust, unsettled by Bill's vigorous efforts, was falling through the shaft of light created by the opening. Inside there was an atmosphere of doom, a sinister mood that Bill could sense. Others would have shut the door and walked away, but he entered the hut, eager and exhilarated.

Against the back wall stood an old iron bedstead, just wide enough for one. To the left of the door, a small wood-burning stove with a large, ancient kettle upon it. On the floor next to it, a copper cooking pan, the remains of some long-forgotten meal still clinging to its rusty sides. A wooden box, next to a rocking chair, contained twine, and what looked like shearing clippers. A number of hessian sacks were folded and stacked under the box.

First, he used the sacks to cover the springs of the mattress, then he cut three lengths of twine, and finally he dragged the rocking chair outside and sat in it, testing its sturdiness. After this he picked up his semi-conscious daughter, carried her inside and placed her on the bed. The pony tried to follow him into the hut. He shouted and waved his arms at it, and it backed away, but did not leave.

He tied Lilly's tiny wrists to the bed frame and then looped twine around her neck a couple of times before securing it to the frame. Then, with the help of the knife, he ripped a small piece of sacking free, rolled it into a ball and stuffed it into her mouth. This action caused her eyes to open in terror; he liked that. Even though they were a long way from anywhere he didn't want her to have a chance of being heard.

Outside, the pony waited, head down, saddle crooked. Bill took hold of its reins and, after some strong persuasion, was able to lead it away. After about a mile of travelling in the opposite direction from the farm, Bill slapped the animal on the rump, shouted at it and waved his arms. Still the pony would not go. Lying nearby was a short but hefty oak branch. Bill picked it up and stabbed it into the animal's soft underbelly. Shocked, the pony bolted off at breakneck speed. Bill watched it gallop away through unknown countryside and thought it unlikely the creature would find its way home.

It was mid afternoon by the time he returned to the old shepherd's hut. Once he had seen off the pony, he'd had to pick up essential supplies. It had been a long walk back to his car, parked near the Sutcliffes' farm. Then he'd driven into town to make his purchases, and on his return parked nearer the woods. It was still a long walk, but it was worth it.

In a minute he'd go in and give his daughter a drink, but for the moment he wanted to stand in silence and sense his surroundings. He was in control, and it felt good. All around him was silent; even the voices were quiet. Looking about him, he noticed a shepherd's crook trapped under the ivy. An uneven smile moved slowly across his face, never reaching his eyes. No one had been here in years.

O N THEIR WAY home from the police station, Adie and Jack were silent, each with their own thoughts. Accidentally, Jack drove over a deep rut. Adie winced in pain and Jack put an apologetic hand on her shoulder, but that was the only communication between them.

Back in the farmyard she tried to walk straight-backed from the vehicle to the house, but her body stiffened in protest. Reaching the door of the boot room, she caught her gaunt reflection in the window: grey skin and hollow, terrorised eyes looked back at her.

Jack could not watch her lonely agony any longer and left Vera and Sam to look after her. He went to the study to telephone the hospital – Thomas had to be told. After that he would find Rupert.

In the kitchen, Adie eased herself onto the sofa. Sam put a cushion behind her head and a blanket over her legs.

'You lie there and don't move. I'm going to take care of everything,' he said, stroking her hair. 'Would you like a cup of tea?'

'Yes, please.' A weak smile crossed her lips. Once again, her son had to be more mature than his years.

'Any joy?' Vera asked.

Adie met her friend's eyes and shook her head.

'Right, well, I'll let you two have that cup of tea alone; I've got jobs to do upstairs.'

Vera disappeared from the room to clear away the evidence that would not be needed. When she returned to the kitchen, carrying contaminated laundry, she swept through, taking the lot outside. Next, she set to cleaning blood from the floors and doors.

Sam was sitting by Adie's side, holding her hand and smiling. She could see he was hoping for a smile in return, but she just nodded and closed her eyes. It was Sunday morning and Sam should be somewhere playing with friends, not here nursing his damaged mother. And Lilly, spirited Lilly, who could not be kept down, would surely be bewildered by this turn of events.

Adie felt ended, closed down. How could she keep putting her children through this? They would be better off fostered, adopted, away from her and their father.

When Vera had finished cleaning, she announced, 'Today, for Sunday lunch, I am going to cook you my famous sausage, egg and chips, and you, young man, are going to help me while your mum has a snooze.'

Jack and Rupert returned, and when the cooking was done, they ate lunch from trays perched on their knees. Adie managed a few chips dunked in egg and then cradled her cup of tea in both hands for comfort. The others did not fare much better.

'What did Thomas say?' Vera asked.

'Well, obviously he was shocked. He hopes to be discharged from hospital tomorrow morning.' Jack was not prepared to divulge the full conversation.

Without warning, Adie made a statement. 'We will leave, the children and I,' she said, in a flat voice, 'in a couple of days' time, when I am on the mend.'

Her words shocked them and left them speechless. Except for Sam, who could not contain his emotions. Love, anger and frustration boiled over.

'So that's the answer, is it?' he shouted in her face, tears streaming down his. 'You'll just run away again, until the bastard finds you once more.' He stood dropping his tray onto the floor with a crash. 'And what will he do to you next time? Probably kill you that's what!' His arms waved about in exasperation. 'And then where will Lilly and I be? Dead alongside you is where we will be! You have to stop running, otherwise our whole lives will be ruled by that maniac – ruled and wasted!'

He slumped down on his chair and buried his face in his hands, regretting his outburst. 'Sorry. I did mean to say those things, but in a different way; I didn't want them to come out like that.' He stood again, looking down at his mother, waiting for her to rebuke him. But nothing happened, she had no resistance; no shouting back, no argument, nothing.

Staring at her broken egg, Adie knew she was beaten. 'But if we stay, he will do it again, to you as well as me. At least if we run it will take him time to find us, and there is always a slim chance that he won't.' She looked up at Sam now, not believing her own words, but hoping that he would. 'How can we stand up to him?'

'I'm not sure yet, but we'll find a way. You have support now. Jack and Rupert and Thomas—'

'I cannot put this on Thomas's shoulders. He expected to take on a housekeeper, not a whole heap of trouble.'

'I can assure you that is not the way Thomas sees it. You misjudge him; he greatly appreciates all that you do,' said Jack.

Adie searched Jack's eyes, still unable to believe she had worth. What she saw was undisguised frankness. Looking away, she considered his words.

Jack continued. 'Listen – the police may be useless, but our little community is strong. We know how to pull together in a crisis. I don't know all the answers, but you do have support now. We will protect you and the children until this is over with.'

'Adie, you should believe Jack. All of us in this room are family. If anyone is an outsider it is me, and I can assure you Thomas, Jack and Vera have saved me many times, but never intruded, and I am just a tramp,' said Rupert.

'But, Rupert, you are a man. It's different for women. How will I explain my life to Thomas? How can he have respect for me when he finds out the things that have happened, and that I have lied to him?'

'I have told him, this morning,' Jack interjected, 'what has happened to you. He understands why you didn't tell him what was going on in your life. His respect for you has increased with the knowledge of your bravery, your instinct to survive and the way you protect your children—'

Abruptly, the telephone sprang into life. Vera picked it up. 'Beckdale Farm, Vera speaking.'

'Hello, Vera, how are you?' said Jenny.

'Hello, Jenny, I… I'm fine. How are you?' said Vera, trying to make her voice sound normal.

'I'm good. Actually, I wanted to speak to Adie, is she there?'

'That's a pity, you just missed her. She's gone with Jack, to see Thomas.'

'Oh, that's good of her. How is he?' Jenny's voice showed genuine concern.

'Due to be discharged tomorrow, I believe.'

'Good to hear he's on the mend. Well, actually, I just wanted to check that Lilly arrived home all right, and that she isn't too upset. The girls had a tiff this morning, and she decided to take herself off home early, without telling me. I only found out when I went to call them in for lunch.'

'What time was that?'

'Oh, she left before lunch – about a quarter to eleven, I think.'

Vera glanced at the clock; it was just gone 3pm. 'She's not here. Are you sure that was the time she left?'

'Hold on a moment, just let me check with Sara.' There was the sound of Jenny's receding footsteps and then just the crackle of the line. A cold shiver ran down Vera's spine and she rubbed the back of her neck with her free hand.

'Is everything all right?' Jack asked.

Vera could hear Jenny's footsteps returning, so she waved Jack's question away.

'Yes – about a quarter to eleven, at the latest. Maybe she's fallen off Prince. It should only take her thirty minutes at the most to ride home from here.'

'You're probably right; we'll start looking from this end. Will you start from yours?'

'Yes, I'll send Jim out straight away.'

When Vera told them the news, Adie feared that her mind would slip into a place from which she would not be able to retrieve it. She struggled to contain her body, expecting it to burst at any moment into a crazed frenzy. In her head, she lectured herself on the facts. Of course, she'd always said Prince was too much for Lilly to handle.

She expected that he had bucked her off and she'd broken something.

Even though she told herself these sensible things, when she tried to speak, she couldn't; she was frozen. Looking down, she noticed she was gripping Sam's hand so hard that it was turning white. She couldn't let go. Sam gently stroked the skin of her forearm, where bruises and broken blood vessels revealed the previous night's traumas.

'Jack, Rupert, take Sam with you and go and see where she's got to,' said Vera, gently easing Sam and Adie apart.

Adie watched them go. Distant and numb, afraid of going mad, she observed the room.

S AM AND THE men went to search for Lilly. The route she would have taken was not suitable for a car, and besides, being on foot would make it easier for them to check every ditch and bramble patch. They walked in silence, praying they would find her, perhaps injured, but otherwise safe and well.

Jack had tried before to get Sam to open up about their past, but the boy seemed to think he was protecting his mother and sister by not telling. Now, as they searched the foliage, Sam began to speak, and it spewed from him. He told the history of his and his sister's life. About how they would often share a bed and hold each other tight, hoping to protect themselves. But still their father had abused them and secured their silence with threats of death by knife. He told all that he knew about his father.

When Sam finished talking, Jack could think of nothing to say except, 'We'll find her.'

Inside, Rupert was reeling. First there was Adie's beating, and now Lilly was missing, God only knew where. With the knowledge Sam had shared, his fears for Lilly grew. His new-found stability was being stretched.

They saw Jim ahead on the footpath and rushed to meet him. He did not move towards them, but stayed on the spot where they had first seen him, continuing to search the area.

'Looks like there was some sort of struggle here,' he said. 'See how the grass and edges have been trodden down, and this hedge crushed and flattened here?'

Silently, they examined the area.

'You not found anything, then?' Jim continued.

'Nothing,' Jack said.

They stood in silence, scratching their heads and looking about. Then Sam said what Jack was thinking. 'He's got her, hasn't he?'

'It's looking that way,' said Jack.

Rupert was looking away at the horizon, trying to hang on to a thin thread of sanity.

'Who? Who has got her?' asked Jim.

He listened intently while Jack gave him a short version of the events. They'd known each other for years, and Jim knew that his friend was not prone to overstatement.

'I'm off to tell Jenny to keep Sara indoors. Then I'll drive up to yours; there must be something I can do to help,' he called over his shoulder.

When the three of them got back to the house, they spoke quickly, breathlessly and over each other, in their attempt to explain the situation and waste as little time as possible. Darkness was approaching.

'Vera, you get on that telephone to the police; maybe you'll have more influence than me.'

She lifted the handset and asked the operator for Haybeck Police Station. The connection was almost instant.

'Haybeck Police Station, Sergeant Wilson speaking.'

'Hello, Sergeant, Vera Jeffery here. Jack attended the station this morning with a Mrs Lewis to report that she had been attacked by her husband.'

'Ah, yes, that's right. What can I do for you, Vera?'

'We have, in this last hour, become aware that Mrs Lewis's daughter, Lilly, has gone missing. She left her friend's house on her pony this morning at about a quarter to eleven and has not returned home. We believe her father has abducted her and we are worried that he will harm her.'

'The child could have fallen from her pony and be lying injured somewhere – have you not been out to look for her?'

'Yes, we have, and we did not find Lilly or her pony, but we did find an area where it looks as if a struggle might have taken place. The ground and surrounding area have been disturbed, crushed. Due to the nature of what happened to Mrs Lewis last night, you can understand that we, and especially Lilly's family, are extremely concerned for her.'

'I can see why you are concerned, but surely the man will not harm his daughter.' There was an incredulous tone to the sergeant's voice.

'That is exactly our fear: that he will harm her. We have just learnt, from her brother, that he frequently abused him and his sister when the family lived together.'

'And how old is the child?'

'Seven.'

Still unwilling to believe what Vera was saying, the sergeant continued. 'In my experience, little girls, and possibly boys, who see their parents having a fight, often say things they don't understand. And, if the mother is telling her children that their dad is a bad man, then the child is even more likely to tell untrue tales about him.'

Vera was becoming angry and her voice raised a few octaves, but she tried to reply in a calm manner. 'With all due respect, Sergeant, you do not know enough about this family to make that judgement, and what I want to know is—'

But before she could finish her sentence the telephone was snatched from her hand.

'This is Jack here, who am I talking to?'

'Oh, 'ello, Jack, Sergeant Wilson here. What is Thomas doing having a woman like that in his home? I know he's been on his own a long time, but there are plenty of decent women about.'

Seething with disgust at the sergeant's intimations, Jack cut him off. He knew that, at some point in the future, he would put the man straight, but right now, Lilly's need was greater. 'Never mind that – when are you boys gonna get off your arses and get out there and look for Lilly? That girl is in danger!'

'Now, steady on, Jack. You've looked and not found her, and you know the area better than we do. It's nearly dark now and searching would just be wasting police time, especially as she has probably gone off with her father. Poor man must be desperate to see that his daughter is all right. Undoubtedly, he's heartbroken. I'll bet you a guinea that he returns her tomorrow morning, unharmed. Look, it is almost dark now; any evidence there is will still be in place tomorrow. We'll be over at first light to inspect the area your wife mentioned. Of course, you will let me know when she returns.'

Jack slammed the handset down and studied what was left of the daylight. His logical mind got to work. They could fix the shooting lamps to his pickup, but then they'd have a fight to get the vehicle down that narrow track, and doing that would destroy evidence. Besides, the lights were meant to shine in the distance, not close to. They had oil lamps that they sometimes used out in the fields, but they wouldn't give enough light to look for tracks. The bloody man was right about one thing: they would not be able to see much until daylight returned.

———※※※———

THAT SAME EVENING, about 7.30, Lawrence was sitting in his car at the entrance to Beckdale Farm, planning what he would say when he got to the farmhouse.

Since his arrival in Cumbria, tiredness had enveloped him. It was a tiredness of the mind caused by the battle he'd been fighting alone for too long. The open land he found himself in, the friendly people, their way of life; these things gave him hope that everything in the world could be all right. Even though it was April, and a cold evening, the surrounding raw beauty made him want to climb the hills and see the views from the top. He felt the need to throw his demons to the wind, to get the business done and get on with his holiday. Admitting to himself that his passion for the Lewis case was waning, he hoped to find them safe and well. If he could see the family at their home this evening and convince himself that everything was all right, then there would be no need for the school visit in the morning.

But he was having doubts about his original plan. His car, for one, would never pass as one belonging to a welfare officer. In the end he decided to be a tourist; it was half true. He'd ask if they did bed and breakfast; maybe they would let him stay for the night.

Turning his vehicle onto the farm road, he slowly navigated its narrow width, thinking about what he would say when he reached the house. Then headlights appeared behind him, catching him up at an alarming rate. The vehicle slewed off the road and overtook him on the uneven verge. Lawrence reminded himself that, this evening, he was not a policeman.

After turning a corner, he could see the farmhouse in front of him; it was ablaze with light. Approaching an open five-bar gate, he made out the neat lines of a well-cared-for garden. Passing through the gate, the scene that confronted him astonished him.

Several dogs were milling about, barking and unsettled. A woman, bruised and battered, and a boy, her son by the look of him, were involved in a heated conversation with three men and another woman. The vehicle that had just overtaken him, out on the farm road, was there.

It took Lawrence only a few moments to fathom who the bruised woman and the boy were. He did not know the others. Where was Lilly, the daughter?

Neither dog nor human had noticed his arrival. In the next few seconds his holiday crashed into oblivion. The reluctant detective in him took over; it would be a little longer before he could be free. Picking up his file on the Lewis case, he stepped out of his car, leaned against it and listened.

'My daughter is out there, with him,' the bruised woman yelled, her face contorted. 'The dogs will find her; I know they will.' The boy, crying, held on to her.

'Adie, you are not strong enough, and besides, it is dark now. These dogs are not trained for this kind of work; they might lead us completely astray and we'll end up wasting precious time. At first light we will go and search for her and, maybe we'll take Fern.'

'You don't believe that any more than I do.'

The woman called the dogs to her and tried to leave with them, but the man she had been talking to ordered them to heel and they obeyed him. At this point the woman collapsed.

Lawrence had seen enough. Reaching into his inside pocket for his ID, he walked towards them. All of them, except the small, older woman who was tending Adie Lewis, stood motionless, surprised by his presence.

'I am Detective Inspector Lawrence Appleby from Sussex Police, and I think we should get this lady inside.'

For a moment all was still, then Jim squatted down and lifted Adie from the cold earth. Vera ran ahead, opening doors to allow him easy access to the house. Jack escorted the inspector. Rupert ushered the dogs into their kennel and then went to the kitchen. He no longer cared what happened to him; Lilly was all that mattered.

When they were all in the kitchen, it was Jack who spoke first.

'Thank God. I'm glad the force has seen sense at last.'

'Well, don't get too excited, it's just me at the moment. And you are?' Lawrence asked.

'My name is Jack Jeffery, and this is Jim Sutcliffe. I work for Thomas Elliott Lambton, as does Mrs Lewis.' Jack indicated Adie. 'Jim runs his own farm on the other side of the valley. This is Sam, Mrs Lewis's son, and this is Vera, my wife. And Rupert, who also works for Thomas.'

Lawrence acknowledged each of them as they were introduced and then said, 'And where is Mr Elliott Lambton now?'

'He is in hospital, after an accident on the farm. He is due to be discharged tomorrow,' replied Jack.

'And the accident, is that anything to do with the situation in which you find yourselves now?' Lawrence asked.

'No, at all. And what do you mean, it's just you?' asked Jack.

Lawrence looked at them, their faces turned to him expectantly. Even Adie Lewis, recovered from her faint, was paying attention.

'As I said before, I am from Sussex CID. I am here with regards to events that took place back in January on my home patch. I have not been informed by the local force about this current state of affairs. So, you see, I have just walked into this situation. If one of you would kindly tell me the circumstances now, of Mr Elliott Lambton's accident and what that commotion in the yard was all about, I will be able to assess whether I can help you.'

Jack took it upon himself to give Lawrence the details. He told the story from the beginning, including what Sam had said about his father. He spoke about the letter Adie had received, their quartered cat, (at this point Sam sat down and began to quietly cry), the attack, the poor response from the police and the disappearance of Lilly. The only part he didn't know about was how Adie had left her husband, but Lawrence already knew that. He listened intently, then took the picture of Bill, as a younger man, from his file and asked Adie if this was her husband. She confirmed that it was. Lawrence had all he needed. There was no doubt that the action he was about to take would get him dismissed, but he had already given up on the police force.

Now it was his turn to tell his story of disillusionment and why he was in the North on a private mission. He kept it short and succinct; his time would be better spent on the girl. The others listened and appreciated his candour, as he told them he would commit every fibre of his body to Lilly's safe return.

As Lawrence was speaking, Rupert stood to gaze out of the window. Usually darkness, with its blank emptiness, eased his troubled mind, but this evening it toyed with him. Should he confide in this wayward copper? Would the night reveal what they desperately wanted to find? He peered into the gloom, searching its every shade. As Lawrence finished speaking, and silence fell on the room, an apparition unfolded slowly from the black, finally revealing a sight that churned Rupert's stomach and weakened his knees.

Prince was approaching the window. The pony's heavy breathing was visible on the warm moist air pumped from his soft nose. Light from the window caused his coat to shine, indicating he was sweating. An involuntary tremble shook him and his crooked saddle slid further down his side; his reins hung loose and broken.

'Oh, my God.' The words exited Rupert's mouth in not much more than a whisper, but everyone heard them and rushed to his side, all except Adie, whose progress was slow.

When she caught up with the others and saw Prince through the window, her hands flew to her mouth. Her knees gave way, she sank to the floor and sat there, motionless, staring into space. Frozen for a moment, all eyes were on her, waiting for a further reaction, as if she might explode.

For Sam it would have been better if she had. Thinking that his father had finally broken her, a roar of inhuman ferocity rose up and escaped his mouth. He swept a vase from the kitchen table and it flew into the wall, sending splinters of glass across the room. Somewhere in Adie's distant mind the glinting debris reminded her of the previous night's horror, and she shuffled frantically across the floor to hide in the corner, believing violence threatened her again. Her son's manic frustrations continued as he punched, first, the table with his fists, then the wall, leaving bloody smudges and his roars turned to sobs.

Adie, was empty, a husk and the sound of her suffering child was in the far distance. With hopeless eyes she looked over her shoulder at him, and even though his pained face stabbed somewhere deep in her heart, she could do nothing. She faced the corner, hugged her knees and tried to rock it all away.

Jack enveloped the boy in his powerful arms and smothered his punches. He drew him down onto the sofa and cradled him like a small child, holding him until his physical eruption was reduced to sobs.

It was not the first time Jack had held a sobbing, broken young man. Back in the war years he'd tried to mend the shattered minds of many young conscripts and return them to the fight. As he held Sam, he watched his mother. Vera fed her water laced with a tincture of hops. But it was of little use; she had closed down, become robotic. Like Sam, Jack would have been happier to see a different reaction.

When Sam appeared calmer, Jack held him at arm's length, his hands on the boy's shoulders, heavy and anchoring.

'Now, boy,' his voice was hard and demanding, 'I expect better than this from you. Your mother and sister need you to be a man.'

'But what if he—?'

Jack silenced the boy's trembling mouth with his hand before he could say the words. 'We'll have none of that talk. That little sister of yours is going to be back here pestering you before you know it. Now, promise me you'll never utter those words or have thoughts like that again.'

Sam nodded his head, not believing himself. Jack removed his hand.

'And what about Mum?' Sam asked. 'Will I ever get her back?'

Jack looked at Adie. She was rocking like a metronome, her skin the colour of a stone statue. He wished he believed the words he was about to say.

'Don't pay too much attention to how she is now,' he said in a gentler tone. 'Your mum is a strange mixture of gentleness and steel. She'll be up and fighting again before you know it. Now, remember what I said: they need you to be a man.'

Silence fell again. Each person, except Rupert, who had left the house, was overtaken with their own thoughts and avoided the others' saddened eyes. The room, laden with fear, rage and frustration, bore a heavy burden.

RUPERT REMOVED THE tack from Prince's trembling frame. Several pieces of foliage had been caught up in the strapping; all thrived in the local hedgerows and woodland. Next, he examined the pony from head to hoof. Across his knee was a gash where the skin lay open like an envelope, blood traced down his leg. As well as the cut to his knee, there were numerous scratches, probably caused by brambles. The lacerations did not worry Rupert, but Prince's obvious distress did.

Finding the kit Thomas used for stitching back the uteri of ewe's damaged while giving birth, he cleaned and stitched the gashed leg, all the while talking to the anguished pony. Before leaving the stall he washed the sweating animal, rubbed him down and filled his hay net. As Rupert walked away, Prince began to kick the stable door and whinny.

Jack, Jim and the inspector approached.

'I've checked him over and stitched that leg, but he's in a right state, all wild-eyed. He's been through a lot of woodland,' said Rupert.

'Do you think it possible he could lead us to Lilly?' asked Lawrence.

'Definitely possible,' said Rupert.

'You know, no one could handle that pony until Lilly came along. Let's face it, that animal knows more about where she is than we do,' said Jack.

'Then, as soon as we can see, we'll give Prince his chance,' said Lawrence.

Back in the house they found Vera and Adie sitting together on the settee, their arms about each other. Vera was awake, but Adie's eyes were closed.

Jack mouthed, *Is she asleep?*

Vera shook her head in reply and said, 'What are you going to do now?'

'There's not a lot we can do until daylight,' said Jack.

'Do you chaps have some sort of powerful light that you shoot with?' said Lawrence.

'I do,' said Jim.

'Could we use it to get a look at the spot where you think Lilly was taken?'

'I thought about that,' said Jack, 'but the light runs off the car battery and we can't get a vehicle down that pathway.'

'Does it illuminate the distance or close to? Could we get your vehicle in a position where the light will shine on the spot, but the vehicle doesn't have to be on the pathway? If we can do that and I can get a look at the sight then at least we'll know we're starting from the right place when daylight turns up. It might give us a bit of a head start.'

Jim began to outline a plan. 'If we fix the searchlight to the pickup, we'll get some good vision. I can try parking up on my side of the valley, directly across from the spot. Sam, you can operate the light.' He thought it best that Sam stay with him, in case they found something it wouldn't be good for the boy to see.

Sam was already getting his boots and coat on. Jack showed Lawrence to the boot room, telling him to kit himself out. Lawrence chose a waxed coat belonging to Thomas and, after a little searching, found a pair of boots in his size. From his jacket he transferred his trusted handcuffs to the pocket of Thomas's coat. Rupert went to get the dogs. They followed him back to the house, noses and tails down, sensing the mood. Inside, subdued, they sat in a bunch.

'We'll leave the dogs with you, just in case,' Jack said to his wife. 'Don't open the door to anyone unless it's us or the police.'

Rupert looked at Adie, hoping she would say something, or even just give some sort of facial expression. There was nothing, except that her eyes were alert with the same wildness he'd seen in Prince's.

———※※※———

OUTSIDE, NO MOON or stars lit the way. The night was still, as if brewing a storm. Small rustling sounds could be heard in the undergrowth, and night creatures called through the air. A rush of shivers ran up Lawrence's neck; he was not used to this rural expanse. Here in this sinister stillness, Prince's kicking and calling were clearer; his anguish haunted them.

Glad of work to do, Jim fired up the engine of his pickup and he and Sam drove off into the darkness. Jack handed Lawrence the torch and the three of them passed through a hedgerow into the black night.

When Jim reached his house, the lights were on, and as they turned around in the yard the front door was thrown open. Jenny ran out with a flask in her hand.

'You've not found her,' she declared, shoving the thermos into her husband's hands. Her contorted face was wrapped in guilt. Silently she cursed herself for not reacting sooner to the girls' childhood spat. 'I've just made it, it's hot and sweet.'

'Thanks, love. We've got to get on.'

'I knew you'd be out looking,' she shouted after them as they drove away. 'Good luck.' But Jim and Sam could not hear her, and nor did they see her tears.

Using the headlights of the vehicle to illuminate the barn, they worked quickly, connecting the wiring to the battery and fixing the powerful spotlight to the roof of the pickup. In no time at all they were on their way.

When they arrived at the place where Jim thought he could shine the light on the pathway, he parked and joined Sam in the bed of the vehicle. Knowing it would take the others a while to reach the spot, he began to use the light to illuminate each piece of surrounding land. Even though he could not see the detail he scanned the ground methodically with the powerful beam and tried to scrutinise every leaf, bush and patch of earth. And, although he saw nothing definite, he was fairly sure he knew in which direction they had gone. He thought Prince must have been in Flimby Forest. Neither the land nor the woodland had been managed for decades, not since old Flimby died with no one to leave it to.

Sam was becoming impatient, so Jim handed control of the light over to the boy. He swung it around to the designated spot and, as Jim had suspected, Jack, Rupert and Lawrence were only just approaching the place. They waved their acknowledgement of the light.

Getting to work immediately, they picked through every blade of grass and inch of hedgerow. For nearly an hour they searched, then Lawrence found a pink hairclip. Jack said he had seen Lilly wear that type of clip but couldn't confirm that this particular one was hers. With heavy hearts they continued their slow work, covering the whole area. Nothing else was found, but Lawrence agreed with the others that this was probably the place where she had been taken.

When the five of them were back in the farmyard, Jim said, 'I think it might be best if we have a chat before we go in – you know, so that it's not in front of Adie.'

They murmured their agreement and Jim continued.

'I reckon they've got to be somewhere in Flimby Forest. I had a good look at the lie of the land before you got there and there's nowhere else that pony could have got in that state.'

'Why this particular woodland? Are there no others around here?' Lawrence asked.

'There are, but not like Flimby,' said Jack. 'Thinking about it, I reckon you could be right, Jim. The other woods are all well managed, and Prince would have been able to get through them at a pace without the sort of damage he received.'

'Can't we go now?' asked Sam.

Lawrence looked at his watch. 'It's three o'clock; less than three hours until dawn. I suggest we get some rest and be ready to go at 5.30. We'll take Prince with us; hopefully he'll show us the way.' Placing a hand on Sam's shoulder, the detective steered the reluctant boy towards the house.

THE WOMEN WERE not in the kitchen. Leaving the others, Jack went to find them. From the hall he could smell that the drawing-room fire was alight. Opening the door, he peeped into the room and found Vera sitting on the settee, fast asleep, her head hanging at an awkward angle. Next to her, Adie was lying on her side, hugging her knees, her head resting in the older woman's lap.

Although her eyes were closed, Adie was not asleep. She had been listening to Prince's desperate calling and it gave her comfort. Somehow, she felt that all the time he called and kicked, Lilly was alive. She prayed he wouldn't stop. When she heard the door move, she didn't open her eyes. She knew, by the reaction of the dogs, that it was Jack who had entered the room. He was still for a while, and then she felt him, very near. From under her eyelashes she looked at him. He didn't see her watching him place a cushion under his wife's head and stroke her hair lovingly. This simple gesture cracked Adie's heart open. She closed her eyes and let the silent tears fall.

Back in the kitchen, Jack found cheese, bread and pickles in the pantry. He placed these on the table and made a pot of tea. Sam was already asleep, slumped in an armchair, pale and drawn. His eyes moved rapidly to and fro under the thin skin of his lids. Jack made him a cheese sandwich for when he woke up and hoped his dreams were not adding to the horrors of the day.

When they had drunk the tea and picked lightly at the food they tried to settle. Rupert spread his jacket on the rug and lay stretched out on his back, Willow curled up beside him, her head on his chest.

Lawrence stood by the window, his hands resting on the sill. 'Jim's gone home; says he'll be back at 5.30.'

Jack nodded. 'Come on, sit down and at least rest your legs – there's nothing to be seen out there.'

Lawrence gave a barely noticeable nod of his head and sat in the other armchair. Jack stretched out along the old sofa. No one wanted to go upstairs, where the taint of evil remained.

Now that the house was still, the hours ticked slowly by, each quarter marked by the muffled night chime of the grandfather clock. Those quarters were filled with another sound. Prince had been rhythmically kicking his stable door since they'd left him. After each thud the door rattled on its hinges. There would be maybe five or six of these in a row and then a single neigh, a moment of silence, then the process started over. The persistent sound of the bereft pony began to unnerve them. It sent poignant, wistful messages, evoking thoughts of the cheeky, candid little girl, the instigator of laughter. It lowered their resistance to destructive thoughts and they began to lose hope.

The three men stayed silent for a long time, eyes open, not talking, while Sam slept fitfully, twitching and moaning unintelligible words. Then, speaking softly, Jack asked Lawrence about his life's work, and how he coped with this sort of situation on a regular basis. Lawrence admitted, for the first time to another person, that he didn't cope with it, and didn't want to pretend any longer. That it made him feel inhuman to act so cold when all around him were devastated. But he didn't admit, considering the poor success rate for saving women and children, or catching their abusers, how helpless he felt.

IN THOSE EARLY hours, on that same morning, Bill was sitting in the rocking chair, his newly purchased Tilley lamp emitting a soft glow. He rocked gently, talking quietly to himself, as he looked at his daughter. She was lying on the hessian sacks he had placed on top of the old mattress springs. Her wrists were tied to the corners of the bed, her neck tied down, her mouth gagged, but her legs were free. He liked the way she kicked him. He thought she was asleep now, but he could not be sure. Taking mental snapshots of the way her hair framed her delicate face and the curl of her eyelashes against her cheeks, he stored them in his mind so he could study them later if he no longer had her.

Earlier, he had tried to spoon-feed her, but she'd spat the food back at him. He'd had to slap her and tape up her mouth. Later, he told her that her mummy would soon be with her, and she shook her head, opened her eyes wide and tried to speak, so he ripped the tape from her lips.

'Don't bring Mummy; you have me. I'll stay with you, I promise. You don't need Mummy if you have me,' she'd pleaded with him.

But he'd told her he did need Mummy. And as he sat studying Lilly now, he contemplated what a pity it would be to kill her. Whether he did or not would be down to her mother; she had to come back to him. But how would he know he could keep her? Could he trust her? He pictured Adie now, so clever, so quick-thinking. How would he know she was being truthful with him? She would say anything to save her little girl. She never felt the need to have power over someone else, and yet she was unaware of the power she had over him.

He had dreamt that one day he would be rid of the evil that stalked through him, so that he could be at one with her. He had tried to contaminate her soul, to bring her closer to him, but had failed. For all of the evil he was aware he possessed, she possessed the same, if not more, of good. After all he had done to her, her strength to resist, to never break, continually surprised him. Still, maybe now that he had Lilly, he could finally bend Adie to his will.

The voices picked up on his flawed thinking; they told him that Adie loved her children more than him, and he could not deny it. He realised then that he was jealous of his children; he loathed their youthful beauty, the happiness he witnessed when they were with their mother, and their innocence. It was hopeless. He would never be able to trust her.

Perhaps it was too late. Perhaps he'd have to kill Adie. It would be his greatest pleasure and his deepest pain.

THERE WAS NO sleep for Adie. In her mind, Bill's lips kept approaching her ear; then his teeth bit down hard and drew blood. Then the vision changed, and it was Lilly's ear he was biting. She sat up and rubbed her brow, trying to push the image away.

Vera remained in an exhausted sleep. Adie stood up and stretched, the dogs watching her from the comfort of the rug. She began to pace the floor. Prince's distress was driving her mad. The incessant kicking and calling felt as if they were meant for her.

Vera had made it clear that, because of her emotional state, it would be better if Adie did not get involved with the search, but she disagreed. Loathing for the man who had taken her child, raped, beaten and battered her one too many times, was consuming her. He had caused her to become this demonic person, full of hatred. She detested feeling this way, was disgusted by her thoughts. Her pace quickened as her other self came to the fore. The years with Bill had given her a sound education in how to bring herself back from the depths of hell. Knowing him better than anyone, she put herself in his mind. It was her he wanted.

If they were going to use Prince to try to find Lilly, she had to go with them. If necessary, she would swap places with Lilly. She had survived everything he'd thrown at her and could live through it one more time.

But what if Lilly was dead? The thought turned her to liquid, and she had to grab hold of the furniture to support herself. Pushing the thought away, she drew down her internal guards and re-engaged her mind. Once composed, she came to a decision.

Feeling guilty, she sneaked away from Vera. She could no longer listen to her friend's meaningless words. How could Vera possibly understand anything about her life?

Indicating for the dogs to stay, she crept out of the room. In the hall she drew back the bolts on the heavy oak door and slipped out into the night. Faint light glowed from the kitchen window as she ducked below it on her way to the stable. There was no time for fear now; all she knew was that they were not going without her. She would get Prince ready and be waiting for them. She would be on his back, and if they tried to remove her, she would go without them.

Approaching the stables, she began to speak to Prince in soft tones. A few feet from his stall, she paused, reassuring him that together they would find Lilly. The pony stopped kicking, snorted and twitched his ears. Adie entered the stable and ran her hands over his shoulders and neck, still talking. He stamped his feet, snorted and shook her off him as he resumed kicking the door.

Recognising that she was in no fit state to hang on to a galloping pony, she trusted that the others could keep him calm.

In the tack room she shouldered his saddle and bridle, hoping Prince would accept them. Touching the bridle to his face seemed to have a good effect on him, and he nudged her chest gently. Slowly, methodically, she slipped the bridle over his head and then placed the saddle on his back and tightened the girth. He stood patiently, although still full of twitches and shivers. When she had finished, she looked out across the valley. In the distance she could see headlights. Jim was returning.

When he had passed the stable on his way to the house, she mounted Prince and his forelegs left the ground in a subdued rear. She talked to him, telling him it wouldn't be long. He quietened and resumed his rhythmic kicking.

Soon she heard voices in the still night air.

Jack: 'Maybe Prince is getting exhausted; he ceased his kicking for a bit, did you notice?'

Lawrence: 'I hope he's up for the job this morning.'

Jim: 'Got my shotgun in the truck; do you think we should take it?'

Lawrence: 'No, I've seen enough tragic accidents when guns get involved with this sort of thing.' A pause, then, 'Is there any reason you think Bill may have managed to get hold of a gun?'

Jack: 'Not that I'm aware of.'

Rupert did not say a word.

In the light of the oil lamp, Adie could see the silhouettes of the approaching men. 'Nearly time,' she whispered to Prince, stroking his neck.

Their faces came into view. They stopped, taking a moment to register what they were seeing.

Lawrence spoke first. 'Adie, I understand your distress, but it's not wise for you to come with us this morning. You could jeopardise things.'

Through her long hours of silence, Adie had thought things through, and she would not change her mind.

'I'm convinced that Prince knows where Lilly is. No one knows my husband like I do. We may have to swap Lilly for me; I am fully prepared to do that. This pony is ready to gallop the moment you open the stable door. Now, I am relying on your skills, Rupert, to not let that happen. But should you decide that you will not allow me to come with you this morning, I will make sure it does happen.'

'Mum should come,' said Sam.

'No!' said Jack. 'She's too weak and we risk losing her to the bloody brute as well.'

'I am in agreement with you, Jack; it's far too risky,' said Lawrence.

Adie watched as her son's overloaded emotions exploded again, and she was proud.

'I am ten and I am Lilly's brother, and you're letting me go. She is her mother; she gave birth to her, and you're not letting her go? She knows my dad like nobody else, except me and Lilly, and she should be with us.'

Jack held Sam by the shoulders and was about to speak when Rupert stopped him.

'The boy is right,' he said. 'The child's mother should be with us. Where are the police? Do you think we will find them at the place where Lilly was taken? I doubt it. Adie should definitely come.'

At that point the distant voice of Vera was heard. 'Adie? Have you got Adie? Jack, is Adie there?' She appeared from the dark and was at once visibly relieved and then anxious to see Adie on Prince's back.

'It's all right, my love, we've decided Adie should come with us,' Jack told his wife.

'You're sure?'

'Yes, I think the right decision has been made,' said Lawrence. 'Vera, we need you to stay here. Phone the police as soon as you get back to the house, and keep phoning until you get an answer. Tell them what we've done and where we've gone. Tell them everything you know.'

Vera was carrying a warm coat for Adie, and she gave it to her now.

It took all of Rupert's skills to let Prince out of the stable and, at the same time, prevent him from bolting. As the search party left the farmyard, a grey dawn was appearing in the east. Drizzle began to fall. It looked as if it would be the relentless kind, and Adie shrank her head into her shoulders, silent and determined.

O NCE THEY WERE on their way the pony seemed more settled until they reached the spot where they thought Lilly had been taken. At this point Prince wanted to be free from Rupert's control. Jim had been right about Flimby Forest; it was in this direction that Prince was struggling to go.

'Right, let's keep this under control; we don't want to lose this pony, or Adie for that matter,' said Lawrence.

They looked at her then, as if they had forgotten she was with them. She stared back at them, trying to convey her grit, not wanting them to see her pain.

'OK, Rupert, let the pony lead the way. What we have to do,' Lawrence added to Sam, 'is leave an easy trail for the police to follow.'

Rupert held on to the reins but gave Prince his head. The pony pricked his ears forward, lowered his head and increased his pace.

They climbed a little way out of the valley and then began traversing the hillside. No one spoke and Adie was glad of the silence; it helped her keep her mind empty. Flimby Forest lay about half a mile ahead. Even from this distance it looked dark and brooding. In the dim early-morning light, with the rain blurring her view, the wall of trees appeared impenetrable.

Prince seemed sure of where he was going and wanted to trot at a pace that was too fast for the humans to maintain. He tried several times to free himself from Rupert's strong hold. At the edge of the woodland he stopped and reared, pulling the reins from Rupert's grip. Adie clung to the pony's neck. He turned, several times, in a circle, sitting back on his hind legs and holding his head high. Rupert was struggling to get hold of him. Silently, steadfastly, Adie hung on. Eventually Rupert got hold of the reins, turned Prince's back to the woods and began to calm him. For a few seconds it looked as if he would be successful. But then the pony reared, fully this time, his eyes wild, whites showing, ears laid flat against his head. He turned in a single bound and, as his front legs touched the ground, his hind legs bucked, sending Sam and the men scattering. At full gallop he launched into the forest. By some miracle Adie remained on his back; her head low, her arms about his neck.

She glanced back and saw the men, and Sam, running, trying to keep up, but the distance between them was increasing. As Prince entered the woodland, she lost sight of them.

A short distance into the forest, the undergrowth forced Prince to slow his pace to a fast walk. He picked his way through the brambles, head down, nodding with each step.

It took all Adie's concentration to keep her battered body on the pony's back. After a while Prince slowed his pace again and she lay forward on his neck to rest. The gentle rhythm and rocking of his broad shoulders had a soporific effect, and her troubled mind struggled to remain alert, it needed to shut down. The pony had freedom to go where he pleased. She hoped he would lead her to Lilly. As he plodded onward through the dead bracken and brambles, certain of his course, she fell into a light sleep.

Waking, she was uncertain of how long she had dozed, and sat up to take in her surroundings. The trees were closer now and there were no clear pathways, except, perhaps, an indication of where Prince had been before. Above, the sky was grey. Rain dripped onto her from the soaked trees. Everything seemed decayed in this damp, misty place. No noise from the outside world penetrated it: no sheep bleated, no motorbike revolutions sped down the lane and, strangely, no birds sang.

A flash of white caught her eye. Prince stopped dead, startled, and Adie sat upright, staring at the strange shape that was moving, and then still. It hovered a short distance away through the trees. After a moment Prince put his head back down and resumed his plodding. Adie was about to rein him in when the white apparition moved again and revealed itself to be a stag. She could make out the white heart of his rump and the fine set of antlers that crowned his head. It seemed that his soft brown eyes looked right through her. They stared at each other as Prince plodded by, the stag not moving a muscle. When he disappeared behind the foliage, she was still looking back at the spot he had occupied, feeling bereft and alone.

T HE SIGHT OF Lilly disturbed Bill. He didn't want to look at her; he wanted her mother – he craved Adie. He'd know when he saw her if she wanted him or not. He was prepared to forget about the boy. But how was he going to get his disloyal wife to this hut, when she was being so closely guarded? He knew there must be an answer; he just had to wait silently and empty his mind, keep the voices away. It would come to him.

But the voices wouldn't let him be. All night they had plagued him with doubts. *You won't be able to let her go now. Even if you get Adie, you'll have to kill Lilly, otherwise she'll tell everyone your dirty little secrets.*

'No, she won't. Adie and I will take her with us. I'll keep them both under control this time. I won't let them go anywhere.'

And how are you going to get Adie? Obviously, she doesn't want you. She wouldn't have run so far away if she wanted you.

'She plays games. She knows she wants me.'

Sneaking about, lying to you, getting money, stealing your car, and, worst of all, having another man. You can never trust her again.

'Shut up!' Bill commanded the voices.

He left them inside to watch Lilly and moved the chair outside. Sitting in it, he gently rocked to and fro. Apart from the creaking of the chair, the world was silent. He continued to rock for a long time, untroubled by the morning damp that clung to his hair and clothes. It helped him empty his mind; that way he knew a solution would come.

Despite the meditation, his senses were acute. He had always been hyper-alert, observant and sensitive to every subtle difference in his surroundings. And now, somewhere at the edges of his mind, he could hear something that he needed to pay attention to. It was a regular sound that had a rhythm to it. Opening his eyes, he stopped rocking and sat straight-backed, straining to hear the distant noise. After a minute he realised the noise was getting louder, and after another minute he knew it was a horse. A flare of alarm in his mind. Was that bloody pony returning, and was someone following it? He had to know.

After checking Lilly was still fully bound and gagged, he shut the door of the hut and made his way towards the sound. Every few yards he stopped to listen and confirm he was moving in the right direction. The fourth time he stopped, he could tell he was getting close. When he stopped for the fifth time, he decided to stay put and use his eyes. After several minutes of examining the grey-brown mass of wood in front of him, he was becoming frustrated. He could hear the sound coming closer, but still he could see nothing. Then, a little way off to the side, he noticed a tiny movement. A few more seconds and he made out the head of Lilly's pony.

And then he saw her. She was lying along the pony's back, her arms dangling. Oh, what a gift. The Devil had been good to him today. Her head was turned away from him, but he knew it was her; he would recognise any part of his wife.

Her body lay as if melted into the pony; she was either asleep or unconscious. He had to get her to the hut, preferably without a struggle. He would like to capture the pony as well. If it could bring her here, it might bring others. It would be best to entice the animal towards him; if he could lead it and its rider, he would have both of them. But if Adie woke and kicked up a fuss, he would grab her, even if it meant losing the pony.

The animal was obviously tired. Covering the ground at a slow pace, its chest, forelegs and nose dripped with blood where so many brambles had clawed at him. Some had attached themselves to his body, their large thorns embedded deep into its skin, but still it kept going, its head nodding and held low. What a stupid animal, Bill thought, to bring his victim to him.

The pony was now only a few yards away. Slowly, carefully, Bill stood and revealed his presence. The creature stopped its weary walking and looked up. Bill spoke quietly to it and held out his hand as if there was something good there for it to eat. But the pony ignored him and carried on with its journey.

'Hey, boy, it's all right; I can take you there,' said Bill in a honeyed voice. All the while he was taking steps, getting closer. 'I can take you to see your little friend.'

Still Adie had not moved; she was balanced precariously on the pony's back and likely to slip to the ground.

When he was close enough, Bill took hold of the rein as it trailed through the undergrowth. 'Come on, boy,' he crooned, barely audibly, and began to walk in front of the pony, expecting it to follow.

But the rein was wrenched from his hand. The pony had inhaled Bill's adrenaline scent. It flung its head high and flared its nostrils. When recognition hit the animal's brain, its eyes rolled, showing their whites; its ears lay flat, and it bolted. As the pony turned and fled from the scene, brambles trailing behind it, Adie was thrown from its back. She landed on her side with a thump and a deep groan. Bill shrugged his shoulders; the pony was no great loss, now that he'd got Adie.

While she was still confused, he grabbed her from behind, clamped a hand over her mouth in a vice-like grip, and dragged her through the brambles to the hut. Once there, he threw her into the rocking chair, her head colliding heavily with its back. Using some twine from his trouser pocket, he tied her hands to the chair and then dragged it into the hut.

———※※※———

ADIE WATCHED LILLY'S eyes widen in horror, then saw the tears begin to fall. She knew Lilly would screw up her eyes in an effort to stop crying and be brave, but it didn't work.

'Look, you have me now, you can let Lilly go. She can't harm you; she'll never find this place again. Just keep me and let her go. I'll do anything you want,' pleaded Adie.

He was tying her feet to the chair. 'How do I know you mean that?'

'I do. I've missed you so much. I made a mistake, Bill; I realise now it was foolish of me to leave you.'

He placed his hands on the arms of the chair and leant forward. With his face a few inches from hers, he studied her eyes. 'My head tells me you are a lying bitch. Talk as much as you like, dear; you will not be able to talk for much longer, so you'd best make the most of it now.'

'What do you mean?'

'Have you forgotten our last passionate lovemaking, when I told you why I stole the carving knife and who it was for?'

Terror invaded her reeling brain, triggering her thoughts into overdrive. 'But, Bill, you know I love you. I thought you liked the chase. I'll stay with you and we can play all your games. Please don't hurt Lilly. I'm here, whatever you need to do, do it to me.'

'I'm not going to cut your beautiful skin my love; I'm going to cut Lilly. It's your punishment for deserting me, for being disloyal to me.'

Adie looked at Lilly then, expecting a scream, a cry, some sort of reaction. But there was nothing. Lilly lay there, passive, staring at them. While her mind reeled, Adie turned back to Bill, and tried again to convince him.

'But I haven't had any men. I'm just a housekeeper. We have our own separate living quarters. You could live there, Bill, with us.'

'It's not the men; you could have had as many men as you wanted, if you hadn't left me. But you did leave me. And you meant it. You saved money. You rented a flat. You stole my car. You took the children and came all the way up here. You don't want me, so stop lying to me.'

Abruptly, he shouted at the air – 'Go away!' – and Adie knew he was shouting at his voices and that he was far from reason. Whatever she said, she would not be able to pacify him. Where was he going to cut Lilly? How much was he going to punish them? How far was he going to take it? She had to stay silent, otherwise it would be worse.

'I'm going to punish you by making you watch Lilly die.'

'No!' she yelled. 'You haven't got time; they're on their way. The police, that is; they're right behind me, following the trail that Prince left.'

Bill glanced at the open door, then picked up the carving knife from the top of the stove and brandished it in Adie's face. 'Shut up, bitch.'

He went to the door and listened for a long time, taking in the gentle rustlings of the forest. When he turned back into the hut she continued to talk.

'You'd better be gone. I told you they are on my heels and they'll be here any minute.'

He swiped the back of his hand across her face, splitting her lips open against her teeth. She went to spit out the gore, and something vicious with spiteful spikes was shoved into her mouth. The hideous thing sparked pain in every place it touched. When she tried to relax her jaw, spikes pierced the inside of her mouth. With sudden, shocked realisation, she knew it was barbed wire. If she moved a tiny fraction its razor-sharp points would impale themselves deeper into her flesh.

Bill went back to the door to listen. Adie's eyes met those of her daughter, and in expectation of death, she felt a bond with her that went beyond age, maturity and kinship. Adie was truly amazed at Lilly's courage. Inside Adie's own mind, panic was taking over, making her lose all reasonable thought. Then she looked at her daughter more closely and saw peace in her eyes. This horrified her beyond anything she had witnessed before. She wanted her little girl to fight, not believe that this was her fate. She tried to convey to her child that they must not give up, but Lilly seemed to be resigned.

Adie made a last attempt at rational thought. Surely, when she had ridden Prince through the forest, they had left enough of a trail to be followed? Help had to reach them in time. But then Bill was approaching Lilly, the knife in his hand, and Adie's courage failed her. She was lost in a living nightmare.

BILL HAD LISTENED for distant sounds that did not belong to this terrain. He had thought he'd heard nothing, but then he was not sure. Adie had instilled a molecule of insecurity in him that wormed its way through his mind. Still, if they were coming it would be her downfall, he told the voices in his head. He'd just have to kill Lilly sooner and be away.

Stopping his rambling thoughts, he listened again. Then he thought he heard something a long way off. It was a human noise.

He'd have to do it straight away. She'd done him a favour, given him time to escape.

He wanted to talk to his daughter now, to explain to her what was going to happen. He sat, with care, on the edge of the bed and lay the knife down the length of Lilly's chest, taking trouble to align it with the centre of her ribs. Then he began to stroke her hair.

Staring at the knife on her daughter's ribcage, Adie felt her own chest threaten to burst open as her heart punched her ribs. She tried to draw attention to herself, moving as much as she could within the constraints of her bonds; she no longer cared that the barbed wire dug deeper. But Bill seemed to be in a kind of trance and nothing she could do would draw him out of it.

He talked to Lilly in soft tones, like a father who had been too strict and now felt guilty, saying goodnight to a child who had been naughty. 'Daddy is going to send you to heaven now,' he said. 'It will take a little while, and it will be a bit painful at first, but that will soon pass, and then you will fall asleep and the next thing you know you will be in heaven. Mummy will be with you the whole time.'

Lilly's eyes were big and wide and full of innocence as she looked up at her father, believing his every word. Adie's heart was splitting open, spilling its blood and falling apart, bit by agonising bit.

'I'm just going to talk to Mummy and then I will be back to send you on your way.'

Standing, he arched his back and stretched his arms high above his head as if getting ready to perform some task of physical endurance. He stepped across the hut towards Adie and stood in front of her. Placing his hands on her wrists, he leant his whole weight on them, crushing them against the arms of the rocking chair. She thought her slim bones might break, but the pain did not bother her. Bending forward, he placed his face directly in front of hers. His breathing was ragged and uneven, his breath foul, and as he exhaled, she not only smelt it, but tasted it on her spiked, open mouth. Unable to close her lips and wash away the odorous coating with her saliva, she tried not to breathe.

'Lilly's death is your doing,' he whispered. 'If you had stayed, she would not have to die.'

For the first time in all their years together his words did not fill her with guilt. Now she knew how mad he was, and that none of this was her fault. He had his face no further than an inch from hers, and as their eyes met she was stunned to see sadness in his gaze. Not since the first weeks of their relationship, when he fooled her, had she seen anything that resembled a gentle human emotion in this man. Hatred, lust and murderous intentions, maybe; but now, as she looked on, tears welled up in his eyes and, in a voice thick with remorse and deep sorrow, he told her how he was going to punish her.

'I am going to cut Lilly's wrists and her life will run away. It will flow from her little body and her death will come. You are going to have to watch her die, knowing it was all in your hands.'

Tears were falling from her eyes now; there was nothing she could do. There was no way she could fight this, and she tried to look round Bill to see if Lilly had heard his words. As she moved her head, barbed wire pierced the inside of her mouth and blood began to trickle from the corners of her lips.

Bill laughed loudly, stepped across to Lilly and lifted the knife from her chest.

H E WAS STANDING outside the shepherd's hut; the door closed behind him, the cutting done. The knife was still in his hand, smeared with Lilly's blood.

The voices were laughing, chatting happily with each other.

Did you see the knife slice the skin?

And the way the blood slowly oozed?

And then it started to pump; little jumpy pumps.

I'd like to go back in and watch, but he won't; he's a snivelling coward.

Bill did not care what they called him; he could not go back in there. He didn't want to look at Lilly. He would have gone back inside and tried to save his daughter if he'd thought it would get Adie back. He still craved her, but it was finished. He knew now that she didn't need him; she was unfaithful and did not care about him, just like his mother.

He hadn't realised how much pain losing her would cause him. These were feelings he had never experienced before. His face was wet and his legs were weak. He tried to stop crying, but could not. The voices, back in full flow, ridiculed him. He supposed that, now, they would be his companions for life.

He started to walk away from the hut, giving no thought to his direction. After a while – he was not sure how long – he changed his mind and decided to go back and plead with Adie. He turned around and began to head back towards the hut.

Then the ground erupted as if a giant mole was digging up from underneath. Lilly's perfect face appeared through the crumbling earth and looked up at him; then it morphed into Adie's face and his knees buckled under him. Crawling through the undergrowth, a pain, so strong, rose through his chest. Bill collapsed and lay there sobbing into the wet earth.

When the sobbing subsided, he knelt and looked down at his upturned hands resting on his thighs. *I still have the knife*, was the one thought he had; then he stayed that way for a long time, empty-headed and numb.

Eventually, he stood up and tried, once again, to walk in the direction of the hut. But his legs were bloodless from kneeling, it took a while for any sensation to return. After a few minutes he expected to see the ivy-clad shack, but it failed to appear. Trusting that it must be nearby, he turned around, looking for it. It was nowhere in sight.

That bitch had done this. The bitch had confused him, made him angry again. When he saw her he'd punish her for it. He spun around several times, looking in every direction, but the hut was still nowhere to be seen. He thought about Adie, and remembered the barbed wire he'd stuffed into her mouth. He laughed. Then her face filled his mind and he started to sob again.

He began to run fast, dashing past trees and crashing through the undergrowth, mustering as much speed as he could in an attempt to leave the pain and the visions behind him. But they followed him, and every time he stopped, they caught up with him, so he continued to run. The voices were having a wonderful time.

B Y MID MORNING the light in the woodland was still dim. They picked their way through like pioneers in an untouched place, following Prince's trail in silence. Rupert led, Lawrence was behind Jack and Sam, and Jim brought up the rear. The pace was slow and uncomfortable, each of them bleeding where they had been snared by thorns. With every step they had to lift their feet high above the undergrowth. Often, they passed high-hanging brambles hand to hand as they navigated the dense foliage.

Rupert had his eyes on the ground, concentrating on the path left by Prince. Lawrence noticed that Sam was agitated; at every opportunity the boy scanned their surroundings. It didn't surprise Lawrence; he wouldn't have admitted it to the others, but for some reason these woods gave him the willies. He felt as if they were being watched.

When he glanced at the boy again, he saw that something to their left held his attention. He followed Sam's gaze and saw, in the distance, a light shining through the trees. It fell in shafts of misty grey and Lawrence wanted to go there, to be out of this dank place.

In front of them Rupert stopped, with his hand raised as a signal to the others that they should do the same. Jack complied, but Sam, Lawrence and Jim were looking at the light, not paying attention, and stumbled into Jack, knocking him to the ground. He scrambled to his feet and looked back at them, annoyed.

Sam pointed towards the light. Silently, Rupert acknowledged the boy's find and then continued with his painstaking task. After about three yards he stopped and indicated their new direction. They could all see the disruption underfoot. Lawrence was grateful to be heading out of the woods.

Reaching the edge of the trees, they realised it was a small clearing surrounded by forest. Jack pointed out a run-down shepherd's hut, so overgrown with ivy, brambles and bindweed that it was almost impossible to spot.

Rupert indicated for them to stay put, out of sight, while he went to investigate, but Lawrence insisted that he lead the way; it was time to take over. They stooped low and, on bent knees, ran quickly and smoothly across the clearing, leaving the others hidden. When they reached the hut, they stood with their backs against the weed-covered walls, then slowly took sideways steps in opposite directions. Lawrence reached the door before Rupert and knew he had found something. Here the foliage had recently been ripped away and the grass had been trodden down. Whipping the door open, he stepped inside and scanned the hut. It contained only two people: the ones they wanted to find.

In a second Rupert was by his side and they assessed Adie. She was injured, but alive. Both men knelt by Lilly. Lawrence took her pulse while Rupert undid the bindings. There was no beat at her wrist.

'Shit,' said Lawrence.

'Try her neck,' said Rupert.

Lawrence pressed his fingers to her throat and acknowledged a weak pulse. 'I want to get after the bastard who did this; can you look after her?' he asked.

Rupert did not answer; he was already at work. Lawrence yelled out for the others. Jim and Jack appeared in an instant. Sam was not with them. Jack had told the boy to remain outside, but then he appeared at the door and a barrage of voices ordered him to leave. Sam did not go.

Adie saw her son come into view and knew the sight confronting him would stay with him forever. His feet grew roots and his mouth twisted in horror. She softened her eyes in apology. His head moved with a jerk as he tried to see his sister's face. Lilly's eyes were closed, her lips had the same deathly pallor as her skin. To Adie she looked dead. She had watched her daughter's blood seep into the ground, and now Rupert was kneeling in it.

'Can you stop the bleeding?' asked Lawrence.

'I can, with tourniquets, but I have to loosen them at intervals, and I'm not sure how long they should be. I've used tourniquets before, but that was on soldiers, not a child,' said Rupert.

'Do your best. Jim, get out of these woods, go the way we came, as fast as you can. Call an ambulance and tell them to get as close to where we are as possible; we'll be carrying Lilly out of the woods. After that you can tell the police. Go now. Jack I'll need you with me as a tracker and a witness.' said Lawrence. He cursed the fact that they were in this godforsaken place.

Jim was gone in an instant. Rupert had removed his shirt and was tearing strips from it. Lawrence talked to Adie as he removed the barbed-wire monstrosity from her mouth.

Jack could see that Sam was a lost boy, completely alone as hell reigned all about him. With a gentle shake of his shoulders, he said, 'Sam, listen', and watched as the shocked boy tried to focus his eyes and hear the words coming from his mouth. Twice more Jack tried to get a response. Slowly clarity came, and he saw Sam's pupils dilate and knew the boy was coming back.

'Stay with your mother until help arrives. We all have to leave. Stay here with her and talk to her; don't let her go to sleep, keep her warm. Help will come – don't worry if it seems to take a while, it will come.'

Sam took off his coat and wrapped it around his mother.

They all watched Rupert as he got to his feet carrying Lilly. The little girl looked like a corpse with her arms bent at the elbows and crossed over her chest so that her fingers rested on her shoulders. Seeing their faces he held her close to him. On each upper arm was a tourniquet, and each wrist was bandaged with strips of shirt in an attempt to stem the flow of blood.

'I hope I've done it right', he said.

'You follow Jim; we're after the scum who did this', said Lawrence.

Without another word the men ran from the hut; Rupert to follow the trail back through the woods. The path Lawrence and Jack took would be unknown, unpredictable.

—✳ ✳ ✳—

E VEN THOUGH HE was running, crashing through the forest, Bill could not get rid of the voices. The faster his heart beat, the more excited they became. They told him he was a coward; he hadn't done the job properly; he hadn't done Adie.

Bill didn't want to do Adie. He hated her, but he also loved her. He couldn't kill her, couldn't stand the thought of her not breathing in this world. But then he couldn't stand the thought of life without her. How could he be rid of this agony?

Through the trees, a glimpse of something caught his eye. He stopped running and stood motionless. At first it was just something brown; then it grew a head, legs and arms. The farmer stood staring at him in silence. This was what he needed. His veins pulsed with invincible energy.

'I doubt they'll ever find Lilly, and if they do, they'll be too late. I expect she's already dead,' Bill told him.

The farmer did not move or speak.

Even though this was the first time Bill had seen him close to, he thought he recognised his face. He was a slight man, wiry, but it was definitely him; he'd seen him wearing that jacket. Still he didn't speak. Why didn't he speak?

Lawrence had no doubt who he was looking at, only now, instead of the meek man he had seen down South, desperate to get his family back, Bill was pumped up, overstimulated, and with a frenzied look in his eye. He decided to play dumb and let Bill take the lead.

'And that bitch Adie watched her die. She deserved that; she's been worse than a whore, living with you.'

Bill hawked saliva into his mouth and spat it out towards the man. Still he didn't speak. Bill hit his own head, slapping himself with his open palm. Was the man really there? The voices told him that he was, and that he should kill him. 'I'm going to,' he told them.

'I left her there watching our Lilly die because she doesn't want me any more,' he told the farmer. Saying this sent tears streaming down his face. 'If it wasn't for you, I would have got her back.' He pointed the knife at the farmer. 'You took my wife and my kids. It's your fault that I had to kill Lilly. With you dead, one day I'll come back for Adie. She'll want me then.'

He ran at the farmer, growling, crazed. The farmer did not speak or flinch.

———✳✳✳———

ADIE WATCHED HER son take a clean handkerchief from his pocket and spit on it, then try to wipe away the dried gore from her face. His hands shook, and he stopped what he was doing and remained still until the shaking ceased. It hurt her very core to see her son so traumatised. It hurt when he dabbed her pierced and bruised face, but she did not mind; she knew it was occupying him, helping him to stay sane. Having him here, touching her, was more than she could possibly have hoped for. They did not speak or look too closely into each other's eyes; neither could bear the agony.

She was astonished that Bill hadn't killed her. She knew she would probably still be alive tomorrow, in a month's time, and in a year's time. But, by the time Rupert had arrived, she had thought that Lilly was dead.

When she saw him working on her, it was as if life had returned to her heart as it pounded with hope, but then she had glimpsed his face as he tore from the hut with Lilly clutched to his chest. Graphic pictures ran through her mind: her daughter's blood pulsing out of those hideous slashes and pooling on the ground; her skin and lips so ghostly; the moment when she had shut her eyes and not opened them again. It felt hopeless.

Adie indicated for Sam to help her leave the hut, she could no longer remain in this place of evil.

Outside the clouds were lifting and shafts of sunlight began to shine through the canopy. Sam found some logs piled up against a tree. He rummaged through them, looking for dry ones. Selecting the best, he helped her sit down. Sitting beside her, he put his arm around her, and they leant against each other. For a fleeting moment she allowed herself to marvel at her eldest child, before her mind slipped back into torment.

She felt naked and vulnerable, afraid that Bill would return and kill Sam. If he did, she hoped he would kill her at the same time. If she was to lose Lilly, it would only be for Sam that she could go on.

She kept telling herself she had to be strong for him. She tried to ignore the awful weight that sat in the pit of her stomach and hung on her heart. It wanted to rise to the surface like a black tide, to say, *She's dead, accept it.* But she pushed it down, knowing that if she listened to it, she would be finished.

They sat, locked together in the strange silence of this woodland, for several minutes, and then Sam spoke.

'I've been praying, Mum; in my head, I've been praying for Lilly. God won't let her die, will he? That's got to be right, hasn't it?'

She could not answer straight away. Praying was all they could do now, but Adie had given up on that a long time ago. Her thoughts drifted to her childhood and her father. He used to say that the best way to get the things you wanted in life was to be grateful for the things you had. And she did have things to be grateful for: their life on the farm and the trusted friends they had made. And most of all Sam. What would Lilly say if she gave up on all of that now? She'd scowl at her and tell her how wrong she was. Maybe now, if she prayed in a truly thankful way, just maybe, her prayers would be answered.

'I can't speak for God,' she said, 'but I am going to start praying.'

They did not know it at the time, but from the edge of the forest they were being watched. Nearby, the sound of a horse's gentle breath startled them. Sam tightened his hold on his mother. Their eyes tried to penetrate the trees where the sound had come from; the animal was coming towards them. Was Bill there?

Then Prince emerged, alone, his long mane and tail matted, his head still down. Despite their devastation, they allowed themselves to smile.

'Maybe our prayers are being answered,' Adie said through her pain as she tried to look at her son.

But he was looking at something else, pointing towards a different part of the forest. 'Look.'

A stag, like the one she had seen on her journey into the woods, was standing, motionless and regal, his head crowned with antlers due to shed. Prince walked softly towards them, stopped in front of them and blew again through his velvet nostrils. By the time their eyes returned to the stag he was, almost magically, melting away into the trees.

'Do you think you can get on Prince's back?' Sam asked.

'With your help I can.'

Once Adie was on the pony, Sam sat behind her. They had been unsure how they were going to guide the weary animal as his bridle was missing, but they needn't have worried. As soon as they were settled Prince picked up the trail, returning the way they had come.

JACK COULD HEAR someone nearby. He knew the sound was human; wildlife wouldn't make that sort of noise. It had to be Bill. The rustling noises and the crack of breaking wood seemed to move away and then come closer. Occasionally, he thought he heard a human voice, but he couldn't be sure.

Then all went silent. He picked his way forward, straining his ears, trying and failing to be noiseless in these impossible surroundings. He knew the man was unhinged; nobody did what he had done unless they were beyond irrational. This knowledge made Jack wary; people like Bill were unpredictable.

The voice came before he saw him. 'I doubt they'll ever find Lilly, and if they do, they'll be too late. I expect she's already dead.'

Jack stopped in his tracks. He looked in the direction of the voice, but the forest was dense and the shadows dark. The man was still talking, enabling him to hone his senses towards the sound until he could make out a different shade and shape among the trees.

'And that bitch Adie will have watched her die. She deserved that; she's been worse than a whore, living with you.'

Jack realised that Bill thought he was talking to Thomas. Creeping forward until he could see his face, he saw Bill spit at Lawrence, slap himself and shout at the air. Then he started to cry, babbling through great sobs. Jack was nervous. He knew action would follow, though whether it would be violent or whether Bill would collapse in remorse, he didn't know.

Lawrence saw that Bill was going to come at him with the knife, but he was confident he knew exactly what to do. Knife pointed towards you; the two-hand slap, bending the wrists; knife would be dropped; arm twisted up the back; push him to the ground and you've got your man.

Only it didn't work like that. His reactions must have been slow. Instead, Bill's superior weight crashed both of them to the ground. Lawrence could not believe his own errors. He had to start thinking straight. They were grappling, Bill on top, the carving knife at Lawrence's throat. Bill could have cut him then, but something changed in his eyes and he started to talk.

'You're that bastard copper. Thought you had me, didn't you?' he said.

Lawrence did not waste energy on words; fear was taking over. He didn't want to die here in this forgotten, soulless place. Clear thinking and physical strength were deserting him. He could feel the knife touching his skin.

'If you had got Adie back for me, like I wanted, you wouldn't be in this position now. Instead I had to punish Adie, and kill Lilly, but I still lost her. So, now my friends have come back, and they tell me to do things. They're telling me to kill you now. And when I've done that, I'll be off doing things to women and girls that you won't like. You won't be able to stop me, and it will be your fault.'

And then Bill's head snapped to the side, and he slumped and rolled off Lawrence. Jack had come to his rescue, but something dark and frenzied rose up in Lawrence; a powerful surge that roared inside his head. He straddled Bill's chest. The knife was in his hands. He held it to Bill's throat. He wanted to kill him, to make him suffer as Adie and Lilly had done. He cut his skin. It surprised him how sharp the knife was. Blood began to seep through the slit. Jack watched, astonished.

'Do it,' Bill sobbed. 'Kill me. Go on, kill me. Please.'

Lawrence watched as Bill's eyes lost their glittered mania, as his body became slack and his power left him. He threw the knife aside, flipped Bill over and handcuffed him. In the pocket of Thomas's coat, he found twine. The two men secured Bill to a tree. Leaving Jack to guard him,

Lawrence walked away. The sound of Bill's sobs faded away behind him.

———✳✳✳———

L AWRENCE FELT SOMEWHAT disorientated as he made his way out of the woods. When he finally saw blue sky, the sun was fairly high, and when he looked at his watch it had just passed 11.30. To his right, up the hill, he saw a group of uniformed policemen. Finally, the local force had turned up. He began walking towards them. Then, amongst them, Lawrence noticed the peaked cap and physical posture of DCI John Holdstock, his superior officer. Looking further up the hill he could see Vera and a man with crutches; Thomas Elliott Lambton must be home.

As he approached the policemen, the DCI took Lawrence aside.

Lawrence felt calm, as if a great burden had been lifted from him. His career and life as he had known them were finished, and he was glad of it. He could be arrested for what he had done, but he was prepared to face any consequences.

'I should have kept a closer eye on you. What the hell do you think you're playing at?'

'I'm sorry, sir, but I couldn't stand by and let him get away with it.'

'Well, he obviously has got away with it; clearly you haven't caught him.'

'I did catch him, sir. He's back in the woods.'

'What have you done, tied him to a tree?' The DCI's voice was incredulous.

'Yes, sir.'

'Christ – have you harmed him?'

'Well, we did fight. He came at me with a knife. I messed up trying to relieve him of it and we ended up grappling on the ground. He nearly had me, sir. Then he said stuff… I don't know, I lost it…'

'And?'

'I cut his throat.'

'Shit. Is he dead?'

'No, sir. I thought about it, but in the end, I just cut him a little bit.'

The DCI took off his hat and ran his fingers through his hair, then put it back on. Various blasphemous words left his mouth. Lawrence watched him, knowing that he'd brought a whole mountain of trouble down on his boss.

'Sir, I'll take what's coming to me. There's no need for you to be dragged down with me. I'll make sure they know it was all me, and Jonesy, he's—'

Lawrence was about to say, 'innocent', but his boss cut him off.

'Shut up, stay shut up, and let me think.'

The DCI paced in circles, occasionally shaking his head and muttering. 'You're a lucky bastard,' he said, eventually standing still and facing Lawrence. 'Firstly because I sent two local officers into the woods to track you and Bill Lewis down. They returned just before you showed up, having been unable to find you. Secondly, I came up here alone to talk sense into you, because when Jonesy slipped up and I found out what you were up to I felt you were worth the effort. You could have a brilliant career ahead of you, if you just stay on course. And, thirdly, you're lucky that the local DCI happens to also be a very good friend of mine.'

'Sir, please, I don't want you to put yourself in any jeopardy on my behalf.' Lawrence saw that his boss was about to explode.

'I already have, you idiot, by coming up here and not telling anyone in our department about the situation!'

There was silence for a moment.

'When I've finished talking you are going to walk away in the opposite direction from me and disappear. You will not speak to anybody about this except me. I, hopefully, will be able to instigate a cessation of your service for medical reasons. I will be in touch if this is not possible, or when I deem it suitable for you to return.'

'Sir, I want to thank you for all that you have said, but I do not want to return to the force.'

Lawrence noticed the look of sadness that entered his superior's eyes.

'I didn't realise it had got to you so bad, Lawrence.'

'I wouldn't trust myself out there any more.'

'I'm sorry about that. I know the force has its faults; I was hoping you would be one of those who could bring about some changes.'

'No, sir, it won't be me; I'm finished.'

'In that case, stay away from the department. Don't talk to anyone, not even Jonesy; you don't want to get him even more involved. Make sure I can contact you. I hope to swing it so that you appear to have resigned, but if I can't you may have to attend an enquiry, and, if that is the case, our stories will have to match.'

Both men stood in silence for a while with their hands in their pockets. Lawrence was looking out over the valley, searching for the right thing to say, but the words didn't come, so instead he asked, 'Will you charge him with Maureen's murder?'

'I'll do my best to get him to the gallows,' the DCI replied.

O N   T H E   F I R S T   day of Lilly's stay in hospital, Adie was told her daughter was in danger of going into shock due to severe blood loss. This, added to the other complication of dehydration, made her a very sick child. Lilly was kept sedated.

After she had received her own medical treatment, Adie was told to go home and wait to be called, but she refused. Instead, along with Sam and Jack, she was shown into a grey room with high windows that they couldn't see out of. It was a room away from other visitors; the room where relatives received bad news. Sitting on metal-framed canvas chairs, Adie held her son's hand. He leant in towards her in a protective manner. Jack sat opposite, patient and strong, dispensing sweet tea from a flask, and cheese sandwiches.

For two days they waited, and Adie knew that sometime soon she would be either on clouds of happiness, or in deepest grief. She feared that losing the little girl who'd helped them build their new life, and whose innocence and honesty had brought them all closer together, would be something she could not endure. But she knew that Sam was afraid of losing his mother as well as his sister, so she tried to appear strong for his sake.

The door to the room was held open by a hook and every time a nurse walked briskly down the corridor, the three of them stood and prepared themselves for news. But, so far, no medical staff had entered the room and their wait continued.

———✳—✳—✳———

I T WAS NINE in the morning on the third day. Jack had been back to the farm for more supplies and they were ready for another period of waiting. Once again a brisk walker was coming down the corridor. As they had before, the three of them stood.

A nursing sister entered the room. 'Would you like to see your daughter now? She's waiting for you.'

'She's alive? She's awake?'

'She's very weak, but she'll be fine. She's asking for you both, so come along, with smiles on your faces for her, please.'

Adie did not need to be told; her smile was so broad it would have hurt the muscles in her cheeks even without her injuries. She glanced back at Jack as they left the room, feeling guilty that he could not be included. He nodded his encouragement, his face displaying his joy.

'You can have fifteen minutes. I'll come and escort you out when your time is up.' The sister turned on her heel and strode away down the corridor.

Slowly they opened the door a little and peered through. Looking back at them, smiling weakly, her eyes and cheeks sunken, was their daughter, sister and beloved friend. Words were not needed. They sat, one on either side of the bed, and the three of them soaked up the sight of each other, unable to believe they were there together.

It was Lilly who spoke first, tapping a delicate finger on each puncture wound that marked her mother's bruised face. 'Is Daddy with you?'

'No, sweetheart.'

'Where is he?'

'Daddy has been taken away. I hope we shall never see him again.'

RUPERT WAS STANDING at the paddock gate. He had turned Prince out and was waiting for him to do his usual buck and canter around the field. But this morning was different, the pony trotted to the opposite fence near the entrance of the farm and stood there, unmoving.

Curious, Rupert began walking across the field towards the pony. Behind him, Thomas had also noticed the pony's strange behaviour and, using his crutches, was picking his way over the field. When Rupert was nearing Prince and Thomas was halfway, Jack's vehicle turned onto the farm road and stopped. The door opened and

Adie emerged to help Lilly climb out. As she made slow, tentative progress towards the fence, Prince pranced backwards and forwards, then came to a standstill in front of her and the two men, with tears in their eyes, watched them reunite.